**monsoon**books

# SINGAPORE RED

William L. Gibson is a writer, educator and occasional sound artist based in Southeast Asia. His fiction and nonfiction work has appeared in magazines such as *Signal to Noise*, *Black Scat Review* and many others. His regular column on Asian art and media, 'Opium Traces', can be found at *popmatters.com*.

The album *Chillout*, by Gibson's experimental music project Third World Skull Candy, is available on BitPulse Records.

*Singapore Red* is the third book in the Detective Hawksworth Trilogy of hard-boiled crime novels set in the rough-and-tumble frontier of 1890s Malaya, that includes *Singapore Black* and *Singapore Yellow*.

Learn more about the author at: *www.williamlgibson.com*.

Also by William L. Gibson

TRANSLATIONS
*In the Land of Pagodas* by Alfred Raquez
(with Paul Bruthiaux)

NONFICTION
*Art and Money in the Writing of Tobias Smollett*

FICTION
*Singapore Black*
*Singapore Yellow*
*Singapore Red*

# SINGAPORE RED

WILLIAM L. GIBSON

**monsoon**

**monsoon**books

Published in 2017
by Monsoon Books Ltd
No.1 Duke of Windsor Suite, Burrough Court,
Burrough on the Hill, Leics. LE14 2QS, UK
www.monsoonbooks.co.uk

ISBN (paperback): 9789814423670
ISBN (ebook): 9789814423687

Cover design by Cover Kitchen.
Frontcover photograph of Singapore business leader Hoo Ah Kay,
also known as Whampoa, seated at his mansion, c.1865.

Printed in USA

*The lords of the mountains and the earls of the seas*
*shall all join its retinue, when the spirit of*
*our deceased imperial father descends from on high.*

*Posterity will smile upon your deed as time passes;*
*and your sons and grandsons will have*
*limitless good fortune.*

Emperor Zhu Di to Sultan Parameswara,
the last king of Singapura

# Contents

Rendezvous at the Plum Pavilion   9

Two Become One   28

Scissors, Paper, Stone   46

The Chinese Protectorate   67

Red Threads   81

Outbreak   92

Winchester 1893   113

Johor Bahru   131

Father, Mother, Orphan   151

Quarantine   166

Fizzy Water   181

Attacked!   197

Golden Lotus   210

Family Ties   228

No Deposit, No Return   246

HISTORICAL NOTE   267

MORE BY WILLIAM L. GIBSON   272

## CHAPTER I

# Rendezvous at the Plum Pavilion

THE ICE ON THE WIND cut through her clothes, searing the tender skin beneath the shapeless mass of coarse material. She had never been so cold before, and did not know that the air itself was capable of causing such pain. With each inhalation, she felt as though her ribs were splintering. She held her hand to her face in horrible fascination, watching as her exhalations turned crystal in the darkness, her breath falling chilled around the fingers that would not move and could not feel but that were still part of her.

One of the wardens saw her standing mutely breathing on her hand, and being from these parts, knew the lethal danger of pausing in a blizzard. They needed to find a temporary shelter to wait out the worst of the storm, otherwise they would never make it to the Plum Pavilion. The warden snatched the woman's hand, jerking the prisoner out of her trance. Their gazes met in the frigid darkness, panting slowly beneath the heavy wool swathing their heads so that only their eyes could be seen. The other warden, wrapped in great bundles so that she moved like an old man, appeared beside them, gesturing into the billowing whiteness ahead. She had found a place where they could hide from the merciless wind.

Once out of the gale, the prisoner began to blow on her hands.

Her breath was no longer visible and as the warmth returned to her fingers a new pain formed, as though hot needles were sprouting under her skin. This was also a new sensation for her, and she tapped her fingertips together, feeling the needles ricochet up her forearms.

In the safety of the shelter, stamping the sensation back into her feet, she wondered if this climb through a treacherous blizzard was worth the effort. Would Jin Long meet her as promised? Now that he was an Inspector of Justice, would he still love her? Would he believe that she was innocent of the murder for which she was condemned to die?

He had been such a gentle boy when he came to visit her in her younger days, spending so much of his money on her favours that often his pockets were empty. Then she bestowed her favours without charge. The stone-faced man she saw in court so little resembled that sweet boy that she was not sure at first whether it was the same person. And now he had arranged this secret rendezvous with her, on this night when the frigid air was like a malevolent entity who wanted to take from her toes and fingers and nose.

In the silence of the shelter, the exhausted wardens had fallen asleep in their bundles, leaning against each other in a heap that looked like stacks of old horse blankets. Seeing that she was alone for a moment, Su San's heart overran with despair, and she began to sing,

*A howling snowstorm in bone-biting winter.*
*My fate is unpredictable, as the path ends in this*
*pitch-dark night.*
*The snowflakes fall, like desolate tears.*

Facing the audience as he sang, the boy felt his mouth getting dry. The heavy headdress pinned to the wig began to wobble; he shifted his thin neck uncomfortably so it would not slip off. He could feel the heavy makeup running in the heat and hoped that he still appeared true to the character. This was only his second time playing the coveted role and he wanted to leave a strong impression, if not on the audience seated on wooden folding chairs in the torpid night beneath red paper lanterns strung across the lawn, fanning themselves as the perspiration rolled down their temples, then on the manager of the troupe who was out there somewhere in the steamy darkness, watching him. Under the dim scarlet light and shadow of the lanterns, the audience appeared ghoulish, and his recurrent nightmare of being shackled to a stage, straining to defecate while a crowd cackled and pointed at him, suddenly seemed all too real. He skipped a cue then picked up the lyric on the next beat, hoping no one noticed, feeling the wetness under his arms begin to dribble into his costume.

Adding to his nervousness was a face in the audience that watched him with the avidity of a shark circling prey. The man was seated in the second row, his dark eyes glittering as though he were seizing up which chunk of flesh he wanted to bite off first. He had a fat face and neck, though there was, the boy noticed, a certain elegance to him. His long queue had been freshly braided for the special occasion, and his silk *changshan* was immaculate. Even his nails appeared polished, glinting as they did like claws when they reflected the bright lanterns of the stage. But that bloodthirsty look on his face as he studied him made the boy sweat even more. He missed another cue, and cursing to himself, wilfully turned away from the audience for a moment to regain his composure, hoping the wig and headdress did not slip off while he momentarily looked upward.

Low Teck Beng suppressed a sigh when the *dan* broke form to turn his face upward, away from the audience. The boy's smooth neck was graceful like a swan, the long contours of his thin body just teasingly visible beneath the costume. His hips and thighs were especially luscious, he noted, tracing the lines in his mind. He shifted his bulk in the narrow, uncomfortable chair. Up until now he had been bored by the *wayang* opera performance. He had seen the story a thousand times, it seemed, and he sat here now only to appease his father and older brother, the insistent wooden clack of the *ban lei* percussion block boring into his brain.

But once the *dan* began to twist and turn on stage during the blizzard scene, using a thin white blanket to signify the snow, he noticed the boy's suppleness and now his interest was piqued. It had been awhile since he had got himself something special. He was too busy these days to make the necessary arrangements, and so he stuck with the usual fare, the *ah kus* in the bordellos his cousin ran down on North Bridge Road, the high-end brothels for the Teochew elite. The girls were fun, no doubt, but the *dan* on the stage sparked other ideas, and now his mind drifted over those possibilities while he fanned himself with the folded sheets of the *Lat Pau* Chinese daily paper. The cheap ink came off in the perspiration of his hands, staining his palm and fingers black, which made him angry. But even he acknowledged that it did not take much to make him angry these days.

It was the ninth day of the lunar new year, the fourth of February by the European calendar. It was the year of the Wood Goat and he had already been warned by the family geomancer that the animal was not propitious for him. It would not be a prosperous year, and he should be very wary this year of fornication, wine, gambling and travel, the geomancer had told him without a trace of irony while holding two withered fingers to his wrist, listening to his pulse. Did he not know that these were the requirements and hallmarks of his trade? How could he avoid such stuff? The geomancer continued, eyes closed, feeling the pulse. His body was too hot, he should cut back on alcohol and ginger and other heaty foods. He recalled the old man suddenly stopped and opening his eyes wide, stared directly into his own, a look of shock on his face, and immediately dropped Low Teck Beng's hand as if it were made of poison. Then he had quickly looked away, rubbing his liver-spotted hands together as if rinsing them. What could the old coot have seen in there? 'On the ninth day, ask Tiangong for protection and benediction for the coming year,' he had said gravely. 'Make plenty of offerings of sweet meats and rice wine.' He elaborated no further.

But Low Teck Beng had been busy all day, the ninth day being both the birthday of Tiangong, the Jade Emperor of Heaven, as well as the day of the big family gathering and *wayang* opera performance on the makeshift stage they had setup on the lawn of the family estate, Panglima Prang.

With all the activity, he did not have time to go to Giok Hong Tien temple, dedicated to the Jade Emperor, down on Havelock Road. It would be overrun with Hokkien anyway, for they were especially fervent in worship of Tiangong, and as the headman of the criminal gang of the most powerful Teochew *kongsi*, Low Teck Beng avoided crowds that might harbour potential killers. However, he did make prayer to the idol on the home altar and offered rice wine and a roasted suckling pig, though sweet meats he could not find. There was also an outdoor bonfire and altar for guests to make offering, and he was sure to burn extra incense there as well. He made a note to head down to the temple tomorrow, if he were not busy, or the next day, to make the specific offering the geomancer had suggested.

*How could he have the cold heart to pretend that
he did not know me,
Forget so easily all the warmth of our past
romance?*

The hypnotic sound of the three stringed *sanxian* filled space between the boy's voice and the serpentine sigh of the bowed *erhu*, all pinned together by the incessant clacking of the wood block.

*The questions and doubts I have on my mind will
not be answered.
Tears and blood stain my lovely clothes.*

The gathering was about more than celebrating the new year. His father had called together their family and related *kongsi* from as far as Bangkok and Kuching to discuss, in a friendly and non-committal fashion, a business proposal. His brother, Low Teck Seng, the favourite son, whom his father had always treated as the smart one, the one with promise, had a grand idea, which the whole family needed to hear.

'Your brother thinks ten years ahead, twenty years ahead,' his father had chided him that very day, as he did most days. 'All you do is gamble and drink and whore, while your brother works hard to keep the family business profitable.'

Never mind that he, Low Teck Beng, oversaw the entire criminal wing of the organization. Never mind that he, from almost nothing, built up the illegal traffic in coolie labour that kept the legal plantations running, the gambier plantations in Singapore and Johor, the tin mining in the Klang valley, the pineapple lands on the coast near Muar. Never mind that he, Low Teck Beng, was the one who smuggled in the girls for the houses in Singapore, who arranged the payments to the insufferable *ang-moh* officials who always had their hands open. Between paying the police in the motherland and paying the police in Singapore he barely broke even on most trades, not to mention the loss of product en route, and still he managed to turn a profit.

But his brother, his exalted brother, was the one who got the opium and spirit license concessions under Low family control and so he was the hero, the good son. He was the one trained in English, the one the respectable members of the family dined with publicly in town.

Yet when they needed Low Teck Beng to oversee the removal of a Hai San strongman, then they did not tell him he was a weak-willed profligate. No, when they needed him to twist the knife for them, to slice off fingers or gouge out eyes, to spill the blood that they were afraid to spill, the blood that needed to be spilled in order to keep the family business on an even keel, then they came on to him with milk and honey in their voices.

Now his grand brother had devised a new business scheme, and once again he, Low Teck Beng, was being scolded by his father as the good-for-nothing wastrel of the two. Why are you not more like your brother? All you do is drink! And fornicate! And waste money!

Of course he spent every night drinking with whores and gamblers: it was his job. How was he supposed to stay on top of the organization if he was not out every night with gangsters? Surely his father understood and appreciated this situation?

The hollow, brassy sound of the gong called his attention back to the makeshift stage, the boy prancing in the humid night, his slender body acting out the ache symbolized by the blowing cold that stung Su San to her heart.

It was his brother's grand idea to open a bank. A bank, for

heaven's sake! What the hell did they know about *banking*? It was, his brother had said, going to be a bank for Teochews so they would not have to use the banks of foreigners. As though the remittance houses that the *kongsi* ran now were not good enough! Now they had to mimic the *ang-mohs* and open a bank. They even had a name picked out: the Nanyang Banking Corporation. And his father, incredibly, had taken this stupid idea seriously and called together the entire family to try to sell them on it. It would take years to get everyone to agree, to pool funds, to get licenses from the authorities. It was best to start now, during the lunar new year celebrations, to underscore that this is not only a family effort but a clan effort, his father had said.

What a pile of monkey shit! It was just another instance of his brother wanting to be *ang-moh*, another example of his cursed adoration of all things European; European ideas and European clothes and European attitudes. And for this they loved him? Praised him? Sought his advice? While he, Low Teck Beng, was given the dirty work, the muck that no one else wanted to sling. And where was their appreciation?

He did not need any more aggravation. Already his cousin, Xiao Hun, was giving him no end of grief. Despite his misgivings, he had allowed her to run the disbursement of the newly arrived girls into their various establishments. Letting a woman do this had been a mistake, he realized, not because of the shame it brought to the family but because women are ruled by their emotions and true to form, she had fallen in love. And he did not approve of the match. So now she was angry with him and had disappeared, abandoning her work, absconding with the Cantonese scoundrel who had seduced her. A Cantonese! She did not even show up for the family new year festivities! And she had always enjoyed *wayang* opera! Now he had to find someone else to run the girls while he looked for her, putting him, Low Teck Beng, in a bad spot while she let her emotions run wild. He had adored her since they were young and he had trusted her, against all his better instincts, with the important job, which she had begged him for time and again, and now she had betrayed him. It was enough to make his blood boil.

> *Tonight,*
> *I will sing my heart out to no one but the snowflakes.*
> *Let the snow bury my integrity, for my grudge will never be resolved.*

The aria was finished and the young *dan* was about to leave the stage, which frustrated Low Teck Beng further. Watching the supple boy exit, he resolved to make special arrangements for that very night. He would need to get word to the mamasan on Spring Street, and though it would not be easy on short notice, especially during the new year celebrations, she could get him the goods. He would need to get his bodyguards together, send someone to prepare the hotel suite, and then he, Low Teck Beng, would politely slip away to take his pleasure in secret. The family be damned!

He worked hard, after all, and deserved his delights from time to time.

*   *   *

Detective Inspector Dunu Vidi Hevàge Rizby could not remember ever having seen so much blood. It smeared a bright red film across the plum wallpaper that had been badly pitted by the gunfire. It pooled across the floor in a sticky violet morass that stained the feet of the ornate rosewood furniture. It drenched the corpses, six in total, strewn about the room like children collapsed in a game of ring-a-ring o' roses. There was blood splashed across the opaque glass, turning black in abstract patterns as it dried. There was even blood smattered across the ceiling, in spots like bright red stars. There was gore everywhere. White shards of bone blown into the upholstery of the cushions, shreds of pink skin splattered across the soaked carpet, slabs of muscle meat and hunks of organ flesh the size of silver dollars dotted the room, which reeked of the brassy stench of blood.

They were in parlour room of the Plum Suite, tree branches with faux blossoms glued to the ceiling, in the Hotel Formosa on Club Street. One of the better hotels on the edge of the Chinese Quarter, it nonetheless functioned as a place for clandestine rendezvous of the furtive sexual variety for high rollers. It was not the easiest place to commit mass murder.

The furniture and cushions and lamps were shattered and shredded and pocked as though the entire room had been chewed then spat out. The dead were three well-muscled Chinese men dressed in Western-style suits, two Chinese women dressed in cheongsams, and one fat Chinese man in a silk *changshan* and matching brocaded waistcoat. The suited men and the women were mangled beyond recognition. Not since he had seen a body mauled by crocodiles had he witnessed such trauma to human tissue.

But crocodiles do not murder, they merely feed. Scattered across the floor of the room, half submerged in the pond of blood, were brass shells of the type usually found in fowling guns. Counting by eye, Rizby tallied up fifteen empty shells.

The two women were seated side-by-side on a purple velvet

love seat, the plush material now soaked crimson and flecked with pulped flesh. They appeared to have raised their arms to protect themselves. Now, one had no arm below the elbow, the other was missing half her head.

Of the three men in Western suits, two lay the floor on either side of the body of the sixth victim. Both had taken multiple shots to their thorax and abdomen; Rizby surmised that they dropped where they stood flanking the sixth man. A third suited man was half seated in a chair by a round rosewood side table; he had been knocked backward by a shot to the head that all but decapitated him. His knees had caught under the edge of the table, so that he appeared to be titling back casually in the chair, his face erased and skull staved in while he contemplated the ceiling. A revolver lay on the floor where he had dropped it.

The sixth victim, the fat man in a fancy *changshan*, lay in the middle of the room, his body folded back on itself, face down in the half-inch pool of blood. His corpse was not mutilated like the others and appeared untouched save for the little fierce face staring up at Rizby from the side of his neck, as though the man had grown a second head which faced backward. It was the red-faced, black bearded immortal Guan Yu, much worshipped by gangsters and bookies and other men of the night. Despite such veneration, someone had smashed the idol and stabbed a long jagged piece into the man's neck, burying Guan Yu to his ceramic chin.

A copy of the *Lat Pau* Chinese daily was crumpled in the hand of the dead man. Rizby squatted in the blood that was a deep as his heels and tugged the newspaper from the clenched fist, folding the sheets into his jacket pocket.

Only inches away, the face of Guan Yu stared disconcertingly at him like an infuriated gnome crawling out of the man's fat neck. Gingerly, in an effort not to contaminate the crime scene and to save himself from slipping into the blood, he rolled the heavy body over. Guan Yu's ceramic head rotated face down into the coagulating pool as the human head rolled into view. A film of sticky red fluid covered the corpse's face, which was frozen in a scream, the eyes and mouth wide open. Despite the discoloration and the contorted face muscles, Rizby recognized the familiar features of the dead man. It was Low Teck Beng.

He tugged at his earlobe thoughtfully, then pushed the corpse back the way it had been when he first walked into the room. The oleaginous purple fluid that now coated Guan Yu's immobile face began to drip as Rizby looked down at it, and he felt his stomach heave. Luckily he had not had time for breakfast so there was nothing to come up except acidic coffee and bile which he choked back down, a fist over his mouth.

Rizby glanced at his pocket watch. It was early morning, the first rays of light streaking the grey sky outside, the broiling heat of the day already rising. The story was that a uniformed foot patrol, two young Malays barely more than boys, had been hailed by the hotel manager who in stricken words said that an attack had taken place. One patrolman rushed upstairs, forced open the doors to the sitting room, which had been locked, and saw the brutal scene. He then vomited – it was now congealing by the doorway, not more than five feet from where the Detective Inspector stood. The patrolman next ran to the Central Station to summon help, leaving the other to guard the entrance to the suite. It was at least another hour before word got to Rizby and he was able to arrive at the hotel. During that time, the second patrolman assured him, no one else had entered the room.

His own preliminary survey complete, he motioned for Dr. Robert Cowpar to enter. It was the duty of the coroner, whenever practical, to visit a murder scene in person. The inquest report required his detailed observation of the scene. Often he interviewed witnesses and friends of the deceased, conducting his own investigation alongside the police. It was law in the colony that no one found dead in a brothel could be buried without the coroner's inquest report first being filed.

Once Cowpar had made his notes, three detectives from the Native Crimes Squad – Rizby's squad – entered the room to collect evidence. The bodies would be removed to the dead house, escorted by uniformed patrolmen. Then the nauseating business of cleaning up the putrefying pulp and fluid would fall on the hotel staff. And given Chinese superstition, it would be a long time before the room was used again – if ever.

As his men began combing through the room, Rizby headed down a creaking staircase to the narrow lobby to begin taking witness statements. The identity of the person who appeared to be the main target of the attack meant that this case would get priority. Usually the police would not bother to investigate the murder of a prostitute: they would let the coroner perform the investigation to complete the necessary paperwork then let the *kongsi* enact their own rough justice on the perpetrator. But cases involving Europeans or high-profile locals would mean that the police investigation superseded the coroner. Rizby wanted to get to the witnesses before Dr. Cowpar started asking questions, for the Detective Inspector knew that first statements were usually the most accurate, while any follow-ups were watered down or had become formulaic in the telling.

As most witnesses at the Hotel Formosa spoke only Chinese and he knew only a scatter-shot number of words, he had a translator in police pay, Heng Kee Yann, waiting for him in the lobby. The man was Hainanese, and it was known that he often passed police information to his own people, but

21

his fluency in dialects was unsurpassed, so his indiscretion was tolerated.

The witnesses, not surprisingly, were few and far between. Those he could muster were reluctant to the point of uselessness. No guests would consent to speak to the police. Their reticence was only to be expected – they had probably not been up to the most salubrious activities themselves, and given the violence of the murder, they did not want to open their big mouths. The only thing he could get from any of them was the time that they heard the shots, about four-thirty in the morning.

Other than the night manager, only two hotel staff, a maid and a bellboy, had been on duty. He spoke with the bellboy and the maid separately in the vacant lobby. Both were teenagers, *sinkehs* fresh from the Chinese mainland, and they were as scared of the Singapore police, especially a fox-faced, brown man such as Rizby, as much as by the violence they had witnessed.

The boy, who called himself simply Yu Sang, had bad acne and looked as though he weighed about fifty pounds. His voice was so soft at first that Rizby and Heng could not hear him. His voice quavering, he told them the attack happened at 4.36 am.

'How do you know the time?' Rizby inquired.

The boy froze up, fearful to answer. The translator spoke smoothly, soothing him. Apparently he had been sneaking a snack in the kitchen when he heard what he at first thought were fireworks, then quickly realized was gunfire. He had glanced at the kitchen clock before taking cover behind the icebox.

'Can you tell me how many shots you heard fired?'

The boy responded with a single syllable mumble that Heng translated as 'There were too many to count.'

'And how long did the attack last?'

Again the answer was a mumble. Heng said without inflection,

'He says it seemed to last a long time. In fact, the word he used means "forever".'

'He was obviously scarred out of his wits. When did he come out from the kitchen … did he notice the time?'

'He says he stayed there until the night manager discovered him and chased him out.'

'When was that?'

The boy mumbled again and Heng said with a touch of mirth, 'Thirty minutes ago.'

The maid, a Miss Ong, was more composed than the boy, though she too was shaken and fearful. She told them that the murdered group had checked in late, about two-thirty in the morning. They requested food and drink be sent to the room.

'What did they order?'

'Two bottles of Bisquit Dubouche Cognac and a platter of pastry and fruit.'

'How many people were in the party?'

'Two women and four men. They all arrived at the same time.'

'Did you notice anything strange about the group? Were they tense or nervous?'

No, she said, they were having a good time. She did notice that one of the women had a husky voice. At first she thought it was a man speaking, but when she saw how pretty the woman was, she knew it could not be.

'Where were you when the attack happened?'

'In the downstairs parlour, drinking tea with Mr. Loo, the night manager.' The girl looked demurely at the floor as she said this, and Rizby wondered if maybe the two had been doing more than sipping tea together. The girl was moon-faced and plain with heavy eyebrows and pale lips, but with the right cosmetics, he could imagine a type of symmetrical beauty emerging.

'Did you see the attackers?'

She nodded in the negative. She had stayed in the parlour when the night manager went into the lobby after they heard them arrive. After a few loud words were exchanged, she heard the group walk up the stairs.

'And then?'

She grew upset, patting her hair and fussing with the hem of her apron.

'It will be alright, Miss Ong, please continue.'

There had been a few loud shouts from the Plum Suite on the second floor, directly above the parlour. She heard what sounded like a fight – scuffling feet and loud thumps. At this point the night manager returned to the parlour and then the shooting started. Both of them took cover under the heavy rosewood table and waited until they heard the men leave before they emerged. It was the night manager who went upstairs to investigate.

'Did he say how many men went upstairs before the fight?'

'Three.'

'And how long were they in the room before the shooting started?'

'Perhaps two minutes, perhaps less.'

'Could you say how many shots you heard?'

Like the boy, she told them there were too many, too quick, to count.

'And how long did the shooting last, do you think?'

'About a minute,' she said flatly.

Rizby could not believe his ears. 'Are you certain it was such a short amount of time?'

She gazed at him as if wondering why he would doubt her, then nodded her head gravely. 'One minute.'

After she left, he said to Heng, 'It makes no sense. That amount of damage caused by only three men in less than a minute? No one can reload fowling guns that quickly.'

'Perhaps one had a revolver?' Heng suggested.

'Perhaps, but that would not account for the mutilation of the bodies and the large number of fowling shells.'

Rizby hoped the night manager could shed some light on the situation. Between the boy's 'forever' and the girl's 'one minute' there must be an accurate time frame.

Mr. Loo had bad halitosis that matched in smell the sallow colour of his skin. His hair was thinning, teeth crooked, and his Western suit jacket soiled, but he carried himself with an arrogance that all hotel managers learn to be a necessity of the job when speaking to recalcitrant staff, or nosy detectives. Loo also spoke English well enough to converse with Rizby – he told the detective that he had been in Singapore more than twenty years. He was Teochew, from the mainland and had been working for Mr. Foo ever since he arrived as a boy.

'Foo?'

'Foo Hee Keng. The owner of this hotel,' Loo glanced at the clock on the wall. The sunshine outside was already bright. 'He should be here soon, I think, if you would like to speak with him.'

'Foo is Teochew?' Rizby asked, knowing that the dead Low upstairs was a Teochew. The dialect groups tended to stick to their own kind.

'He was born in Singapore, but he is Teochew.' Loo groped for the right turn of phrase to explain complex origins, finally saying, 'Foo is Straits-born Teochew."

'Can you describe the attackers?'

Three Chinese men, twenty to thirty years old, Cantonese speakers, plain black *changshans*. They each carried a burlap bag.

'They asked for Low Teck Beng by name?

25

'Yes, they said they were friends delivering a favour for his party.'

'You let them upstairs?'

Loo shook his head negatively, 'Of course not. I asked them to wait in the lobby while I fetched Miss Ong to go upstairs to tell Mr. Low he had guests. I wanted to stay here to keep an eye on them.'

'But they did not wait,' Rizby said. It was not a question.

Loo simply stared at him before looking away. The first of the bodies was being carried on a stretcher down the stairs on its trip to the morgue. Though wrapped, the body was leaking bloody fluid on the polished marble floor, which he had just had scrubbed the previous day. Loo winced.

'What happened after they went upstairs?'

'I heard shouts, but could not understand the words clearly. There was the sound of a fight, something crashed on the floor, then the shooting started.'

'How many shots did you hear?'

'I cannot be sure, but more than a dozen.'

'And how long did the attack last?'

'The fight was about two minutes, the shooting about one.'

'One minute? Are you certain you heard more than a dozen shots in one minute?' Rizby could not keep the incredulousness from creeping into his voice.

'I am absolutely certain, Detective Inspector. I listened closely because the shooting was happening in the room right above me…and I was afraid for my life,' Loo said flatly.

Fingers tugging on his earlobe pensively, Rizby said he would return to speak with Mr. Foo. His top man, Detective Mohamad Anaiz Bin Abdul Majid, would stay at the hotel until he returned, he explained, and he asked Mr. Loo not to leave until that time.

He did not say that given the important stature of the dead man in Singapore's underworld he felt it necessary to get his Superintendent involved as quickly as possible. News of the murder would soon spread quickly among the Chinese and the police would need to take pre-emptive action to avoid a bloody war of retribution between the top *kongsi*.

Rizby rose to go, but then recalled the newspaper he had taken from the dead man's hand. He pulled the coarse pages of *Lau Pat* from his jacket pocket, saying to Loo, 'Forgive me, but I cannot read Chinese. Would you mind telling me the date of this newspaper?'

The manager reached for it but Rizby held on tightly. After squinting, Loo shrugged and read out the date: Monday 4th of February, 1895.

Rizby recognized the date of the ninth day of the lunar new year; yesterday's edition.

## CHAPTER II

# Two Become One

POLICE SUPERINTENDENT DAVID HAWKSWORTH stiffened as he felt the sharp edge of the blade against his neck. One wrong move and he would bleed out on the pavement, clutching his hand to his severed jugular vein while the warm blood spurted out and his brain starved and his heart thumped twice as hard as the pressure dropped. No doctor on earth could save him. One minute, perhaps, not more than two, and it would be done, his forty-odd years of life pooling on the street around his still twitching corpse.

Luckily, the white-haired barber Khoo Soo Tun did not slip and the razor scrapped harmlessly over Hawksworth's skin, taking with it merely whiskers. Not many Europeans, and fewer police, would dare to let a Chinese street barber put a straight razor to their neck but Hawksworth had been having his face shaved and hair cut by old Soo Tun for years. It was a point of pride with him, a public indication of his trust in the mutual respect between himself and the Chinese *kapitans*, the headmen of the criminal *kongsi*.

The barber's lean-to was set between two pillars of the five-foot way in front a chandlery on the ground floor of a shophouse on North Canal Road. A cheval mirror was set before a stool; another stool held a case containing the implements of the craft, the scissors and razor and strop and soap and brush and towels.

In one bucket was clean cold water; in another, dirty, soapy water. In the late afternoon, when the sunlight became oppressive, Khoo unfurled a black and white *chickchak* curtain across the space between the pillars, so named for the sound the bamboo slats made when being rolled. Khoo paid no rent, but he did pay tribute money to the Spring-Blossoms, the Hokkien gang that controlled the street, who in turn answered to the most powerful Hokkien *kongsi*, the *Ah Boo-Hway*, or the Mother-Flowers.

It was a hot morning, cloudless, the sky a brilliant cobalt blue. The heat seemed to magnify sounds and smells so without moving his head an inch, Hawksworth knew what was happening on the street. A hackney carriage passed within a foot of the barber's stall, kicking up dust, the horse whinnying as it clopped. A rickshaw driver cursed in Cantonese as he passed, the wheels of his chair rattling. A bullock cart lumbered by laden with green *kangkong*, water spinach, fragrant for being freshly cut.

In his lap now was yesterday's edition of the *The Mid-Day Herald* (published '2 pm daily,' it claimed). He was not reading it: Khoo merely placed it over the white apron to catch stray whiskers. The advertisement on page three caught his eye:

*Kupper's Beer*
*Chop 'Payong',*
*The only beer which received any award*
*at the Chicago Exhibition.*
*Huttenbach Brothers and Company*

The Huttenbach Brother's company was a recent arrival in Singapore, he knew. They were a German firm based in Penang. Kupper's was their latest imported product and they were trying to create a groundswell of interest, publishing the advertisement in every paper in the settlement. They even published ads in Malay, *Minum Kupper's Punya Beer*, Drink Kupper's Beer, with the same catchphrase, Chop 'Payong'. But for the life of him, Hawksworth could not puzzle out what Chop 'Payong' was supposed to mean. Chop could mean 'hurry' as in 'chop-chop', or it was the colloquialism for the type of rubber stamp, like a company seal, that businesses used on official documents. *Payong* was Malay for 'umbrella'. Yet there was no umbrella on the beer's label. How could one chop an umbrella? Such trivial puzzles irritated him to no end.

Without moving his head or neck, he flipped the newspaper over in his lap, reading down the end of his nose while Khoo made his final strokes with the razor.

> The S.S. Carmarthenshire, *which arrived here on Saturday morning with gunpowder, anchored outside the harbour limits off Pasir Panjang. After offloading the powder, she went alongside the Tanjong Pagar Wharf. This morning, two Kling coolies went into the afterhold to remove cargoes, but they both suddenly fell down and fainted, and, before assistance could reach them, died through suffocation.*

'Detective Inspector,' Hawksworth spoke loudly while facing forward, giving Khoo a sudden fright, 'Do you know if the deaths of the Kling coolies who perished suddenly at Tanjong Pagar yesterday were investigated by the coroner?'

Rizby was standing in the five-foot way behind Hawksworth, a bewildered look on his face. 'I saw you approaching in the cheval glass,' Hawksworth explained. Khoo pulled away the white apron with a snapping flourish and the Superintendent paid by dropping coins into the old man's hands.

'Ah, of course, the glass. The answer is yes, Dr. Cowpar has issued his report on the dead Klings, who it seems suffocated on residual fumes from the gunpowder.'

'Bad luck. Poor sods.' Hawksworth stood, steadying himself with his cane. The metatarsal bones of his right foot had been smashed in an accidental explosion at the police station several years before and had never been given a chance to heal properly. Now, his foot throbbed whenever the weather changed – which during the rainy season was every afternoon about four o'clock – and he had trouble balancing without support. Made of a single piece of Bornean iron wood, hand-carved by an Iban head hunter, with geometric patterns along the shaft with a hard round knot at the top, the cane was now Hawksworth's constant companion. In addition to providing support, it was also useful as a weapon: he had become adept at balancing on his left foot while swinging the cane as a cudgel.

They were about to cross the street in the direction of the Central Station when Rizby began to speak, forcing the tall Hawksworth to bend toward him to hear. 'There has been a massacre at the Hotel Formosa. Low Teck Beng is dead.'

Hawksworth paused a moment, then asked innocently, 'Is that the fat brother, the one in charge of the criminal activities? Or the skinny one who runs the legal operations? I can never remember which is which.'

'The fat one.'

The Superintendent sighed. The top clans had called a truce and been quiet for years, to the benefit of everyone. Each kept to its own enclave with the result that street level crime had decreased, small businesses flourished, and generally an air of peace and prosperity dominated. At least this was true in the administrative centre of Singapore – in many of the Malayan states the turf wars continued unabated. Now this murder risked total war in the colony, the jewel in the crown of the Straits Settlements. The new Governor had made it his sworn duty to sweep the secret societies out of Malaya once and for all, which meant, Hawksworth knew, that his job would be made that much more difficult by pressure from blockheaded bureaucratic officials who never set foot in the field but nonetheless issued policies and procedures to the police.

'You have visited the crime scene?' Hawksworth said, stepping back from the glare of the street.

'I have just come from it.'

'Tell me what you saw,' he said grimly, pulling Rizby with him further into the shadow of the five-foot way.

'Low Teck Beng was lying in the middle of the room, with the head of a shattered Guan Yu idol protruding from his neck. There did not seem to be any other injury to him. Three men who appeared to be bodyguards and two women, most likely prostitutes, were killed with shotguns.'

'Any indication of who died first? Low Teck Beng or the others?'

Rizby tugged at his earlobe, recalling the scene. 'It is difficult to say. The killings all happened in the same room, the outer parlour of the Plum Suite, at 4.30 in the morning. The ladybirds were both seated on couches and both had wounds that suggested they were trying to shield themselves. Two bodyguards would seem to have been standing when they were shot. The third was seated. Low Teck Beng appeared to have dropped where he was standing.'

'They were taken by surprise?'

'Doubtful. According to the manager, the killers – there were three – were allowed into the room. They knew that the party was in the hotel.'

'So they knew where to find their target and the target let them in. Most likely a traitor.' Hawksworth rapped his cane ruminatively against the pillar. Two chattering coolies squeezed past, their long queues swaying. 'A statue of Guan Yu, you said? One does not sneak up on someone with a broken ceramic statue with intent to kill. That is an act of passion. Yet assassins do not show up with fowling guns with the intent to merely startle their victims. Are you sure there was no one else present?'

'The manager and night maid said they heard shouting and fighting before the shooting began.'

'Someone was there to confront Low Teck Beng, then lost his temper and smashed the statue, plunged it into his neck, while the others fired on the bodyguards and ladybirds...'

'Or they shot the others first then stabbed the victim.'

'Perhaps they showed up without the intent to kill?'

'To judge by the way they...the sheer number of times they fired...the supposition is that they came intending to slaughter.'

'What do you mean?'

'There were fifteen empty shells in the room.'

Hawksworth paused for a moment, imagining the carnage. 'Good lord. You said that three killers entered the room?'

'That is what the manager indicated. Each had a burlap sack, which I assume held the shotguns. He also said that they spoke Cantonese. Another point, Superintendent: witnesses claim that the shooting occurred in less than one minute.'

'One minute? Incredible! Are you sure?'

'That is what they say.'

'How can three men fire fifteen shells from fowling guns in less than one minute?'

Rizby's response was merely to frown and shrug. Hawksworth tapped his cane twice more then spoke quickly, 'Return to the hotel and gather more evidence and assist the coroner if he is not through with his investigation. I will go to Panglima Prang and speak to the Lows directly to try and forestall what will surely be bloody retaliation.'

'Yes, sir.'

'As I see it, someone inside the Low organization must have helped to set up the killing. In fact, he may have been expecting their visit. We are to pursue the identities of the bodyguards and the ladybirds. One of them is the key.'

Hawksworth seemed about to launch himself into the street when Rizby restrained him with a quiet, 'Superintendent?'

'Yes?'

'Are you formally assigning the case to me, to the Native Crimes Squad?'

In the heat of the moment the tall man had forgotten that he was no longer a detective, but was indeed the superintendent of both the detective and native crimes branches. All plainclothes officers fell under his purview and he now spent most of his days seated safely behind a comfortable desk, shuffling papers and reading reports. This change in position suited him fine: since the birth of his daughter Fenella a year and a half before, he had become less keen to take risks. But the desk life was often stifling and he could not deny to himself that he was excited about taking on a new investigation.

He smiled at Rizby, a sparkle coming into his eye, then spoke with casual authority: 'Given the prominence of the victim, who we will assume was the target of assassination, I will personally oversee this case. You and your squad are to act directly under me for the duration. I am sure Inspector-General Fairer will agree...I will inform him when we are at tiffin today.'

Rizby smiled up at Hawksworth. It was the first time in nearly two years since they had worked together on a case, and it was also the first time in nearly that long he had seen his superintendent brimming with energy.

*   *   *

The rickshaw wallah wore a wide-brimmed hat that bounced up and down as he pumped his legs, panting in the heat. He wore no shirt and his dark skin was slick with sweat as he pulled Hawksworth up the hill along River Valley Road to Panglima Prang, the family seat of the Low dynasty. The Superintendent did not know what to expect when he arrived. He was sure the news of the death would have already reached the Low family through the Chinese gossip machine. For something like this to happen during the lunar new year festivities presented twice the calamity: there was the shock of the immediate loss, then fear of what the inauspicious event portended for the coming year.

Since he had last visited Panglima Prang two years prior, the Lows had embarked on a project, he knew, to control all the legal opium trade in southern Malaya. They had gained control of the opium and spirit farms – the licensed concession to sell British opium – for Johor and Malacca, and they had cut a deal with the Dutch to gain the farm in the Riau Islands, part of the Dutch East Indies, to the south of Singapore. However, the Cantonese Hai San *kongsi* still owned the opium farm license for Singapore itself, which is what the Lows now needed most. Singapore was the biggest market and the main transhipment point for the product – without that prized license, the other territories were little more than satellites. Of course all the *kongsi* were also involved in the illegal opium trade which, by all measures, was equal in total revenue to the legal trade, but if the Lows could gain control of the Singapore opium farm, not only would this give them a monopoly over the other *kongsi*, but it would also make black-market smuggling easier for them. They would dominate the opium trade across the South China Sea. Perhaps the massacre of Low Teck Beng was the first indication that the Hai San would not let go of the Singapore opium farm all that easily.

The rickshaw rolled to a halt outside the tall hedgerow that separated the Low property from the main road. Hawksworth paid the panting wallah then strode toward the front entrance, which was barred by a high metal gate set in concrete pillars with Chinese characters in bright red: he could not read them, but knew that they spelled out the Low family name. Two guards came to attention as he approached. Each wore only loose pale-blue cotton *changshans* and straw boater hats with black bands. One held a *parang* at his side – a short machete-like sword – the other, Hawksworth noted with alarm, held a large-bore revolver. The Lows were expecting bad company – the news of the son's death had definitely reached them.

The tall man did not break his stride, heading directly for the one with the pistol. The guard held up his palm to stop him, but he merely barked out, 'Superintendent Hawksworth, Straits Settlements Police. Open this gate.'

Neither guard moved, not from obduracy but confusion: neither spoke English. Hawksworth sighed as he pulled his leather wallet from his breast pocket, then flipped it open to show them the brass shield inside. The one with the *parang* nodded then spoke quickly to the other, who called to someone inside. Another guard appeared on the other side of the gate – he had been standing behind the concrete pillar – and swung the gate open.

Once through, he took in a view of havoc. Groups of Chinese of all ages, men and women and children, were roaming the grounds, many of them holding travelling valises; some of the women were wailing, some of the children were sobbing. He noted that the lawn that led to the edge of the hill, which usually provided a stunning view up the Singapore River, across the colonial and Chinese districts, to the ships bobbing in the maritime roads and Batam Island beyond, was now blocked by a portable wooden *wayang* stage. There were folding chairs stacked on the lawn and red lanterns strung above, useless in the daytime glare. They had been celebrating the new year, he realized, and now the celebrations were over with the death of the fat son. He took the milling bands of Chinese to be the extended family.

A thin Chinese man dressed in a Western suit, his hair cut and set in the Western style, approached from the house. Hawksworth recognized Low Teck Seng, the son who ran the legitimate trade of the *kongsi*, the mastermind behind what was already being called in the press and on the street the Low family's 'Grand Opium Syndicate.'

'Superintendent Hawksworth, thank you for coming,' the thin man said before Hawksworth could get a word out. 'It has been a most terrible day for us. The news of my brother's passing could not have come at a worse time.' He spoke perfect English with an Oxbridge accent that indicated years spent, at great expense, with a personal tutor.

'I see you were celebrating the new year…do you have many guests?'

'We do, family from as far away as Guangdong province. Now we must find accommodation for them all beyond the confines of the estate.'

Hawksworth was about to ask why that was necessary when

he surmised that it was because they were expecting another attack as brutal as the first – but to mention this fact directly may be interpreted as an insult since it was openly acknowledging the fact the Lows were involved with illegal trade. This fact was an open secret, but one that would have to be treated delicately in their own home, lest they lose face.

'I am sorry to hear of your loss. Would it be possible to speak inside? I have some information about the case that I think you would like to hear.'

Teck Seng nodded, looking grave, then led the way toward the main house. The building was famous for its combination of Eastern and Western architecture, combining a Grecian portico with a Chinese roof as though the Pantheon and a pagoda had been smashed together and the resulting jumble piled on a hill in Singapore. The interior, as he knew from previous visits, resembled a rummage sale of antiques and curios from across the Orient mingled higgledy-piggledy with Western furniture and fixtures.

Once inside, the thin Low excused himself to find his father. The normally quiet home was now filled with a tumult of Chinese families flinging themselves about, children scampering over Persian rugs, young men standing in corners speaking quietly, old women with their personal belongings tied in bundles collapsed on over-stuffed Western sofas, muttering to themselves. A servant appeared noiselessly by his side, motioning him toward a hallway off the main entrance. Hawksworth had been there before – it was a reception hall.

It was silent and calm inside the room, the chaos and noise of the outer rooms kept out. As during his previous visit, Hawksworth sat in a chair before a dais on which were three chairs where the father and brothers would receive visitors. The only words Low Teck Beng had ever spoken to Hawksworth were from that chair in that room two years before, and they came back to him vividly now, almost like the echo of a living presence, '*Wah! Maybe he bringing ice.*'

'Superintendent Hawksworth,' a low voice rumbled behind him and he rose to find the head of the family dynasty, Low Hun Chiu, addressing him from across the room. The old man was walking toward him, one hand outstretched in greeting, the thin son directly behind him. A third man, a thickset mass of muscle with a short queue, followed; he pulled the door shut then took up position at the back of the room. The Lows were not taking any chances today.

The tall man rose to greet the elder Low who shook his hand in the Western fashion, gripping his palm and pumping. Hawksworth could tell the patriarch had not had much practice at it. 'I am sorry to hear of your loss, Low Hun Chiu.'

'It has been a most upsetting morning, Superintendent. We thank you for coming,' the elder Low said in Teochew, the son translating smoothly.

They took their seats on the dais facing Hawksworth, the third chair empty where the dead brother usually sat. He noticed that the elder Low looked haggard, his eyes red-rimmed either from lack of sleep or weeping or both. The thin son had a rat-like face that even in these circumstances seemed to twitch as it sniffed the air. Despite everything, he appeared well rested; his eyes betrayed no sign of tears.

'I do not want to take too much of your time this morning,' Hawksworth spoke slowly for the translation, 'but I wanted to let you know that I am personally overseeing the investigation into the death of your son.'

Both faces remained impassive at the news – they had

expected no less.

Hawksworth continued, 'Your son was not alone when he...
took his leave. There were three bodyguards and two...ladies...
with him.'

'We know about the others and feel sorrow for their families.
For us Chinese, to suffer a loss at this time of year is especially
difficult.'

'Whoever...met...your son knew both where he was and
when to find him. We suspect that one of the bodyguards or
perhaps one of the ladies might have passed information.'

'Passed information to whom?' the father croaked out, eyes
narrowing. He could flick his wrist and have a dozen men killed.

'That is a question that we are working very hard to answer.
In the meantime, I would like to ask about the bodyguards. Had
they been with your son long? Were they trustworthy?'

'All three had been with us for many years, in fact two grew
up with my brother and myself and we considered them members
of the family.'

'And the third?'

The son shook his head, tugging at the French cuff of his
shirt, 'We do not suspect him – he was our nephew and had been
with my brother for a long time.'

Hawksworth was not even aware that there was a Low sister
who had married and given birth. But he also knew that Low could
mean any number of tangled relations. Given the complexity of
Chinese names for familial connections, they often reduced the
English translation to the simplest designation. 'Nephew' could
mean the son of an uncle's daughter's marriage as much as the
progeny of a sister's marriage.

'And the ... women? Were they his regular ... companions?'

The Chinese faces remained immobile, the hint of impropriety ineffective. 'We do not know who the girls were, but we are looking into it ourselves.'

'And hotel staff? My understanding is that the Formosa is owned by Teochews. Did your brother often visit there? Was he a regular customer?'

'It is indeed owned by Teochews and we do know the owner, who is an old family friend. My brother was known to use the hotel regularly for meetings and kept the Plum Suite for himself.'

'Did he tell you that he planned a meeting last night? Who would have known where to find him?'

This time the father answered, 'Last night we had the entire family together, as you can see, and paid an opera troupe to come all the way from Ipoh to perform....' he trailed off, restraining his emotions.

The son began to speak his own words, 'My brother did not tell us he planned to go to the Formosa last night. It appears to have been a spontaneous decision.'

'Who could have known his whereabouts? The hotel staff, his personal assistants, the girls....'

'To us it is immaterial who knew where he was. What we want to know is who murdered him!' the father suddenly thundered, half rising from his chair, before collecting himself and sitting again, the veins in his neck bulging.

'We understand that the killers spoke Cantonese,' the son said calmly.

How do they know the assailants spoke Cantonese? Hawksworth wondered to himself, never ceasing to be amazed at the intricacy and efficiency of the Chinese information networks. 'That is what the hotel manager claims,' he said firmly. 'Until we find who did this, it is only a claim, made by one witness, and uncorroborated.'

'We do not have to follow police regulations, Superintendent. Our people believe that it was the Hai San who are responsible for this outrage.'

It was the son who spoke but Hawksworth now addressed the father, 'Low Hun Chiu, I beg of you, do not take any retaliatory action until we can uncover the true culprits. I deeply appreciate your loss, but I assure you that going to war with the Hai San will simply lead to more killing and the disruption of business... for everyone.'

'You expect me to simply wait for the police to bring me my son's killers?' the father asked gruffly. 'Then what will you do, put them on trial? Parade this insult against my family through the public courts? That is not the proper way to handle this.'

'Low Hun Chiu, I urge you to consider this from the point of view of the colonial administration. If you go to war with the Hai San and cause further death and disruption, then when the opium farm license is next awarded, the Low *kongsi* will most surely not get it. The colonial administration will award it to the *kongsi* that is most steadfast and law-abiding.'

'The Hai San hold the current license....'

'And it will be taken from them as well if you decide to take the course of revenge. Then it will be awarded to another *kongsi* altogether, perhaps a Hokkien or Hakka *kongsi*, and all the effort of the Lows to build a grand opium syndicate will be lost.'

The father and son conversed rapidly in low tones, weighing what Hawksworth had said. Finally, the son addressed the Superintendent in measured tones. 'We thank you for this advice and will weigh it with great care.'

Cursing inwardly, Hawksworth remained stern in his speech, 'I will of course employ every means at my disposal to catch the killers as quickly as possible and bring them to justice.'

Cutting him short, the father said in a harsh voice, 'When will my son's body be returned to me?'

'Once the coroner's inquest has been completed and the public report accepted by the court, all the bodies may be returned to their families or surrendered for burial by the authorities.'

'And when will the inquest take place?' the son asked.

'As quickly as possible, most likely in two to three days, at most four,' Hawksworth said, the son translating. 'I assure you that that the body of your son is being cared for....'

The father now rose, followed quickly by Low Teck Seng. Passing by Hawksworth, he said simply 'Good day to you, Superintendent, your concern for my family is very much appreciated, as always,' before walking away. The son lingered for a moment longer, 'A servant will show you out, Superintendent, but please do not feel the need to hurry. I wish you best of luck with your investigation. Please find me in my office if you need to speak with me further.' The implication was that the Superintendent should not come back to Panglima Prang. Low Teck Seng looked past Hawksworth, staring expressionlessly into space for a moment, then scurried after his father. Hawksworth was alone in the quiet room.

Now that Low Teck Beng was dead, the thin brother would run the entire organization, both criminal and non-criminal. Power was now consolidated inside the Low organization itself, and for a fleeting moment he wondered if the thin brother had ordered the execution of the fat one. It was an intriguing possibility, but his best lead, he recognized, was still the dead prostitutes. The ladybirds would mean a mamasan would have to be found, and then an entire procurement network from rickshaw boys to deliverymen. Someone within that network had to know where Low Teck Beng had been last night and they knew who had been sent to kill him – if he could find that person, he could find out who ordered the execution. To do so, Hawksworth knew that he would have to delve deep into the world of the brothels to uncover which network Low had been using. It was not a task he was looking forward to.

The servant entered the room to escort him out. As he turned to go he noticed the family altar in the foyer. He recognized the three gods Fu, Lu, and Shou, the gods of Wealth, Prosperity, and Longevity, arranged in a row, as they were in every Chinese home. He saw a red-faced Guan Yu, who only hours before had been used to kill Low Teck Beng. There was a Goddess of Mercy, Guanyin, her face wearing the beneficent smile of a Bodhisattva. There were more he was not familiar with, though he had seen them countless times on countless altars. The Chinese pantheon was large and although he knew the stories of many of the immortals placing names to figures was not always easy.

The servant was motioning for him to go when he noticed, tucked away in a corner, a type of statue he had never seen before. The head was made of clay, but the body was constructed entirely of gold coins. String had been run through small holes bored in the centre, so that the body of the idol appeared like a coat of chainmail hung on a wooden frame. It was not more than a foot tall and most of the coins appeared tarnished with age, though one or two appeared to have been added to the body fairly recently. There was one so new that it was gleaming.

He felt the weight of the gold half-sovereign coin in his own pocket and his fingers instinctively went to it, tracing the edge. It had been forcibly placed in his hand during a case and at the time he assumed it was part of that investigation, for he had been jumped and beaten by the same men who pressed the coin into his palm. Later he had been told of an old superstition of the Straits, that a gold coin or other valuable object could be used as an evil eye to keep watch on an unsuspecting victim. Hawksworth had dismissed such stories as nonsense and kept the coin as a souvenir of a successful investigation, a good luck charm.

Staring now that the empty clay eyes of the little idol made of coins, he was not so sure the luck his half-sovereign would bring would be good.

## CHAPTER III

# Scissors, Paper, Stone

As with most of the secret society *kongsi*, the Hokkien Mother-Flowers had responded to government crackdowns by splitting their legal and illegal activities and fragmenting their clan into smaller semi-autonomous gangs. Thus the Mother-Flowers were both officially registered as a 'friendly society' with the government bureaucracy, meaning that they were a benevolent group, while simultaneously being feared and respected on the streets as the most powerful Hokkien clan.

While the Hai San and Lows fought over the control of the opium farms and plotted to open banks, the Mother-Flowers had headquartered their vice trade in the town of Johor Bahru, the nearest settlement across the narrow straits in the independent Sultanate of Johor on the mainland peninsula, beyond the reach of the Straits police. It was in Johor that the *kapitan* of the Mother-Flowers, Chong Yong Chern, spent most of his time overseeing the most lucrative vice the *kongsi* operated: the black market lottery. The official Straits Settlement Annual Report for the previous year estimated that the lottery netted the *kongsi* nearly one hundred thousand dollars per month. The money bought the Mother-Flowers power and prestige that no other Straits-formed *kongsi* could reach. Only the much older Low and Hai San clans were stronger.

That afternoon Hawksworth was looking for the second-in-command of the Mother-Flowers, Tan Yong Seng. The two men had known each other for years and had developed a friendship that even the great difference in cultures and professions could not breach. In fact, as often as not, the two sides assisted each other in practical matters like trading information and, occasionally, more material means. Over the years, Hawksworth had found the clandestine support of the Mother-Flowers to be invaluable in his investigations; that he occasionally had to bend the rules to assist them in return was merely the cost of realpolitik.

Tan Yong Seng would know where a man like Low Teck Beng would get his prostitutes. But finding Yong Seng was proving to be difficult, for he was not in the usual places. The fancy house on Neil Road that the big boss Yong Chern had bought for his beautiful yet vicious young sweetheart Shu En several years prior was now an upscale brothel and gambling den. Shu En and her entourage had moved near the coast to a commodious new bungalow house in Katong, a suburb where respectable Peranakan families were now building homes. A decade before the entire area had been rural, ramshackle kampongs and fishing villages along a scrubby strip of land between the sea and the far edge of a palm plantation which stretched into Geylang, where Hawksworth lived. Not far away was Fort Tanjong Katong, where 8-inch Armstrong guns pointed out at the ships bobbing at anchor in the maritime roads. It was said that the presence of the fort made the Peranakans feel more secure, which is why they chose Katong when they left the city centre to move into more spacious surroundings.

Hawksworth hoped that he did not have to travel that distance to find Yong Seng. After asking at one of the godowns the Mother-Flowers operated as part of their legal trade, he was able to trace the elusive man to one of the Japanese brothels on

Malay Street. Unlike the Chinese *ah ku* prostitutes who tended to serve only other Chinese, the Japanese prostitutes, the *karayuki-san*, would take allcomers, regardless of race. Why Yong Seng should choose a Japanese brothel over one of the houses run by his own *kongsi* was anyone's guess, but Hawksworth was sure he would soon find out.

The brothel he was looking for was housed in a plain two-storey shophouse. He vaguely recalled that only a year or two previously it had been a dry goods shop. Now the whole street was overrun with bordellos, nearly every shophouse converted to the purpose. There was even one that boasted European women, mostly from Russia but also from Turkey and the Caucasus. Unfortunately for the Superintendent, all these houses looked the same from the outside and despite the wilting heat, he had to walk the entire street looking for the one the boy at the godown had mentioned.

It was nearly noon by the time he found the correct one. In the front parlour a group of drunken British sailors were singing a beer hall song, accompanied by one of their mates banging on an out-of-tune upright piano.

> *Oh! Cunt is a kingdom, and prick is its lord;*
> *A whore is a slave, and her mistress a bawd;*
> *Her quim is her freehold, which brings in her rent;*
> *Where you pay when you enter,*
> *and leave when you are spent.*

He showed his shield to the servant who came to offer him a drink. The mamasan was swiftly summoned, complaining before he could open his mouth that she had already paid the police this month and she was not due to be raided for another two weeks, and why was he here, could they not leave a poor struggling businesswoman in peace for a while?

Assuaging her, Hawksworth explained that he was merely there to find Tan Yong Seng and no arrests would be made. Yes, he would like a drink, a *stengah* of whisky and soda water. Compliments of the house for our friends in the police, of course, he was assured.

A smooth-skinned Chinese servant, a buck-toothed boy in a blue smock with a luxurious dark queue, led him upstairs to the second floor room overlooking the street. The boy rapped gently on the wooden door.

'Go away! We are busy!' came the gruff reply, shouted in Hokkien.

Hawksworth stepped forward and pounded on the door with his fist while shouting, 'Tan Yong Seng, this is the police. You are to open this door at once!'

The door opened slightly and Yong Seng's face peaked out. He was obviously drunk, his eyes blazing red, his face a deep shade of puce. But what was most remarkable were the peanut shells dangling from the tip of his nose and earlobes.

'Ah fuck you!' he yelled in English, a new phrase he had learned from American sailors, then focused on Hawksworth's face and broke into a wide smile. 'Oh, Superintendent Hawksworth, my old friend! I am so happy to see you! Please do come in!' he shouted with joy, throwing the door wide. He wore only a dark blue silk kimono. It hung loosely, revealing his nude body beneath. The clam-shaped pincer of an empty peanut shell was clipped to one nipple and, Hawksworth noticed with a quick glance, at least one more was attached to his testicles.

On the bed behind him were two Japanese girls in their early twenties, one plump, the other thin, also nude with peanut shells clamped to erogenous body parts. As Hawksworth entered, they made desultory efforts to wrap themselves in their kimonos, though both remained recumbent and exposed. The pungent smell of rice wine mixed with sweat and other body odours hung heavily in the room.

Yong Seng sat on the edge of the bed while Hawksworth took an armchair beside it, his cane propped within easy reach. They spoke in the lingua franca of the Straits-born, a mish-mash of Malay and English with the odd Cantonese or Hokkien or Tamil phrase tossed in.

Pulling his short kimono tight around his nakedness, Yong Seng eyed his friend and spoke in a serious tone. 'Since the birth of your daughter and your promotion, I have hardly seen you, though I hear that you are doing well, which makes me happy,' he wagged his finger at Hawksworth. 'You look prosperous,' he added. Hawksworth knew that the compliment meant he was growing chubby.

Hawksworth leaned forward and pinched the peanut shell hanging from his friend's nose. 'What on earth are you doing here?'

Grinning, Yong Seng plucked the shell away but left the two dangling from his ears. 'Having a good time during the new year celebrations! We are playing *suit*,' he used the Malay word.

'*Suit*?'

Thick fingers went through gestures to illustrate the conflicting elements.

'Ah. Scissors, paper, stone.'

'The Japanese girls call it *janken*. The winner of each turn gets to place a peanut on the bodies of the losers...anywhere they like,' he added mischievously, raising his eyebrows.

'I see you have developed a taste for Japanese,' Hawksworth

said, eyeing the rumpled bed and dishevelled women. To judge by their reactions, neither could comprehend a word of English.

'I like *variety*, my friend,' he said, using the English word. 'Not all women are the same. The master *zegen* of this bordello is from Kyoto and he tells me that the Japanese distinguish between three prized types: there is the *kinchakubobo*, "the purse," which is tight,' as he spoke he grasped his middle finger with his fist to demonstrate the action, 'and there is the *todatebobo*, or "trapdoor," which grips.'

'I see.'

'But the most precious, the one that offers the most pleasure, is the *takobobo*, "the octopus," which sucks. Very rare, indeed,' he spoke in the knowing accent of a connoisseur.

'You forgot one.'

Yong Seng looked at him quizzically, 'Which?'

'The one that bites.'

Both men stared at each other for a moment then burst out laughing. 'It is good to see you again Yong Seng,' Hawksworth said before turning sombre. 'You have heard the news of Low Teck Beng?'

'I have. It is not a great loss. He was a mean and vindictive man.'

'Do you have any idea who killed him?'

Yong Seng shook his head, causing the peanut shells to quiver. 'No, but he had no shortage of enemies.'

'This is not some street level thug who was killed, it was the headman of the Low *kongsi*. Whoever killed him knew they would be starting a war.'

'We heard that the killers were Cantonese. Ask the Hai San,' Yong Seng said defensively, looking cross.

'I intend to,' Hawksworth spoke archly, then softened. He

had not come to start an argument.

The two Japanese girls were visibly bored, frowning at the conversation they could not follow.

'But first, let me ask what you know about the Lows,' he continued, 'They had a large gathering the night Teck Beng was murdered. There were many out of town visitors, but the Singapore family merely said they were here for the holiday.'

Yong Seng scratched behind his ear, giving a longing glance at the plump girl to his left. 'We too heard about this gathering of Teochews. Our information is that they want to open a bank.'

'A *bank*?' Hawksworth sounded sceptical.

Yong Seng shrugged the Chinese shrug that denoted accurate information yet total indifference. 'Perhaps Teck Beng was killed because he did not want to open an account,' he added sarcastically.

Hawksworth spoke sharply, 'Five people were murdered with him, three bodyguards and two prostitutes.'

'They should have been more careful of the company they kept.'

Hawksworth looked at the two Japanese girls in the bed. The thin one was studying her cuticles, her high breasts pointing toward the ceiling, peanut shells clamped to her dark nipples; the other was staring absently at the wall, scratching her vagina beneath the kimono. 'The girls were innocent. They only died because they were witnesses.'

'Are you certain that they were girls? The rumour is that Low Teck Beng liked *ah kuahs*.'

Hawksworth pursed his lips at the unfamiliar expression. 'Meaning?'

Yong Seng thought for a moment, stroking his chin while formulating his response. He finally decided on a literal translation,

'Boy becomes girl.'

'What! You mean the ladybirds with him....'

'Maybe the birds were not ladies.'

Whistling low, he said, 'Female impersonators? That does put a different complexion on the matter. Not many brothels would be able to supply such a specialty item for a high society client and keep it secret.'

'It was not much of a secret,' Yong Seng said dryly, 'But I will ask around for you, although now that he is dead I do not understand why you care to know.'

'It is my job to know.'

Replacing the peanut shell on the tip of his nose, Yong Seng looked Hawksworth in the eye and said with sincere exasperation, 'Now, will you join me for a drink? I have not seen you in such a very long time. We can have a girl sent up for you, play more *janken*, and have a good time.... If you are lucky, she will possess a rare *takobobo* for your delectation. You never know until you try. What do you say?'

Hearing Japanese words, the girls sat up, looking lively. The slender one's face was nicely proportioned yet marred by acne.

'I will join you for a drink and a quick game, but then I must go. I have much more work to do today.'

Smiling, Yong Seng rang the bell for the servant to enter the room with whiskey and more wine.

'And Yong Seng...,' Hawksworth added.

'Yes?'

'No peanuts for me, thank you.'

\* \* \*

His head buzzing slightly like a bee in a jar, Hawksworth made his way to his next stop, the Beach Road Police Station. He wanted to telephone the coroner to confirm that the ladybirds found with Low Teck Beng really were female impersonators.

The desk officer led him to the back of the storefront station house to the telephone room, where the phone box was mounted on the wall, the speaking trumpet protruding forward, the listening bell connected by a short cable. The desk officer smiled as Hawksworth assumed the uncomfortable position – the box was mounted for users considerably shorter than himself – and began to crank the handle.

The commercial network was operated by the Oriental Telephone and Electric Company, which also provided apparatus for electricity in homes, but the equipment and installation was very expensive, and only a few could afford the modern wonder and worse, rumours of people being electrocuted were still rife. However, any business operation or private person who fancied themselves to be part of the elite of the settlement was on the OTEC exchange.

Despite the rapid modernization of the settlement's telephone network, rural police stations beyond the central district, in places like Bukit Timah and Bedok, were still not connected by exchange to the Central Station, and runners were still dispatched with messages. To make matters more complicated, the colonial administration ran their own exchange separate from the municipal exchange that the police used. For Hawksworth to call outside his exchange network required calling the switchboard of the municipal exchange, which would connect him to the colonial administration exchange, which would in theory at least connect him to the Office of the Coroner. Often the connection system failed and it was simply more reliable to travel for face-to-face conversation, but today he was in a hurry. If Yong Seng was correct, he wanted to forestall the information about the *ah kuahs* becoming public.

The listening bell suddenly cackled, and the disembodied voice of the switchboard operator located several miles away in the telephone building in Tanjong Pagar was suddenly in his ear.

'Municipal exchange. With whom may I connect you?'

The voice sounded female but the noise on the line, and the compression of the sound, made it difficult for him to be sure.

'Coroner, number 24,' he said, feeling decidedly uncomfortable. Who was he talking to? Did they know who he was? Could they listen to the conversation?

'Please wait while I connect you,' the tinny voice came back.

Static was in his ear, then a series of clicks as the operator switched him to the colonial administration exchange, then another disembodied voice, this one more tinny and distant than the last, was speaking into his ear.

'Office of the Coroner.'

'This is Police Superintendent Hawksworth, telephoning from Beach Road Station,' he spoke definitely to mask his uncertainty. Did it matter where he was calling from?

There was a pause, then the voice said, 'How may I help you?'

Now it was Hawksworth's turn to pause: was it not clear that he wished to speak to the coroner? Why else would he telephone? 'I would like to speak to Dr. Cowpar, please,' he said, but a burst of noise, like gulls shrieking, smothered his voice.

'I am sorry, there was interference on the line. Did you say that you wished to speak to Dr. Cowpar?' the voice asked once the flocking noise had passed.

Interference on the line? 'Bloody nuisance! Bloody telephone!' he muttered to himself. Restraining himself from speaking too quickly out of anger – for then he would only have to repeat himself again – Hawksworth slowly recited his request.

There was further delay and silence, then into his ear came the familiar sound of Dr. Cowpar's voice, or rather, a very poor reconstruction of the doctor's voice. Nonetheless, it was a close enough impression that Hawksworth could recognize the speaker merely by the sound. The uncanny technology made him shudder.

'Superintendent Hawksworth, how may I assist you?' Cowpar asked, his electronic voice devoid of emotion.

'Have you performed the autopsy on the bodies from the Hotel Formosa shooting?'

'I have. Is this now your case, Superintendent?'

'I am taking it on personally. Detective Inspector Rizby has briefed me and will continue to assist.'

'Then I have a surprise for you.'

'The murdered ladybirds are really boys.'

Cowpar paused, his heavy breathing audible on the crackling line. 'How did you know?'

'A Chinese source told me,' Hawksworth spoke quickly. 'Dr. Cowpar, do not mention the gender of the victims to anyone until I can make sense of all this. Given the prominence of one of the victims, we must proceed with delicacy. I would like to view the bodies and hear your conclusions as soon as possible.'

'I will be ready tomorrow morning,' Cowpar said, then the line went dead in Hawksworth's ear.

\* \* \*

The office of the Low Import and Export Company was located not in the Chinese Quarter but further east, on Waterloo Street, nestled amongst the gingerbread facades of the offices of European companies. This was intentional: it announced to the Europeans as well as the other Chinese that the Low company was serious competition for the international trading companies that had branch offices in Singapore. It was only a short walk from the police station in Beach Road, and Hawksworth knew that despite the recent demise of his brother, Low Teck Seng would be found sitting in his office: the machinations of the family empire could not come to a halt, no matter who died.

The lower office was typical of the open space clerical rooms of the settlement. The wooden floor was divided by partitions that set one department from another; a *punkah* swished quietly above, the puller hidden unobtrusively behind a potted palm plant. There were no human voices, only the metal bang of typewriter keys sounded in counterpoint to the pizzicato clack of wooden abacus beads. The Chinese clerks, he noticed, were all dressed in Western clothes, sweating in shirts and pants; some even wore jackets. All had their hair cut in the Western fashion, parted down the middle, the back shaved close. There was not a queue to be seen, not even on the serving boys, all of whom wore short breeches, their thin knobby knees jutting out. One of these approached him and asked in near-fluent English how he could be of help.

The boy led him up a flight of stairs that ran along the wall to the upper floor, where the offices of the managers were located. The furthest door was closed; the boy knocked gently then called out in Teochew. There was a pause before the door opened, Low Teck Seng himself holding the knob.

'Superintendent Hawksworth, I was not expecting to see you again so soon. Please, come in. You are fortunate to find me here. I was about to leave early. Our operations are slow due to the new year celebrations and we have a reduced staff.'

Low's office was small and spartan, a workingman's office, not a showroom for power (they have Panglima Prang for that, he thought). A large work desk of plain design dominated the room, stacked with paperwork, nubs of pens and piles of sharpened pencils strewn in the sort of way that appeared random and untidy to outsiders but evidenced a thorough working method. The only decoration was a hand-painted banner of Chinese characters pasted to the wall behind the desk: no doubt a benediction.

One indication of the wealth and status of the Low family, Hawksworth noted, was that the room had been wired for electricity. There was a tabletop fan with brass blades (no *punkah* and puller in here) and an electric lamp with a carbon-filament bulb, not in use now as the afternoon sunlight streaming through the open window provided enough light to the desk. There was also a telephone; not the bulky contraption fixed to a wall that the police used, but an elegant desktop unit no bigger than a breadbox. The receiver sat neatly in a cradle, the crank-handle beside it small and unobtrusive. Noting that Hawksworth was studying the device, Low Teck Seng said, 'This is a Rikstelefon, a new model from Sweden. Incredibly useful when I need to ring our manager at the godowns.'

'Impressive piece of equipment. It looks expensive.'

'It is,' Low said with a wave of his hand. 'Please do take a seat, Superintendent,' he pointed to a wooden chair. The bright light from the window cast half the room in shadow so that Low Teck Seng's face appeared painted in two tones, like an opera mask. 'Do you have news from your investigation?'

'I do. Were you aware that your brother was with two *ah kuahs* when he was killed?' Hawksworth asked without inflection.

Although Teck Seng tried to show no emotion, Hawksworth could see the muscles in his face go momentarily slack. The information was unwelcome, but not a surprise. The lidded eyes remained impassive, however, waiting to hear more.

'Needless to say, this is not information that your family would like to be made public. There were rumours of your brother's... proclivities...and if this information were to be placed in the official inquest report, then the rumours would be confirmed. A significant loss of face for your operations.'

Low cleared his throat, gurgling his phlegm in such a way as to indicate that what he was about to say would be both precise and indelible, as though he were issuing an edict. 'If my brother was indeed a party to such...unnatural...activities, then the Low family would be forever in your gratitude for helping us to keep such information private.'

'I will do all within my power to keep this unfortunate news, if true, from the public. What I ask in return is that the Low family does not seek any retribution or revenge on the killers, once their identity comes to light. I ask that you let Straits Settlement justice take its course. I remind you that in addition to your brother, the killers are also guilty of the murder of five others. They will surely hang.'

Teck Seng considered this proposal by placing the tips of his fingers together to form a pyramid, which he then pressed against his lips, his coal dark eyes studying Hawksworth's face.

'And if you cannot keep the information from becoming public?'

A peregrine falcon landed nosily on the window ledge, its dark face appearing like a mask as it flapped its wings, adjusting its perch.

In the room neither man moved. Hawksworth spoke into the quiet: 'With your brother's demise, the Low family enterprises will shift to your control. By attacking the Hai San, you would also conveniently remove one of your greatest competitors and the only obstacle between you and the Singapore opium farm license.

Once your father passes, you would then be the uncontested master of the Low dynasty.'

The face half-hidden in shadow did not so much as twitch at the accusation.

'If you do not attack the Hai San but instead allow justice to take its course, your own interests will not be implicated in the murder of your own brother and the police would have no reason to dig deeply into the Low family operations. Bear this in mind.'

Teck Seng remained quiet, though the muscles in his face had drawn tight, making him appear as though he were straining to keep his seat.

'Tomorrow I will visit the dead house and convince the coroner to keep quiet about the presence of the *ah kuahs*. The inquest should be complete in less than a week. If you are already planning retributive action, I would caution you against moving forward until the public inquest is finished.'

The peregrine on the window sill took wing, disappearing in a blur. Teck Seng finally spoke in a low voice, 'Thank you for coming here today to keep me apprised of the investigation into my brother's murder. We will wait anxiously to hear the coroner's report at the inquest, and look forward to having the body of our beloved sibling returned as quickly as possible.' He added in a tone that cut through the room like cold steel, 'We trust that the police force will find the killers and bring them to justice.' Then his face buttoned tight. The conversation was over.

Hawksworth rose to leave, bidding the man goodbye and not expecting, nor receiving, a reply. As he shut the office door behind him, he heard the receiver of the telephone being lifted, the handle of the phone furiously cranked. Low Teck Seng was making a call, no doubt to freeze the murder squad he had prowling the streets.

\* \* \*

Hawksworth stepped into his home in Geylang to find the place filled with the fragrant aromas of Siamese cooking. The pungent snap of lemongrass and ginger was cut through by the sharp scent of chili padi. Along with the smells came strains of Siamese music from the kitchen, feminine voices singing out in a rapid call and response as they fussed over the food and the toddler who stood mutely in one corner, he knew without seeing, watching her mother and aunt as they finished preparing dinner.

Since the birth of Fenella, the bungalow house had become a microcosm of Siam, set in a palm planation a brief ride from the Singapore Straits. When Ni was pregnant, she sent for her younger sister Premrudee to come from their home in Bangkok to assist the local midwife. The older woman who would bring Hawksworth's daughter into the world had been delivering babies in kampongs in Singapore for decades, but she was a Malay and though Ni trusted her, she wanted another Siamese in the house when the baby came. So with some trouble and expense in contacting her and sending the money for the steamship passage, her unmarried sibling sailed to meet the sister she had not seen in nearly ten years and this man with whom she lived, this *farang*, this white man, about whom she wrote in her frequent letters. Premrudee was still with them.

She was as bony and raw as Ni had been when Hawksworth had first found her working as a washerwoman in a brothel the police raided. Now Fon, as she was called, for Premrudee was her birth name and like most Siamese she was known to familiars by her nickname, was putting on weight just as Ni had done when she first came to the house. Hawksworth viewed this inflation of the women – *his* women, as he could not help thinking of them – with a sense of pride. It showed he was a good provider and solid protector of the home.

The outcome of Fon's long stay was that the two sisters not only had the toddler to fuss over but had rapidly turned what had been a somewhat stolid house into a vibrant Siamese home which seemed to the middle-aged man to be constantly filled with sound and colour and smells: how was it possible that two women and a toddler could expend so much energy? He had, without intention or plan, found himself the patriarch of a family and small patch of land. They even had chickens pecking in the garden.

Sometimes he felt like a stranger in his own house, surrounded by women clucking and clacking in a rapid-fire language he could barely comprehend, fussing over the little girl in what sometimes appeared to be a tug-of-war. There was constant motion, planting, pruning, cutting, chopping, boiling, washing, sweeping, cleaning, mending, knitting, ironing. The only time the house became quiet was at night, after the women retired to the bedroom. He had ceded the space during Ni's postpartum *ya fui*, the twenty-five days of confinement in which she was kept warm by means of excessive blankets and fed 'hot foods' such as ginger and spices to make her sweat. He was not to touch her during this time as she was sweating out the fluids of her pregnancy, which could be toxic to a man.

Once the confinement was complete, the three females simply stayed in the bedroom, leaving Hawksworth on an old army cot in the front room. It was comfortable enough: a *charpoy*, a sturdy wooden frame within which was slung a string mattress that hung like a hammock. Along with the father of her child, Ni had banished to the front room the old .577 Snider-Enfield rifle he had kept propped in a corner of the bedroom: there would be no weapons where the baby slept. The big gun, with several boxes of old cartridges of varying degrees of reliability, now rested beneath the *charpoy*, which stood beneath a mosquito net nailed to the ceiling. Thus Hawksworth's sleeping arrangements resembled a camp, albeit set up in the safety of his own home. He had yet to complain about this arrangement, enjoying the quiet and small circle of light from the paraffin lamp as he sipped his nightly arrack, but soon, he decided, the situation would need to change: Fon could sleep with Fenella in the front room and he would sleep in the bedroom with his common-law wife, which was how it should be.

When she first came, Fon had brought with her lotus buds that had been chanted over by a monk in the temple of Phu Khao Thong, the holy Golden Mount of Wat Saket in Bangkok, which housed a relic of the Buddha himself. Consuming them was believed to help ease the pain of birth by ensuring that the mother would open like a lotus flower. As it happened, Fenella's birth had been easy compared to most, the child emerging after a short labour of four hours. They had kept him out of the room during the event, but he stood at the door, hearing Ni yelling in pain – they finally had put a rope in her mouth for her to bite – as Fenella fought her way into the world. He could hear the Malay midwife calling out instructions and was able to follow the events as they unfolded in the closed room. He had seen the statistics on the appalling death rate of mothers in rural births and had fretted from the moment the water broke. She shrieked like pale death when the baby's head crowned, and he nearly burst into the room, restraining himself only when he heard the midwife clap in encouragement – it would all be over soon.

When they finally let him in, he found the midwife tidying up the bloody mess – the birth sheets would be burned and the placenta cut up and buried where animals could not dig it up – while Fon mopped Ni's brow, Fenella nestled on her mother's chest, her tiny fingers grasping her mother's hair, clinging to life in this new world.

She quickly grew into a little beauty, with her father's aquiline nose sitting prominently on the valentine face of her mother. Her skin was like milky tea; she had lanceolate eyes the colour of amber glowing in sunlight. Her hair was dark like Ni's, already growing abundantly, sticking out from her head in an unruly thicket. To confuse any evil spirits who may have been attracted to the beauty of the vulnerable child, they called her Pu, or 'crab', which for the rest of her life would be the nickname by which her family would know her. After three months, during which the baby had no illness or other mishaps, they named her Fenella. Hawksworth had insisted on the Anglo name; he had come across it during a previous investigation and it had struck a cord with him. After she was christened, Fon fixed a thin gold chain, blessed like the lotus buds by the monk at Wat Saket, around her ankle: it was a talisman to protect the girl as she started her journey through life.

A quiet baby then a calm toddler, Ni was convinced that her child's soul was an old one, reincarnated into her daughter, perhaps for its final trip around the wheel of suffering. Dawdling the girl on her knee, she would stare into the amber eyes as though into deep pools, sensing the older presence behind the placid gaze. The child moved with an intensity that seemed quite deliberate, like an adult learning a new, difficult skill. Yet she was a child in body and faced the difficulties of all children, the fears and accidents through which one learned to navigate the world. She scalded herself on the cast iron stove stoked hot for Hawksworth's morning coffee, howling in pain, her face scrunching into a ball of wrinkles as the tears poured down her face, her mother scolding her as she wiped them away.

Hawksworth was there when she experienced her early moments of joy, too. He watched her encounter with a rabbit

Ni had brought from the village market. Fenella had stood back fearfully, staring at the critter pulsing in the grass. Coaxed by Hawksworth, she finally stroked the fur, running her pudgy fingers through the soft warmth, staring up at him in wonder and awe. She put her finger on the creature's twitching nose, causing it to hop away – he remembered her chasing after it, hands held out before her, wanting to stroke the fur again, learning now that pleasure could be as fleeting as pain.

And he was with her when she first learned fear. The towering banyan on the edge of the garden must have seemed an entire world to her small perspective, the dark folds and recesses of the dense roots the lurking place of untold things, centipedes and beetles, and perhaps something more. She kept her distance from the tree and burst into red-faced crying fits the few times Hawksworth had tried to carry her to it, perched high on his shoulders, the tips of the air roots brushing her face as if the tree were trying to snatch her.

Home now in the swirling aromas of cooking, Hawksworth dropped his bag, unbuckled his belt where the truncheon was snug in its ring, and sat to unlace his boots. Hearing the sound of her father's arrival, Fenella bounded in from the kitchen, tripping toward him until he plucked her up and held her close to his face so she could kiss his cheek. He tried to place her down but she clung tightly – as her mother had done all those years before when he had first found her – and it was not until Fon came in to take her away that she let go of his neck.

Ni had the steaming serving bowl on the table, a plate before each chair, Fenella's chair boosted by a box on the floor. Fon served the food into each bowl, Ni uttered a quick blessing in Siamese, head bowed. Then they ate noisily, the sisters chatting, Fenella calmly watching the adults' actions, Hawksworth stroking her tangled hair.

It was a night like any other in his bungalow in Geylang, a lip-smacking meal, a postprandial nap, one last kiss from his daughter and his wife before they retired. He himself was unaware that on nights like this one, he smiled while he slept.

CHAPTER IV

# The Chinese Protectorate

HE STOPPED IN HIS OFFICE at the station to tend to morning paperwork, leafing through correspondence while sipping his second *kopi-o kosong*, black coffee no sugar, of the day. That done, he hailed a passing rickshaw to ride the short distance past Pearl's Hill to the dead house at Sepoy Lines.

The Coroner seemed to grow portlier every year. His live-in Chinese *amah*, whom everyone knew to be his common-law wife, was herself a lady of stout proportions and also, it was assumed, a tremendous cook, for year on year, the good doctor, whom nearly all residents of Singapore would see at least once before the grave, became more rotund – and the more rotund he became, the more jovial his disposition. Despite the warmth of his greetings, an underlying whiff of dead meat, a rank smell of decay, clung to him, which meant that everyone – except his live-in *amah* – kept him at arm's length.

The man now standing before Hawksworth was crimson-faced from toiling in the steamy heat of the morgue. Cowpar's white smock was smattered with dark stains of an unidentifiable nature that smeared as he wiped his hands to greet the tall man warmly, 'Good morning Superintendent Hawksworth, I have been expecting you. The bodies from the Hotel Formosa killing are prepared for you to view.'

In the flat light of the autopsy room, Cowpar's spectacles reflected the brightness from the skylight so that his eyes appeared disconcertingly as two flat discs of white, as though he were somehow less – or more – than a mere human. 'Here is one of the boys who was dressed as a woman,' he said, pointing to the body of a slightly built lad on the slab. 'I must say, with the use of cosmetics and a rather ingenious employ of straps and padding, his impersonation was convincing. It was not until I cut away the clothing that the truth became apparent.'

Hawksworth's gaze travelled across the corpse. He had been slim and young, with coltish legs and a soft, feminine face with full lips, narrow hips and a skinny backside. With the addition of breasts and the subtraction of the little pinkie of flesh nestled in the sparse hair of his groin, he would have made a striking young woman.

'The detective on the case has indicated that the murder weapon was most likely a fowling gun,' Hawksworth said, turning from the body. The boy's gentle beauty was significantly mangled, strips of flesh hanging from the torso, a large ragged hole in his chest from which splinters of white bone protruded.

'Correct.' He reached for a metal pan in which were dozens of lead pellets coated red. He swirled it once so the pellets rolled around the pan, making a rattling noise that seemed especially loud in the silence of the dead house. 'Like your detective, I have no way to account for how so many rounds were fired so quickly, though I can tell you that the shots were fired at point blank range. As you can see, the trauma to the bodies was significant.'

'And Low Teck Beng? He was not shot?'

Cowpar shook his head, the bright light flashing white in his lenses. 'His throat was severely mutilated by the jagged edge of a broken Chinese idol. I cannot determine whether he first died of exsanguination or strangulation; it is possible he choked on his own blood before he bled to death. Either way, his end came fairly quickly.'

'Guan Yu, I was told.'

Cowpar shrugged. 'I would not know. The murder weapon is there,' he pointed to the table where Hawksworth saw the top half of a rather inexpensive hollow ceramic statue of the immortal.

'It appears to have been broken randomly,' the detective noted.

'Yes, that is my assessment as well. It was broken then used as an improvised knife, the head and neck of the statue acting as the handle. The killer slashed several times before plunging it into the neck with great force.'

They made their way to Low Teck Beng's body on the slab. Cowpar pulled back the sheet to show Hawksworth the fatal wound. The skin was tattered and torn, the ends of the arteries and veins poking out like dried tubes. It appeared as though a claw had ripped the jagged gash in his neck. The fat face, baby smooth in death, still wore an expression of surprise and pain.

'Were there other signs of struggle? Who died first, Low Teck Beng or the others?'

'Whoever stabbed Low was standing very close to him,' Cowpar stroked his chin, speaking slowly, 'I would hazard a guess and say that he was stabbed, then, as he was dying, the fowling guns were discharged: I say this because there is not so much as a graze from a pellet on his body.'

'Were the bodyguards armed?'

'Yes, with knives and revolvers…'

'But they were not discharged?'

'With one exception, they were still tucked in their jackets.'

Hawksworth saw it in his mind, Low's body falling as he

struggled in his death throes, Guan Yu's immobile head stuck from his neck, blood spurting outward; his bodyguards reacting but not swiftly enough, reaching under their jackets while the double-barrelled fowling guns opened fire; the boy-girls taking the next rounds, the killers eliminating witnesses. He explained his theory to Cowpar, who agreed with the general outline.

'This information presents a significant problem, then' Hawksworth spoke rhetorically. 'The night manager told Detective Inspector Rizby that there were three men who entered the room. From what we can tell, all three guns were discharged in rapid succession and most likely simultaneously....'

'Are you suggesting that Low Teck Beng was killed by a fourth person?'

'Someone able to get close enough to stab him in a fit of rage while the other three kept the bodyguards in place at gunpoint,' Hawksworth concluded.

'It is a nice piece of conjecture, Superintendent. To judge from the position of the bodies that I saw at the scene, the scenario is plausible. The difficulty is in understanding how the fourth man was able to slip past the night manager.'

'The night manager may well be lying. In any event, I now have a much clearer picture of the case. May I ask when do you plan to conduct the public inquest and file your report?'

'My investigation is nearly done. I was thinking of holding the inquest tomorrow then releasing the bodies the next day after I file the report. There is no great mystery to the causes of death.'

'Dr. Cowpar,' the tall man looked into the reflective lenses above the soft eyes, 'I need you to keep certain information out of the public inquest proceedings.'

The portly man's jowls shook from side to side negatively while he said in a hard tone, 'You know that you are asking me to break the law.'

'No, I am asking you to alter procedure to spare even more lives. I suppose you know who Low Teck Beng is...was?'

'A high level criminal in a Chinese gang.'

'Far more than that: he was the *kapitan* of the Low *kongsi's* criminal gangs and the son of the *kongsi* patriarch. The entire topography of the criminal underworld of Singapore shifted with his demise. I am doing all I can to restrain the Lows from embarking on a mission of revenge that will spill much blood and cause many pointless deaths. I am using the promise of not releasing information that Teck Beng was killed in the presence of what were surely male prostitutes as the primary means of restraint. To avoid an all-out territorial clan war, it is imperative that the information be kept from the public record.'

Cowpar sighed, moving his bulk away from Low Teck Beng's corpse on the slab, the dead eyes staring up at him. 'What specifically are you proposing, Superintendent?'

'I will ask you to report the boys' deaths separately from that of Low Teck Beng and his bodyguards. The hotel staff will report that he stayed with two women. Those women were not found at the murder scene. These two boys were found elsewhere, in a completely separate incident.'

'So, you first ask me to misrepresent evidence. Then you ask me to compound that lie by asking me to lie more boldly at a public inquest.'

Hawksworth clenched his jaw then said quickly, 'If you make public the information that Low was killed with two female impersonators while staying in a private hotel suite, the Low family will loose face and will feel the need to correct that by being all the more vicious in their reprisals. By lying about this now, you will spare much suffering in the future. I do not need to tell you the brutality that the *kongsi* are capable of doing to one another when they clash.'

'Surely the information will surface through other means? The Chinese gossip machine is relentless.'

'True, but if there is no official evidence, then the rumours will die down. However, if the rumours are confirmed in the public inquest, then the Lows will have no choice but to pursue the most egregious course of action.'

The coroner stared without expression into Hawksworth's face for a moment before speaking in a steady voice, 'I appreciate the situation and, may I add, appreciate the position you are in; like yourself, I, too, want to prevent needless deaths. But what you are asking me to do goes against all my principles. Not in all my years have I ever misrepresented evidence or lied at an inquest...' Hawksworth moved to speak, but Cowpar held up his palm to silence him, continuing, 'What I ask is that you give me a day to consider what you are proposing. I may find a better solution.'

'Thank you Dr. Cowpar, but the situation...'

Cutting him short, Cowpar said firmly, 'Twenty-four hours to consider your proposal, Superintendent Hawksworth,' then gesturing at the mutilated corpses laid out behind him, he said under his breath, 'they are in no hurry.'

\* \* \*

The Chinese Protectorate had been founded in 1877 and operated out of a succession of shophouses in and around the Chinese Quarter until it became apparent that it would be more than a sideshow of the system of colonial governance. In 1886, it moved into a larger building on Havelock Road, better befitting its importance to the mechanism that drove the economy of Malaya: an endless supply of cheap Chinese labour.

Freshly disembarked male coolies, known as *sinkeh*, were required to sign in at the Protectorate upon arrival in Singapore. They and their employers would then sign a contract, the contents of which would be explained to the coolie in his home dialect. Systems for redress or reporting mistreatment were also explained. The Protectorate kept a copy of the contract and by this means was able – in theory, at least – to keep track of the legal Chinese coolie labour in Singapore. The black market in labour was fully beyond its purview.

The Protectorate had also been tasked with enforcing the Contagious Disease Ordinance. Newly arrived women and those working in bordellos were regularly inspected for venereal diseases, as were British military personnel. As with the coolies, the Protectorate also acted as a place where women could report mistreatment or other bad fortune, including forced labour, which meant that the agency often crossed swords with the Chinese secret societies that controlled both the coolie and prostitution trades.

Yet under pressure form moral crusaders in London, the Contagious Disease Ordinance was repealed in 1888, followed by the repeal of the registration of brothels a few years later. A large portion of the workload of the Protectorate thus disappeared, for now, hypothetically at least, it could no longer inspect brothels or the sex workers. The resulting spike in cases of venereal disease – for no brothels stopped operating, they merely moved into the shadows – swiftly reached epidemic proportions.

As for the police, whose job it was to keep illegal brothels closed, the Chinese Protectorate had become little more than another colonial bureaucracy. That it required civil servants trained for fluency in the various Chinese dialects and was thereby able to provide translators for investigations was its single greatest virtue.

The several hundred coolies trying to get their contracts signed and verified, long lines of female domestic servants waiting to prove that they were not prostitutes, plus multitudes of low-level bureaucratic factotums from across the colonial administration milling around waiting for information, created a daily pandemonium in marked contrast to the staid architecture of the Protectorate, which was sarcastically nicknamed the 'white house' by the European residents for not only was its very plain exterior whitewashed, but the building ironically existed mostly to serve the largest non-white resident community of the colony.

Hawksworth's rickshaw came to rest on the edge of a throng that spilled out of the front doors of the building and into the wide road. Despite the new year holiday, the machinery of coolie labour did not come to a halt. The *sinkeh* were easily recognizable by their undecorated *towchangs* – their hair queues – which they wore short or braided into buns so as not to interfere with their manual work. Clustered by dialect group, rough-looking employment agents tried to placate them as they broiled in the sun, shouting complaints. Despite his height and Anglo face, Hawksworth had to throw elbows to force his way through the crowd of Chinese, which seemed to increase in density and noise the closer he got to the front doorway. The shouting filled his ears so completely that it was disorienting.

After surreptitiously tripping a rather stout coolie, he managed to slip his way into the front lobby, where the chaos of arm waving and yelling, because it was contained, seemed to reach a critical mass. The air was hot and sticky and stank of stale sweat and mingled with the image of the mangled corpses he had just seen at the dead house, it caused a wave of nausea to sweep over him.

Approaching the administrative desk proved to be difficult, and he was forced to resort to pushing and shoving his way to the front. The distraught clerk was so overwhelmed with the blaring rabble around him that he merely looked at Hawksworth's face when the tall man made his presence known, shrugged his shoulders without speaking, then gestured up the stairs ascending behind him.

He passed through a low-gated fence that miraculously held back the throbbing mob by sheer force of presence and onto the staircase that curled up toward the administrative offices upstairs. From above, the crowd of ranting and arm-waving Chinese looked like a parade gone wrong.

Hawksworth made his way down silent corridors to the office of the Protector of Chinese. An old hand in Malaya, Joseph Brundell had only been recently given the job as the crown of his lifelong service in the Straits Colonies. Despite the somewhat sneering attitude by the rest of the colonial administration, he took his work seriously and proceeded with dedication to his task. The result was a near constant exhaustion as he both managed the staff of civil servants and personally dealt with representatives of British military, police, and customs organizations that plied him for information on the most recent activities of the Chinese. The latest bane of his existence was the various temperance movements that were constantly harassing him to provide otherwise confidential information on the numbers of Chinese taking opium.

When Hawksworth appeared in his office, the Protector was just planning to step out for an hour of solitary quiet over tiffin, and he was none too happy to see the policeman. He greeted the taller man gruffly, offering him the chair opposite his desk.

'Superintendent Hawksworth, I have not seen you since your promotion from Chief Detective Inspector. Allow me to congratulate you,' Brundell said with a forced smile, his stomach rumbling.

'Thank you, Mr. Brundell. I was hoping that today you could be of some assistance on two separate but not unrelated subjects. The first involves banks.'

'Banks?' Brundell asked without curiosity.

'My understanding is that currently, if a coolie wants to send money to China, his options are to remit the funds through an established bank or he can use one of the unlicensed money houses run by the *kongsi*.'

'You are correct, though in practice the two systems are not always separate. Often an unlicensed money house will collect a large sum from clients then use their own accounts at the official banks to transfer the funds. The coolies have much more difficulty opening accounts at registered banks than the *kongsi* do. The Hong Kong and Shanghai Bank is the most popular with the *kongsi*.'

'And if coolies wish to borrow funds?'

'Then their choices would be limited to either the *kongsi* money houses or, if they are long-time residents in Malaya, they might use a *chetty*, a Kling moneylender.'

'So there are, in my understanding, no licensed banks in Singapore owned by Chinese?'

Brundell drummed his fingers on his desk as he replied, 'None. The migrant labour must do with either the services that the *kongsi* money houses provide or what they can find from less reliable sources on the streets.'

'I will tell you that one of the largest *kongsi* in Singapore is actively planning to open an officially registered bank,' Hawksworth said directly.

The fingers stopped drumming. 'If the *kongsi* in question is registered as a "friendly society", then it would only be a benefit to the community, though I imagine the Legislative Council will be very meticulous in their granting of the license. I am sure they will ask my opinion,' Brundell sighed. 'As you are aware, since the enactment of the Societies Ordinance in 1890, the Chinese Protector also acts as Registrar of Societies.'

'And if the *kongsi* were not only registered as a friendly society but was also known to maintain criminal gangs throughout Malaya...?'

'If the *kongsi* in question were to maintain a mixed economy of licit and illicit activities then their opening of a bank would seem to serve largely as a means of using revenue from legitimate business to mask revenue – and expenses – derived from illegitimate business. It would also allow them to better move funds from one location to another across a large business empire. They could open branches of the bank in Batavia or Bangkok or Kuching....'

'Good lord!'

'Yes,' Brundell spoke meditatively, 'the implications are enormous. The *kongsi* would in effect be allowed to control their own economy; transactions would be completely opaque; they could loan money from one enterprise to the other, using revenue from illegal activities to fund legal ones; they could completely blur the distinctions between legitimate and criminal enterprises.' He paused to eye Hawksworth carefully. 'There are only three or four *kongsi* in all of Malaya even capable of considering such an enterprise...'

'It is the Lows,' Hawksworth said, quickly adding, 'and that information is to be kept very close indeed, Mr. Brundell.'

The older man whistled a single drawn out note, then said in a tentative voice, 'So the Teochews are becoming even stronger. Yet, there is a rumour that Low Teck Beng has been murdered.'

Hawksworth studied the man's worn face, creased by a lifetime under the Malayan sun, before replying, 'The rumour is true. And that information you are to keep completely secret until we release it officially. I do not know if his murder has anything to do with this notion about opening a bank, but until we have more positive information about the case we are exercising the highest degree of circumspection.'

'I understand,' Brundell said, running a hand through his mane of pewter grey hair.

'May I ask further, regarding prostitution... Despite the repeal of the Contagious Disease Ordinance, I understand that you still inspect brothels with some regularity.'

At this Brundell's surface of calm erupted in a burst of anger, 'Indeed! And let me tell you, these temperance warriors will simply not understand! The local economy runs on coolie labour and coolies need women. In their enforcing of a morality better suited to London than the tropics, they will simply place the prostitution business beyond our reach. The least we can do is ensure that the women are clean and treated humanely, because I assure you that no one will stop...' he searched for a delicate word and finally finished with a mumbled 'copulating.'

Hawksworth had read the recent Army Health Department report: nearly fifty per cent of all sickness reported in the entire Singapore command was venereal in origin. *The Straits Times* had recently claimed that in the previous year, one hundred and eleven patients in hospital had died of syphilis, making it the greatest killer in the settlement. It was believed that up to eighty-five per cent of the working girls of Singapore had some form of sexually transmitted disease. 'I have seen the rather appalling medical reports and can appreciate your concern, Mr. Brundell.'

'So where will they end, Superintendent? Now after their success with shuttering brothels, the temperance crusaders want to prohibit the sale of opium!' he croaked in exasperation. 'The economic damage from such an action would bring the entire eastern empire to its knees. First outlawing prostitutes, then opium...What outrageous idea will they try next?'

'But you do keep a list of brothels that are still permitted to operate without official sanction, so to speak, yes?'

Brundell eyed Hawksworth warily, his exhaustion apparent. 'Yes, Superintendent, as you know we do keep a list of brothels that we allow to continue to operate largely because they grant us access to inspect the premises and to submit the women to frequent health checks. There is no altruism here. They know that by allowing us this access their own houses will have an economic advantage.'

'You mean that by letting it be known to their customers that they submit to regular inspections, their reputation as clean and safe establishments will be enhanced and thus they will attract a more desirable clientele. Cooperating with you is good for business.'

The Protector of Chinese nodded silently, in effect admitting that he was aiding and abetting criminal activity. The open secret about the Protectorate keeping a list of safe brothels did not sit well with the police commanders, who had the job of closing down all whorehouses whether they played along with the Protectorate or not. But Brundell knew that Hawksworth was of an old guard who appreciated the value of regulation – as opposed to outright suppression – of vice. And despite everything, the brothel trade was if anything increasing.

'Out of that list of safe brothels, would you happen to know which, if any, would be capable of providing a customer with... toffers...specifically, female impersonators?'

The grave expression on Brundell's face waxed to one of bewilderment. 'I am unsure, Superintendent. There are no Chinese Molly houses that I know of, and none of the Chinese brothels of which I am familiar specialize in that particular... inclination. It is not something that we look into when we inspect the places.'

'You do not check male prostitutes for venereal diseases?'

Brundell spoke evenly, 'Such unnatural offenses, should they occur, would fall far beyond the remit of the Protectorate. You should know, Superintendent, it is the official position of the administration that there are no male prostitutes in Singapore at all.'

## CHAPTER V

# Red Threads

THERE WAS ONE Molly house in Singapore that Hawksworth knew of, but it was not the sort of place Low Teck Beng would have gone, for it was a gathering place of European men and though highly secretive, its presence was known to the police, who let it operate largely to spare several highly placed officials and pillars of the community the embarrassment of being caught in a raid. As for travellers or sailors who were interested in buggering native boys, there was plenty of freelance talent available on the streets, if one knew which streets to visit. But Low Teck Beng did not fit into either of these categories. He was unique in that he had the power and access to arrange a rendezvous that suited his own proclivities; finding the people or peoples who facilitated his orgies would be time consuming but not difficult.

Tiffin with Rizby in his office at his desk, both men with metal plates loaded with biryani, the fragrant bed of yellow and red basmati rice topped by a quarter chicken marinated in yogurt then broiled with cloves and cardamom, a boiled egg, and chopped green okra, which the locals called 'ladies fingers,' with thick slices of a sour eggplant known as *brinjal*, all coated with a slurry of yellow curry sauce. It was the Thursday dish in the Central Police Station canteen and the gastronomic highlight of the weekly midday meals, but neither man had much appetite.

'Loo, the hotel manager, has vanished, along with the maid.'

'That happened quickly. Any sign foul play was involved? Or did they get smart and leave town before the killers came back to finish off the witnesses?'

Rizby shrugged, a spoonful of biryani poised before his mouth. 'One or the other or both. Their rooms were empty but the other staff said they did not own much. The kitchen boy was still around, but was obviously making plans to leave. His small kit bag was packed and he was extraordinarily nervous when I saw him again.'

'As he should be. By now it will be known who talked to the police.'

'My guess is that he will have to find a way to scrape the money together to flee, or he, perhaps like the other two, will be at the bottom of the Johor Straits with bricks strapped to his ankles before too long.'

'And there are no further witnesses? No further evidence?'

'Nothing.'

Hawksworth bit into a slice of steaming chicken, chewing while the sweat spread across his back. 'So the evidence we have,' he swallowed, 'is incomplete. We now know that Low Teck Beng was in the company of two female impersonators when he was killed. Witnesses claim that three men arrived, asked for him by name, then proceeded to the room where an argument ensued.'

'The men spoke Cantonese.'

'But was the argument in Cantonese or Teochew?'

'We do not know.'

'And there is no one left to ask.'

'Then the three men fired fifteen rounds in less than a minute.'

'Incorrect. During the course of the argument someone smashed an idol of Guan Yu and slashed Teck Beng's neck with it, killing him.'

'Then the men opened fire?'

'Killing everyone in the room.'

'Was it an assassination or an argument that got out of hand?'

Rizby wiped his fingers then drummed them on the desktop, creating a hollow tattoo. Hawksworth scooped up the last of the rice on his plate. A husk of cardamom seed exploded bitterly in his mouth as he chewed. He fished it out with his forefinger, then examined it abstractly as he spoke. 'Someone was looking for Teck Beng. Someone who knew him, whom he trusted to let into his room, despite the fact that he was with other men.'

'The weapons used indicate that whoever came looking for Teck Beng was expecting there to be a fight, and they were prepared to battle to the death.'

Hawksworth flicked the chewed cardamom husk off his fingertip. The image of the mangled corpses on Cowpar's slabs flickered in his mind. 'My speculation is that there was a fourth person in the room – the person whom Teck Beng trusted. This is the person who smashed the idol and killed him. His murder was an act of passion. The gunmen then panicked and once they started shooting they could not stop.'

'Yet the manager claimed only three men entered the hotel. And he said that Teck Beng was with three bodyguards and two women.'

'Either the manager is lying or the fourth person was already in the hotel. Perhaps waiting for Teck Beng, meaning he arrived before the victim.'

'Every indication is that Teck Beng's party was put together very quickly and in complete secrecy. How did the killers know were to find him?'

'His brother swears to the loyalty of the bodyguards,' he said, standing to stretch his legs, the calf of his bad foot growing stiff.

'Which leaves the female impersonators.'

Hawksworth grunted, turning toward his window. High-end prostitutes meant a sprawling informal network of people, an entire economy fuelled by men paying for pleasurable release. There would be a madam, maids and guards and cooks and staff at the brothel; there would be runners who would bring requests and rickshaw wallahs paid by the madam to deliver the goods intact. There would be flower men and cosmetics men and medical men and sundry deliveries men. There would be the staff at the hotel who would expect a kickback. There would be the police on the beat and the criminal gangs who brought the fresh meat, both groups expecting protection money. Keeping a secret in such a byzantine commercial network would be improbable, but, paradoxically, the echoing rumour mill would also make confirmation of facts nearly impossible. For the time being, he decided to leave it up to Yong Seng to trawl the bordellos looking for information about the *ah-kuahs*.

A knock came at the door and a young uniformed officer entered, 'Excuse me sir, but there is a Chinese man here to see you.'

'I am not expecting anyone. Did he give you his name?'

'Lau Chi Man. He said it is of the utmost urgency.'

Rizby and Hawksworth exchanged amazed glances. Lau was the *kapitan* of the Hai San, the vicious Cantonese *kongsi*. As a rule, the Hai San did not cooperate with the police.

'By all means, send him up,' Hawksworth said quickly, motioning for Rizby to stay. 'And you had better send for Heng as well. We might need some assistance with translation.'

The uniformed officer returned a moment later with an elderly Chinese man. Hawksworth, who only knew Lau Chi

Man by name, was surprised. He had been expecting someone young and robust, with a killer's face. Instead, the man before him resembled in physique and manner nothing more than a prosperous greengrocer. He was attired only in a plain blue cotton *changshan*; his queue was iron grey. On his head was a black silk skullcap without a brim.

'Good afternoon, Superintendent Hawksworth,' Lau said in heavily accented English, struggling with the correct pronunciation of the name.

'Good afternoon to you, Mr. Lau. This is Detective Inspector Dunu Rizby, head of the Native Crimes Squad. How can we assist you today?'

Rizby stood to offer the old man a chair.

'Please, my English is not good,' the old man spoke apologetically, taking his seat. 'I learned some in Hong Kong, but that was a long time ago.'

'A translator is on the way, Mr. Lau, please wait one moment more,' this last phrase Hawksworth was able to speak in very poor Cantonese.

'I will wait but first I will tell you that the Hai San had nothing to do with the killing of Low Teck Beng or his men.'

Both Hawksworth and Rizby were stunned into momentary silence by the old man's proclamation. Hawksworth resumed his seat just as Heng entered the office. Seeing the old man, he kowtowed slightly, then greeted him by name – but even the normally stone faced Heng could not hide his astonishment at seeing the Hai San *kapitan* sitting in Hawksworth's office.

'Mr. Heng, please do take a seat. Mr. Lau came here alone just to inform us that the Hai San are not culpable of the murder of Low Teck Beng.'

Heng stared first at Hawksworth then at Lau; his look of

astonishment had changed to one of amazement. The Hai San *kapitan* walking alone into a police station to defend himself against murder charges that were yet to be made was such an extraordinary experience that he was not sure at first he had understood correctly. He asked Lau in Cantonese to repeat what he had said.

'He said it again, sir, that the Hai San did not do it.'

'I have sent my son to the Low family with the same information,' Lau continued, speaking to Heng. 'The rumour is that the killers spoke Cantonese and the suspicion that the Hai San are responsible for the heinous crime is already hardening into accepted fact. I fear a war of reprisal. We are all prospering under the new secret society regulations. None of us want a war now. I wanted to come personally to tell you this: we have no reason to start a war.'

Heng translated. Hawksworth's fingertips traced the edge of this desk. Rizby tugged at his earlobe, his brow wrinkling in thought.

'Mr. Lau,' the Superintendent spoke first, 'do you have any information regarding the killing?'

The old man shook his head negatively. 'We heard the news only yesterday, not long after it happened.'

'And none of your subordinates would have ordered it?'

He was taken aback by the question and bristled, his eyes flashing in anger, nostrils flaring. He quickly regained his humble composure, but it was too late, the mask had slipped; for the first time since he came in, the old man betrayed the imperial temper required to run a *kongsi*. 'No one in my society had anything to do with this...*murder*.' For emphasis, he spoke the last word in English.

'And you have heard nothing as to the perpetrators or reason for the murder?'

'Nothing! We hear only that we are responsible for it, which is why I am here now, as I said. Further, I want to tell you that the Hai San will offer all the support we can to help in the police investigation.'

'Thank you, Mr. Lau, your offer of help is highly appreciated. I especially want to thank you for coming to see me today. Your words will be taken quite seriously.' Hawksworth rose, as did Rizby and Heng, the latter helping the elderly man out of his chair.

Lau tottered slightly as he stood, then reaching a hand to the wispy grey hairs growing from his chin, he turned his eyes on Hawksworth. They were filled with cataract and turning light blue, but once he gazed into the pupils, the Superintendent saw the iron will of the long-lived gangster. The tiger may be aged, but his bite was still more terrible than his roar.

As if reading his thoughts, Lau's face eased into a smile. 'I thank you, Superintendent. Your reputation as a fair and just friend of the Chinese societies is well deserved. I hope we can meet again under more auspicious circumstances.'

Hawksworth's bowed his head slightly in acknowledgement, then watched as Heng led the old man out of the room; then he exhaled, feeling an immense tension washing from him. 'And what do you make of *that*, Detective Inspector?'

Rizby tapped the end of his nose. 'The Hai San's power has diminished as that of the Lows and Mother-Flowers have risen. I think the fear is genuine.'

Hawksworth's guffaw was short and sharp. 'He all but asked for police protection! I am inclined to believe his protestation of innocence. However, we will keep an open mind. I suspect that Lau knows more than he is telling us,' he sat again and noticed that his dirty lunch plate was still on the table. He shoved it away.

'I wonder what the Lows will make of this, the son of the Hai San *kapitan* coming to them to plead their innocence.'

'Hopefully they will believe it.'

'If the son acts the timid tiger as the father did, then the Lows will simply be even more emboldened.'

'But if the Hai San did not kill Low Teck Beng, who did? The weapons used were not those of a street gang. Shotguns suggest the killers had the backing of a superior force.'

Hawksworth looked into the agate eyes of his adjutant, frowning. 'If we eliminate the Hai San as suspects, then we are left with the Lows and the Mother-Flowers, and neither option is particularly savoury.'

*     *     *

The next morning, not long after dawn, while he was sipping his first black coffee of the day, seated at his desk in the hot room, the sweat already beginning to form a patina of grime on his brow, a clerk knocked on his door to announce that the coroner was on the telephone. Hawksworth followed him down to the telephone room, where the listening bell was in the hand of another clerk. It was no sooner pressed to his ear than he identified himself.

Cowpar began speaking without preamble. 'I have decided to agree to your wishes, Superintendent, to avoid further shedding of blood. However, I want to impress upon you that this is not a decision I have come to lightly.'

'I appreciate what you....'

The metallic recreation of Cowpar's voice cut him short, 'My official report will state that the two boys were delivering food and were caught in the crossfire when the shotguns were fired at Low Teck Beng and his men.'

'That should do nicely.'

'Have you considered that the night manager and other hotel staff will contradict this statement? That they will claim he arrived with two women – women who have now vanished?'

'That is not of great concern now as the hotel staff have themselves vanished.'

Cowpar paused, 'Dead? Or in hiding?'

'We are not sure, but either way, what you file in the inquest report is what will become public record. When do you plan to submit the report?'

'Today. I imagine approval will be swift. The bodies can be collected by this afternoon.'

'Thank you, Dr. Cowpar.'

'Superintendent?' the voice caught Hawksworth as he was about to disengage the line.

'Yes?'

'I hope that never again will you ask me to do such a thing.'

'I hope so too, Dr. Cowpar. I hope so, too,' he said, then disengaged the line.

\* \* \*

After weeks of gorging, the thirteenth day of the lunar new year should be given to depuration and rest. The digestive system should be made clean to avoid illness. Fasting is recommended, but if that is incommodious, for instance if energy for labour or other necessary activities is required, then food should consist of simple rice porridge or lightly cooked leafy vegetables, in small portions. Grease, spices, and alcohol should all be strictly avoided as they increase the body heat and tightness of internal organs. In more practical terms, fasting on the thirteenth day is a way for the body to transition from plenty to austerity.

As a signifier of scarcity, the thirteenth day should be given to worship of the immortal General Guan Yu. Offerings of joss sticks and tobacco should be made before his idol, his red face and flowing black beard and long handled *guan dao* blade, in temples or altars in homes and businesses. It is said that the immortal won hundreds of battles during the time of the Three Kingdoms and his success in combat is believed to translate to success in business for his devotees. That Guan Yu is also the patron god of bookies and smugglers and secret society members should not be understood as an indication of disreputability. After all, they are in business, too.

In his public inquest report, Cowpar had merely written that Low Teck Beng had been stabbed with the jagged end of 'a broken Chinese idol', but the rumours were already in circulation that it was Guan Yu himself that had ended his life, and it was whispered that the Low family should not have started the funeral wake for their son on the thirteenth day. It was decidedly inauspicious. What arrogance! The tut-tutting and tooth sucking gossips muttered. Was it not an insult to the immortal general? Would he not now seek revenge on Low Teck Beng in the afterlife? Everyone seemed to have their own theory about how the gangster had died, and given that the death occurred during the new year celebrations, about how the family should handle the funeral rites.

The wake was held at Panglima Prang. On the same lawn on which the *wayang* opera stage had been erected was now a large canvas marquee, under which Low Teck Beng's coffin had been placed. The wake lasted several days, and family members would take turns to keep vigil all night and day. A life sized photogravure image of Low Teck Beng's pudgy, unsmiling face was propped at the head of his coffin, scowling at the bouquets of white plumeria blossoms and potted spider lilies, the slender flames of candles and smoking tips of joss sticks surrounding the coffin. A steady flow of gold and silver paper money was fed into a smouldering barrel to ensure that the spirit of the dead man would not want for comfort in the other world, the world of shadows.

Low Teck Seng personally presided over the final day of his brother's wake. As the hired priests in brilliant white robes chanted and the incessant sound of the tiny bells filled the air with a tinning drone, he pressed red envelopes into the palms of family members and guests who attended that day. In each was a single, five centavo Mexican silver coin, a token gesture to ensure that they got home safely. The coin was to be spent, not kept, before the guests arrived home – to keep it would bring very bad luck indeed. What the guests did keep was a three-inch-long piece of red thread. It was recommended that mourners tie the threads to the doorknobs of their homes to ward off any evil spirits who may have followed them from the fragrant wake. The red threads, it was believed, should be kept tied on the doorknob until at least three days after the departed has been buried beneath the earth.

## CHAPTER VI

# Outbreak

CHAP GOH MEI came and went, the lantern festival marking the fifteenth day and the end of the lunar new year festivities. Life in the Chinese Quarter returned to the drudgery of hard labour broken by meals of sour yellow noodle soup loaded with garden discards. The rickshaw wallahs went back to opium dens when their workday was done, the dock coolies to the beds they shared with three other men, taking turns to sleep in shifts; the hawker dashed down the street, his portable kitchen of brazier and pot strung across his back on a bamboo pole, boiling water scalding his ankles when he tripped. There would be no more colourful *wayang* operas in the streets, no more the rapid snap of firecrackers, no more rice wine shared generously with strangers; at least not for another long year.

The next day, Low Teck Beng was buried in the Low family tomb in the Chinese cemetery at Kwong Hou Sua. The procession, headed by a blaring *gong kuan* band, banging drums and cymbals, blowing off-key horns in a dirge meant to frighten away malicious spirits, wound its way north from Panglima Prang to the top of the island. Coolies ran ahead of the carriage carrying the coffin, throwing paper money coloured gold and silver on the road, paving the way for the deceased with tokens of wealth for the next life. Metal umbrellas painted gold and silver jangling with coins were carried by two robed coolies directly before the hearse carriage, which was surmounted by a figure of a bearded Chinese lion to signify the gender of the deceased. But such symbolism was merely a matter of form: everyone knew it was Low Teck Beng's final trip. The roads were lined with Teochews as the funeral cortege passed slowly through town, then into the suburbs, and finally into the rural districts. He may have been a murderous thug, but he was *their* murderous thug, and a show of respect was required.

At the edge of the cemetery, six members of the Low *kongsi* bore the coffin to the elaborate family grave, embedded in the grass of the sloping hillside, with a commanding view of the straits of Johor. He would be facing away from Singapore, toward the open sky where the sun rose. One of the last mourners to leave the graveside was his father, who moved listlessly these days, followed closely by the family geomancer, who had lingered, staring expressionlessly at the fresh earth mounded in the bathtub-shaped grave, as if listening to a song only he could hear. Then he, too, departed, leaving the grave solitary. The first downpour of the afternoon started soon after, the fat drops pounding the freshly turned dirt into muddy paste.

Hawksworth had made a point to be at the front gate of Panglima Prang when the procession commenced. He caught the eye of Low Teck Seng, who would walk the entire way under the gruelling sun behind the hearse carriage. The men exchanged subtle nods of commiseration as the *gong kuan* cymbals crashed and clattered, filling the air with brassy shards of sound.

Then he went back to his office, where the stacks of paperwork waited.

At the end of that day, as he left the Central Station, a boy in a short queue and blue cotton smock and pantaloons materialized from the hurly-burly of the twilight street: a messenger from the Mother-Flowers. Yong Seng wanted to meet him personally early the next morning at the tea stall by the park. It seems he had news that was too important to send via messenger.

\* \* \*

Yong Seng appeared surprisingly sober, if not completely depleted. 'I have been working hard for you the past few days, my friend,' he smiled wryly as the two men sipped black tea in the rising light of dawn. The grass of Hong Lim Green had appeared black in the gaslight, but now was taking on a dun colour as the sky brightened.

'What have you learned?' The tea was making Hawksworth feel giddy. His morning beverage was coffee and he missed the earthy aroma and strong bitter flavour that usually grounded his day. The tea merely made him queasy.

'Ah, my *ang-moh* brother, I will tell you. Do you know that in the past week I have visited more than twenty-two separate bordellos?'

'Good lord, man!'

'I have slept with more than fifty-six women.'

'In only twenty-two bordellos you slept with more than…'

'I have drunk more than thirty-five bottles of brandy.'

'Yong Seng, you exaggerate…'

'And I now have a rash on my ass in the shape of Hong Kong island, strange pustules on my cock that itch then burst like zits, yellow snot rolls from the tip of my dick, it is painful to piss, and my urine smells like rotten winter melon.'

Unsure if the man was hyperbolizing, Hawksworth merely said with dead earnestness, 'Your great sacrifice for Her Majesty and the Straits Settlements Police will not go unrewarded.'

Yong Seng shrugged the Chinese shrug that indicated that the effort and work and sacrifice he had endured were really not such a big deal since they were done for a friend. Smiling, he said, 'Now I will undertake a rest cure and heal my wounds. Besides, Shu En was wondering why I was not spending more time attending to important business.'

'But what have you learned of the *ah kuahs* that were with Low?'

His friend's purple lips curled back into a half sneer that burst into a short, loud laugh that caught the attention of passers-by. It was only then that they seemed to notice the sharply dressed Chinese and the linen-suited white man sitting so close their foreheads were nearly touching.

'I know where he got the boys,' Yong Seng said, gulping his tea. 'It is one of the fancy houses in Kreta Ayer. The place is run by a Teochew gang loyal to the Lows but it mostly supplies Cantonese girls. These *ah kus* are not fresh from the boat, mind you, but are known to be especially beautiful and have some, ah, training, in the sensual arts. Very jemmy, high-class establishment; the girls are voluntarily inspected monthly by the Protectorate; the prices are steep. They mostly serve top-rank Teochew businessmen, though some Cantonese go there slyly. No *ang-mohs* allowed. The mamasan is called Koo. She is known to provide "special services" on request, discretion assured. *Ah kuahs* are her specialty.'

'And this is where Low got his boys?'

Roughly clacking the empty teacup on the tray, Yong Seng said simply, 'There can be no place else.'

'Madam Koo's house in Kreta Ayer. I will find it.'

'Why do you waste your time? Everyone knows that the Hai San killed Low Teck Beng.'

'And everyone believes this because the killers spoke Cantonese?'

'Of course, and only the Hai San would dare to kill a Low.'

'But these are only rumours. I need facts, Yong Seng.'

'Facts!' he chortled with genuine mirth. 'Waiting for facts will get you nowhere. Do what you believe is right, not what the facts tell you.'

Hawksworth studied his friend intently for a moment. The distance between the Orient and the Occident was sometimes very great indeed, even when the two were close enough to smell each other's breath.

Yong Seng stood to stretch before scratching vehemently at his crotch. 'Aiyoh! This burning is the devil's torture!' he tugged futilely at the folds of his *changshan,* shifting from one foot to the other. 'I will be recuperating at our house in Katong, should you need me.'

'Good luck,' Hawksworth said, standing to bid his friend good-bye. A smile and a nod, then the two men went in opposite directions, Hawksworth moving slowly with the help of his cane, Yong Seng limping from raw pain radiating from his groin.

The sun had risen fully by the time they left the tea stall; it was already oppressively hot as he made his way past the Police Court across South Bridge Road to the imposing edifice of the Central Police Station. The clock on the tower read 9 am. There would be time for a meal before he gathered some men to take to Kreta Ayer. Like all brothels, Madam Koo's doors would not be unlocked until after midday. The customers would not start arriving until dusk. Koo herself, he knew, was probably still snoring.

*　*　*

Tiffin consisted of sticky steamed white ice and curried *gurame* freshwater fish with chunks of tomato and green ladies fingers floating in red curry; a side plate of green *nai bai,* steamed and tender, with garlic and oyster sauce was followed by a steamed lotus paste bun. He ate alone at his desk, as he often did, setting aside the mound of reports he was supposed to read. Three days' worth of *The Straits Times* newspapers lay on the desk and he idly flipped through them as he ate. The advertisement for Kupper's beer caught his eye. It seemed to be everywhere these days. Chop Payong. What could that possibly mean? he wondered as he did every time he saw it. He tucked the little enigma away in his mind, then rose to gather his men for a visit to Madam Koo.

Rizby was out, working on the investigation. He found young Joseph Jeremiah, only recently inducted into the Native Crimes Squad and given unofficial enrolment in the *burung helang*, as the men most loyal to Hawksworth were known, the name derived from the Malay term for bird of prey.

'Will we need a translator?' Jeremiah asked.

Hawksworth sent him to find one and only a few moments later he returned with Heng Kee Yann, the same man who had been with Rizby at the Hotel Formosa when the shooting was first uncovered. The three men rolled in a hackney carriage the short distance across the Chinese Quarter from the Central Station to Sago Lane, exiting at the well-known red light district near Duxton Hill.

They found Madam Koo's place at the corner of Banda and Spring Street. It was a shophouse with an ornate facade, slightly set back from the street with a faux-Moorish balcony on the upper floor. Two stately lipstick palms, with bright red trunks and dark green leaves, grew nearly as tall as the upper floors. The tips of their fronds brushed a signboard that read 'House of

Koo'. The windows were shuttered and the house was silent and still in the harsh sunlight of midday, but when the men knocked the door was opened quickly by a thin serving boy prepared to receive deliveries.

They flashed their shields, which the boy studied, eyes widening in fear, before running to fetch a beefy male servant. The house muscle, dressed in cotton pyjamas with his queue unkempt and smelling of sleep, ushered them into the front parlour, asking them politely to wait for Madam. They sat in an elegant room decorated with rosewood furniture burnished to a dark satin finish, the in-laid mother of pearl glistening like rain drops.

The altar was off to one side, and Hawksworth spotted a ceramic idol of Pan Chin Lien, patron goddess of prostitutes. Graceful and sweet-faced, yet libidinous and cruel, it was believed that she was sold by her mother when merely eight years old to an Imperial Commissioner, after whose death she was sold again, just reaching her sexual prime, to the man who would deflower her before passing her as a bride-gift to his tenant, a short and ugly, yet wealthy man named Wu Dalang. In short order, she would seduce a page boy, have a running affair with her son-in-law, drive one man to suicide and be implicated in the brutal deaths of several more. The old stories say that her brother-in-law, Wu Song, disembowelled her after he caught her sleeping with another man whom she had convinced to poison her husband.

Another servant appeared, a heavy-set boy, his face freshly washed and hair clean and plated, carried a tray loaded with jasmine green tea. Smiling vapidly, the servant poured the tea into nearly translucent ceramic cups. It was served 'gunpowder' style, rolled into pellets that opened and unfurled as the tea leaves became saturated. Hawksworth noticed that the pellets were small and tightly folded – a sign of superior quality.

Everything about the place reeked of expense. The clients were expected to pay dearly for what they considered to be a classy environment. But the smell was the same as any whorehouse, he noted, the unseemly odours of sweat and bleach. All those bodies spread-eagled and all those bed sheets that needed cleaning. No amount of elegance in the front parlour could cover the gangly human commotions taking place upstairs.

Koo appeared by the time they finished their first cup. It looked as though she had just put herself together. She was corpulent but elegantly attired in a long dress with a high collar, a string of large pearls strung through the folds of fat around her neck. Her makeup was thick and sticky in the humidity, the sweat glistening beneath the pancake; the painted eyebrows were the only solid lines, the rest seemed smeared and elastic, as if made of rubber. Her lips were tight and small, coloured a dark red with lipstick that had stuck to her yellow teeth. In her hand was a folding fan that she flicked open as soon they were seated, stirring the air around her head, knocking her wig slightly askew.

'Thank you for taking the time to speak with us, Madam Koo,' Hawksworth spoke through the translator.

'I am always happy to help the police,' she said, her face creasing into a well-practiced smile.

'When Low Teck Beng was killed the other night he was in the company of two *ah kuahs*, who were also killed. We have been informed that you are the person who supplied them. Is this true?'

Smile frozen in place, she merely sipped her tea, eyeing him over the rim of the cup.

'Madam Koo, this is not only a murder investigation, it is also a favour to the Low family, whom I know personally. They would like to find out who killed their son, as would we. Cooperate fully with me and things will be much easier in the long run for all of us. Tell me, did you supply the *ah kuahs* to Low Teck Beng the night he was killed?'

Letting out a beleaguered sigh, she nodded affirmatively.

'Did he often...was he a regular...' Hawksworth groped for words while Heng translated.

With an intuition born of a lifetime spent soaked in men's needs, she knew what he was driving at and answered the question pre-emptively, 'He would come to me about once or twice a week. As far as I know, he only came here for his *ah kuahs*. You know he liked girls, mostly. But for his *ah kuahs*, he came to me.'

'Girls as well? But that night he wanted only *ah kuahs*, yes?'

She smiled. 'It was a bother because of the new year holiday, but I was able to get everything arranged.'

'He came here?' Hawksworth asked, sipping his second cup of tea. It was deliciously fragrant and light, without a trace of bitterness.

'No, he sent his bodyguard to collect the...girls. It was a secret, of course, so he did not want to be seen in public with the *ah kuahs*.'

'Any idea why he would take such a risk as to...with... boys...,' again, the Superintendent tried to find the correct words and was surprised to find that despite the depthless vulgarity he had witnessed in all his years on the force, he was flummoxed.

'He liked to gamahuche,' she crowed in a voice that sounded like a rusty hinge, freshly oiled.

Hawksworth did not at first follow her meaning, but when Madam Koo made the jerking motion with her fist toward her parted lips, sticking the tip of her tongue obscenely into the opposite cheek, he understood. 'He liked them in his mouth,' she said mischievously, adding, 'but everyone likes something.'

'The boys who were with him the night he died, were they his usual...consorts?'

The translation was far smoother than his question; the answer quick, if evasive, 'One was, one was not.' Seeing where this line of inquiry could lead – and sensing culpability – the mamasan was getting visibly nervous. It appeared as though the hot air were causing her face to melt.

'The new boy, was this his first time with Low Teck Beng?'

She shook her head negatively, 'No, second or third.'

'And where did the boys come from?'

Her lips tightened until they appeared white as she glared at him. How many people had seen the police walk in here? she wondered. Talking to the police could only bring trouble.

'Madam Koo,' he spoke in practiced measured tones, 'if you do not answer my questions now I will close your establishment and toss you in gaol. You are running an illegal operation and all the protection you pay to *kongsi* and the police will not help you if I decide to shut you down. Now tell me, where did the boys come from?'

Sighing again, she spoke low and fast, 'From a young Cantonese named Hoi. All the Cantonese *ah kuahs* come from Hoi. The boy was a *sinkeh*, fresh from the village. He had only been in Singapore for a few weeks. The older boy had been here at least a year.'

'Who is Hoi and where can we find him?'

Koo's rubbery face shrivelled like a desiccated apple. She did not want to utter another word. Hawksworth leaned closer to her and snapped his fingers. 'Help me or gaol for you,' he whispered. There was no translation – none was needed – she knew what he meant.

'Hoi is part of the Claw Fists, a Cantonese gang under the

Hai San. But the *ah kuahs* he brings me are his own business. I usually find him at the tailor's shophouse on the corner of Upper Chin Chew Street.'

'What is Hoi's full name?' Jeremiah asked, asserting himself.

'I only know him as "Hoi". He is about twenty years old with a scar down his left cheek.' She drew a line down her face from her left ear to her jaw to show him.

'You pay protection money to the Claw Fists?' Hawksworth asked briskly.

Koo snapped at him, a string of profanities spewing out, 'I pay protection money to *everyone*, you son of a whore!' She shouted rapidly, 'Police, Hai San, Claw Fists, and on and on and on. Everyone has their bloody hand out, wanting more and more. Low was generous with me so I got him what he wanted. So he liked to suck a little cock from time to time, so what? So do I! It was not my boys who got him killed! Now you go and fuck yourself and all your faggot police boy assholes and leave me alone to run my business, you dripping diseased cunt bastard!' She stopped shrieking, her shrill voice echoing in the room. Hawksworth saw she was shaking with rage, wobbling in her seat, red-faced beneath the makeup.

'She said that she is angry because she pays protection money to the police and she does not appreciate us asking questions,' Heng translated calmly. 'She says Low was a good customer and insists the *ah kuahs* had nothing to do with his murder.'

'Thank you,' Hawksworth politely spoke to Heng. As he stood to take his leave, he turned back to Koo and smiling, said to her in a sweet voice, leaning over the seated woman, 'If you ever call me a "cunt" again, I will have your wrists broken over a table edge you disgusting old sow.' The Cantonese phrase was *chi bai* – no translation was needed for that.

It stung like a wet slap when he stepped outside. It was more humid than usual, the suspended precipitation turning the air into a tepid brew. There would be heavy rain later in the day, he knew, washing the streets clean. But for now, the dust rose to mingle with the stench of dung and slops in the steamy air. His stomach lurched. The green tea was turning acidic in his guts, causing a wave of nausea to sweep over him. He had planned to walk with Heng and Joseph Jeremiah to Upper Chin Chew Street but decided instead to hail rickshaws.

The people on the street moved in a miasma of silence, the enervating atmosphere sapping their strength. The normal velocity of movement slowed to half its regular speed – the rickshaw puller's legs went through their circular actions in slow motion, as though the wheels of the cart were spinning in the opposite direction. Not only the movement of people, but of the animals, horses and bullocks, seemed to be stilled by the humidity. From his rickshaw, Hawksworth looked out on an uncanny world, as though the dust and noise and movement of the crowded streets were somehow suspended in solution. He felt the tea churning in his stomach, the nausea rippling through him.

By the time they had reached Upper Chin Chew Street, the sense of time and motion had returned to normal but he now felt extremely tired and only wanted to lie down, a soothing damp cloth on his forehead. The thought of little Fenella flicked into his mind, and he wished to be in his cool, shaded home. Then, before he knew it, they were alighting at the Cantonese tailor shop.

The front room of the shop was apparently the informal clubhouse of the Claw Fists, who appeared to be little more than a raggedy band of skinny young men lounging around trying to look tough. They were no doubt dangerous in that they felt the need to prove themselves and violence was the quickest route to manhood. They also looked thick as bricks, and were all the more threatening for being dumb. Such little gangs were useful to the big *kongsi* precisely because they provided disposable troops who made up in brutality what they lacked in intelligence. Hawksworth had known their kind his entire life. Hoi, he guessed, was their leader, somewhat entrepreneurial and slightly smarter than the rest.

Even in the gloom of the shop, Hoi was obvious. He was seated in the biggest chair, smoking a cigarillo. There were three other youths with him – the tailor stayed in the back room. Smooth faced and slim, with his scar and short glossy queue, Hoi resembled nothing less than a wharf rat.

Hawksworth waited outside while he sent Jeremiah and Heng into the shop. Jeremiah was nervous – not without reason – but the older officer knew that the only way to overcome such nerves was by being thrust directly into the action. He could overhear the young detective questioning Hoi – and Heng translating – before commanding him to step outside.

Hoi emerged onto the five-foot way, his trio of friends lingering behind in the dimness of the shop. He was young, little more than a teenager, though he already had the bent posture of a street thug. Hawksworth could sense the braggadocio with which the young man would attempt to impress his friends; the young ones were the most dangerous because they had not yet received enough hard knocks. He knew the future Hoi envisioned for himself, rising up the rungs of violence into an established gang then into the firm grip of an established *kongsi*, until someday he would be the boss. All the puppies had the same dream of becoming the big dog.

Jeremiah circled behind the suspect to sandwich him between Hawksworth and the nearest pillar of the arcade. Heng added a fourth element, effectively blocking the young man into a tight square.

'Mr. Hoi, I am Superintendent Hawksworth of the Straits Settlements Police. I am asking you to come with me to the Central Police Station for questioning.'

After hearing the quick translation, Hoi hesitated, his coal black eyes locking on Hawksworth's own. The older man recognized the flickering instant when the flight or fight reaction kicked in, Hoi's brain running probable outcomes of courses of action. Hawksworth braced himself.

With his friends watching him, Hoi stood his ground, tensing his muscles and hissing in Cantonese, '*Sek sii gwei-lo. Diu lei lau mau*!'

In one deft move, Hawksworth shifted his weight to his left foot while twirling his cane like a baton in his right hand. The heavy knob on the end swung upward to slam hard into the shorter man's testicles.

Hoi's hands reflexively cupped his groin, though no sound came from his mouth. As he toppled over in pain, Hawksworth's cane slid from between his legs. A crowd quickly materialized from the throng of passers-by, gathering to watch and point, jabbering at one another, some laughing. His friends emerged from the shop to stare mortified at their boss rolling in the filth of the street, writhing and groaning in agony.

The tall man placed his boot on Hoi's chest, rolling him over and pinning him down. 'Detective, please shackle this man and escort him to Her Majesty's Prison at Outram Road,' he spoke over his shoulder to Jeremiah. 'Toss him in the Stews. We will question him tomorrow.'

He studied the mob as he spoke, searching the dark eyes under the burning sun. Somewhere in the crowd might be the very men who had murdered Low Teck Beng, and if they saw Hoi being taken in, they would realize that the police were getting closer.

Then he felt his stomach churn again from the heat and bitter tea and he turned away from the crowd to lean against the pillar, retching drily. He straightened up and walked wearily back to the waiting rickshaw. There would be no more work today, he decided.

\* \* \*

Detective Inspector Dunu Vidi Hevage Rizby was seated on the hard wooden bench on the top floor entrance of the unmarried officer's dormitory. His work day was finally done and he looked forward to luxuriating in a bath before retiring to sleep. He was pulling off his left boot, his mind drifting to the soothing water that awaited him, when a breathless uniformed officer appeared on the stairs. The appearance of the officer brought a frown to Rizby's fox face. It could not possibly be good news.

The boy spoke quickly in shaky English so that it took several exchanges for the information to be transmitted. Rizby sighed. There would be no bath tonight.

'Who at the scene is from my squad?' he asked the boy.

'Detectives Nair and Anaiz, sir. Nair sent me to fetch you.'

Rizby pulled his boot back on. 'Is there a carriage waiting?'

'Downstairs, sir. I will accompany you.'

The streets of the Chinese Quarter were unusually quiet, he noted as the carriage clattered from one puddle of gaslight to another. As they rolled closer to Macao Street he saw that a crowd had gathered, mostly Chinese, coolies and businessmen and even a few women. They were being held back by uniformed officers so that the crush of bodies formed a ring around the front of a shophouse. The carriage rolled to a stop on the edge of the crowd – he saw that another was coming directly behind his own.

He stepped down, shrugging on his linen jacket to cover the Tranter .32 revolver on his hip. From the carriage behind emerged Assistant Coroner Tatham, looking tired and careworn. Rizby noticed that his nightshirt stuck out from his waistcoat; he had been asleep when roused then came immediately without taking the time to dress properly.

'Good evening, Detective Inspector Rizby. Or should I say good morning?' Tatham asked in a voice that was high-pitched for a man his age and size.

Rizby checked his pocket watch. The hands pointed to just past midnight. 'Morning it is, barely. Dr. Cowpar is unavailable?'

'Down with fever. They got me from bed not less than thirty minutes ago, said it was murder, multiple homicide, but in the rush I forgot to ask who was killed.' Tatham paused, brushing his knuckles against his whiskers, taking in the scene. 'Quite a to do. There must be twenty police here.'

'Lau Chi Man, the boss of the Hai San *kongsi*, and three of his associates were gunned down about an hour ago.'

There was a moment of quiet while the news sunk in. 'Good lord!'

'We had better find detective Rajan Nair, he was first to arrive after the uniforms.'

As if on cue, Nair appeared from the crowd and Rizby and Tatham pushed through to the entrance of the shophouse. He saw Detective Anaiz along with an interpreter taking the witness statement of a hysterical charwoman. They walked up the plain wooden boards of the creaky stairs. For the main house of one of the big three *kongsi* in Singapore, the interior was remarkably spartan, he noted. It lacked any sense of luxury. Compared to the trappings of even a modest hotel, it was as though the Hai San were monastic.

The murder room was, however, depressingly familiar. Lau and the three others were tossed about the room like rag dolls, their bodies chewed by shotgun pellets. Blood soaked into the bare wood of the floorboards, spewed across the unadorned plaster of the gore-splattered walls, pooled around the corpses. Fifteen empty brass shells lay on the floor, half filled with blood and body fluids. It was almost as if someone had recreated the killing at the Plum Suite on a bare stage set with prop furniture. The set-up was easy to read: they had been talking to the killers who then pulled their weapons and fired before the victims had a chance to react. Only here there was no central victim, no Low Teck Beng with a ceramic idol sunk in his neck. But the situation was sparkling clear: someone was removing the top echelon of the leading *kongsi* in Singapore.

Tatham glanced at Rizby then entered the room to begin the preliminary medical examinations.

Watching the Assistant Coroner work, the fox head tilted sideways. Forefinger and thumb rubbing his earlobe, Rizby spoke into empty space, knowing that Nair was beside him. 'They walked in here without a fight? They came in here with shotguns and simply walked up to the head of the most powerful Cantonese *kongsi* in all of Malaya then shot him and his bodyguards?' his voice crackled with wary scepticism.

'There are two more bodies downstairs,' Nair said behind him. 'It looks like they tried to stop the killers and were then shot themselves. The only witness was the charwoman who says she hid in the downstairs cupboard while the men shot their way out.'

Rizby spoke into the room, gazing at the crumpled corpses. 'They shot their way out but they walked in? Tell me Nair, who in Singapore can walk into the private hotel room of Low Teck Beng *and* into the *kongsi* house of Lau Chi Man while carrying large calibre weapons? Who has that sort of access?'

'Police?'

'Or the army,' Rizby turned to look at Nair. 'But in both cases the victims were apparently talking with the men who shot them. They were not suddenly caught unawares by police or soldiers. It is almost as if the killers were invited in.'

He turned heel on the grisly scene then headed downstairs to where Anaiz was speaking to the charwoman. 'Ask her if she recognized the killers.'

'I already have. She said that she had never seen the men before. There were three men, Chinese, aged between mid-twenties and mid-thirties. They spoke Cantonese. To judge by their accents, she suspects they were from China, not Malaya.'

'Did she see the weapons? How did they get them into the *kongsi* house in the first place?'

Anaiz spoke, then the interpreter, then the woman, then the interpreter said to Rizby, 'She says that they carried big bags with them.'

'Were they expected?'

The chain of voices went round again, 'Yes. She says that when they arrived, Lau himself came down to greet them.'

'When you are finished, make sure this woman is given an escort home. We must arrange for her protection. In fact,' he scratched the stubble on his chin, 'so long as she does not make too much of a nuisance, take her into protective custody as a material witness. I do not want her to disappear like the staff of the Hotel Formosa.'

He walked back outside, hoping for fresh air but finding only tepid murkiness. The crowd had thinned but there was still a dozen or so people lingering. He realized that they were waiting to see the bodies – they probably had heard the shots and were wondering who had died. The shophouse had long been the lair of the Hai San – it was no secret. That is was little more than a stone's throw from the Central Police Station had always been a point of pride with the Hai San; they could thumb their nose at the police. Now it made their execution all the more brazen.

The pre-dawn call to prayer was sounding from the mosque on Telok Ayer Street when the first of the shattered bodies were carried down the stairs and into the carriages for the short ride to the dead house. Rizby stood at the edge of the crowd by a gaslight, watching as a stretcher bore away the corpse of what was once one of the most feared men in all of Malaya.

A gurgled yelp caught his attention and he glanced around the street. A Chinese coolie came staggering out of the darkness of an alley, his arms held limply before him, his eyes sunken deep into his head. His clothing appeared to be that of a *sinkeh*, only recently arrived. He shambled toward Rizby, soaking wet, his hands held out before him. Another strangled gurgle escaped from his lips and the Detective Inspector instinctively recoiled. Stepping into the circle of the gaslight, the stinking man clutched as his throat with hands so shrivelled that the skin hung limply, as though it were about to fall away. The coolie took a step toward Rizby then, emitting a wet throaty noise, collapsed at his feet. He shook once then lay still.

Other bystanders had noticed him and, like Rizby, had kept their distance, but now they began to creep forward to peer at the body.

'Stay back!' Rizby yelled. 'Back! All of you!'

Seeing the commotion forming, the coroner's assistant pushed through the crowd to stand by Rizby's side. 'Where did this man come from?' Tatham asked, his high-pitched voice turning into a whine of alarm.

'He came out of the darkness of the street, from that direction,' Rizby pointed down the alley.

'Keep everyone away from this...body. Is he dead?'

Rizby knelt and rolled the man over. Flecks of vomit covered his mouth and dotted his shirtfront. He appeared shrunken, his skin a sickening puce colour. He was not breathing. There was no pulse. A stench of rotten fish was overpowering. 'He is gone,' Rizby said, his fingers at the man's throat.

'He could not have come far in such a condition. We urgently need to discover which house he came from. My guess is there are more like him. They will need immediate medical treatment. And we must determine how long have they been in the settlement and where they have gone, worked, slept. It spreads by contact with air.' The Assistant Coroner spoke so rapidly it was hard to understand him.

Rizby whistled for Detective Nair, whom he saw across the street. 'I will put my top man on it now.' As he was instructing Nair to gather the uniforms to help with the crowd, he heard Tatham say loudly, as if to himself, 'I will wake the Principal Civil Medical Officer personally.'

'For one dead man? Is that necessary?'

Tatham's haggard tiredness had been replaced by an electric excitement. 'He is the only one with the authority to order a comprehensive quarantine of the settlement.'

'Quarantine?' Rizby asked, his voice ringing with apprehension.

'If he appeared on the street like this, it can only mean the worst. If there's one there may be a hundred more. Understand, Detective Inspector, Singapore may well be facing its first cholera epidemic in twenty years.'

CHAPTER VII

# Winchester 1893

HAWKSWORTH WAS NOT COMFORTABLE in his Superintendent's office. He had enjoyed the view from his previous space and grown used to having Rizby in an adjoining room. Then it had been his desk and worn-in chair and an uncomfortable wooden seat opposite for guests. This new room was too big for one man: it felt empty when he was alone in it. And unlike his previous office, here the walls went all the way to the ceiling, which created more privacy but prevented the circulation of air so that this room was perpetually stifling. The office was not yet wired for electricity, either, so he had neither electric lights nor desktop fan.

He leaned back in his chair as he sipped his morning coffee, contemplating the *punkah* swaying hypnotically above, the tassels swishing in counterpoint to the sweeping movement of the cloth. During the day, the *punkah* puller, an elderly Bengali with only one name – Gagan – who was as still and silent as a piece of furniture, was often Hawksworth's only companion. It made the Superintendent feel even more alone when only the two of were together in the room, the *punkah* swishing quietly overhead, Gagan's stick-thin leg moving rhythmically, mechanically, his eyes half shut and mouth half open, as though he were in a trance.

That morning he had discovered a sleek reticulated python curled asleep around the clay bathing jar in the brick-lined bathing room at the back of his bungalow in Geylang. It was more than five feet long, yet a mere baby that had crept during the night into the semi-enclosed space, perhaps attracted to the fresh water. Years previously, he would have thought nothing of it and simply ignored the thing – it would eventually go away on its own – but with little Fenella toddling around the house on her chubby legs, the snake's presence was worrying. He sent Ni to the nearby kampong to fetch one of the boys who lived there to help him dislodge and carry it away. The Malay lad who helped was thrilled at his good fortune, for he could sell the snake to the Chinese butcher's stall in the *pasar malam*, the night market, in Katong for a handful of coins.

The *punkah* swished above, fanning the hot air in the room. His coffee cup was empty but he was too lost in reverie watching the tassels swaying to serve himself more from the pot.

The clay bathing jars had acquired the sobriquet of 'Shanghai jars' and were quite large. It was pleasant to douse oneself with fresh water in the steamy equatorial mornings. There was also a funny story he had heard told many times about a young English lady who, being newly arrived in the tropics, was not aware of how to use the jar and assumed it was some sort of vertical bath. Petite, she managed to slip inside but quickly discovered that she was stuck. As she shrieked for help, her husband and servants burst in, and seeing her head protruding from the top of the jar, smashed the clay. The poor woman was left soaked and shaking, clutching at her pale naked modesty in a puddle on the floor while the native servants smirked down at her. The story was often related as a joke, but Hawksworth could not bring himself to smile as he recounted it now.

The *punkah* swished. Outside, a yell and crash in the yard yanked him from his distraction. He sat upright in his chair and was in the act of pouring himself another coffee when a knock came at the door followed by Rizby, who took a seat in one of the cushioned armchairs across from the Superintendent's desk.

'Good morning Detective Inspector,' Hawksworth spoke first, glad for the company. 'I am afraid I have finished the coffee. Shall I ring for Ah Fong to bring more?'

'Good morning, and no thank you, Superintendent, I have already taken my morning cup at the officer's barracks. I suppose you have heard the news of the murder of Lau Chi Man? And the discovery of the cholera victim nearby?'

'I have. Detective Nair briefed me earlier. My understanding is that you suspect the same killers as in the Low Teck Beng investigation.'

Rizby nodded affirmatively.

'Then we shall treat the cases as linked. Hopefully our Mr. Hoi will provide a lead when we interrogate him today. We need to let him stew a bit longer before we pull him into the light. As for the cholera victim, it appears that the Principal Civil Medical Officer is conducting an inquiry with the help of the army medical corps. This falls somewhat beyond our purview.'

'I have just heard that they found an entire shophouse stuffed with cholera victims, some already dead, only three doors down from the Hai San *kongsi* house. That is most likely where the man came from last night.'

Hawksworth tapped his fingers meditatively. 'If they do decide to enact a quarantine, it may well hinder our investigation.'

Rizby nodded again, then fell silent, distracted.

The only sound came from the swishing *punkah* above them. Neither seemed ready to start the day, their minds' elsewhere. Hawksworth broke the silence, 'You know, they have completed metaling Kallang Road all the way to Changi. Now they are starting on the dirt byway that runs past my bungalow. I will not mind the better road surface, especially during the monsoon rains, but the inconvenience now is very off-putting.'

'Superintendent, may I ask you something...of a...personal nature?'

Hawksworth was surprised. As close colleagues, they had faced life or death situations together, but they rarely if ever spoke of personal matters. 'Yes, of course, please....'

'It is about women...or a woman....'

Hawksworth was at a loss for words. Never before had Rizby shown, even less mentioned, any interest in women. Billiards and beer, yes. Women, no. For all he knew Rizby was utterly asexual.

'You see, Superintendent,' Rizby continued, 'I believe that I... well, there is a woman I would like to ask for her hand...to... matrimony, you see.'

'I congratulate you, Detective Inspector.'

'Thank you, sir. However, there is a complication.'

'Go on.'

'The problem is that while I have known the girl for a number of weeks now, I have yet to exchange more than a few pleasantries with her.'

'I see...perhaps you should tell me where you met...or meet... her? Who is she?'

'Her name is Soe Soe Aye. She is Burmese, a Buddhist like myself. We meet occasionally in Kampong Kapor, at the Pali Buddha shrine on Kinta Road.'

Hawksworth breathed a sigh of relief. For a moment he had a vision of some blue-eyed flaxen-haired European beauty with peaches and cream complexion with whom taut and wiry, short and dark, fox-faced Rizby had fallen hopelessly in love. The chances of such a union coming to fruition were slim to nonexistent. Rizby had already hit the top level a man with his colour of skin would reach in the Straits police force, and though the occasional pay raise or extended holiday may be granted him for his outstanding service, it was understood by everyone, including Rizby, that fair or no, he would see no further promotion. To do so would place him above Anglo officers, and that simply would not do. He took this unfairness in good sport, yet an emotional blow from an unrequited love with a European girl might prove to be too much. But a Burmese girl and a Buddhist, there was much hope for success.

'She is independent? How did she come to be in Singapore?'

'She is the housemaid of the Snodgrass family. They were recently transferred from Rangoon and brought her with them. Her English is tolerable as Mrs. Snodgrass has taught her.'

'How often do you see her? No late night assignations I assume? No impropriety?'

'Of course not, sir,' Rizby said archly, sounding genuinely surprised Hawksworth would even consider such things.

'Then what is your plan? How do you intend to move upon her?' He realized his words could be misconstrued and blustering, corrected himself, 'I mean, to broach the subject?'

'That is exactly the point on which I hoped you could advise me.'

He stared at Rizby, not comprehending. What did he know about marrying women? He and Ni were only in a common-law marriage and that was more or less accidental, an unexpected if completely satisfactory turn of events. As far as he could tell, the woman had made the decision. He had always thought he would remain a bachelor. 'Detective Inspector, I do not know if I am truly the person in whom you should place your trust. Perhaps Inspector-General of Police Fairer would be of greater assistance,' he added without intending sarcasm, 'Fairer behaves as though he were practically born married.'

Rizby began to speak but another knock came at the door, causing him to hold his tongue. A uniformed officer, a Sikh with a bright candy-stripped turban, entered the room and saluted smartly. 'Jolly good morning to you, Superintendent Hawksworth, sir. Please be informed that Sergeant Major Walker requests your presence in the armoury,' the man said with awkward diligence.

Hawksworth and Rizby made their way through the narrow hallways of the Central Police Station toward the armoury in the bowels of the building. The armoury had been wired for electricity; the pale blue light of overhead fixtures kept the worktable in the centre brightly lit while casting the corners in purple shadow. It smelled clean and mechanical, laced with the chemical aroma of gun oil and metal solvent. Keeping weapons from rusting in the tropical humidity required a full-time armorer and gunsmith, a crimson-faced Lancashire man named John Heaton who had been in Malaya for donkey's years. He spent his days in the windowless room constantly disassembling and cleaning and oiling the weapons of the police force; his movement came to resemble a machine, precise, calibrated, and angular.

Seated at the worktable with the police gunsmith was the grimacing visage of Sergeant Major Hardie Walker. Other than occasional random encounters in the station hallways or canteen, Hawksworth had not seen Walker in nearly a year. But it was the weapon on the table that now drew his attention. He had never seen anything like it before. It had a round smoothbore barrel like a fowling gun, yet beneath that was a wooden handle that appeared to slide back to work a mechanism around the receiver. The wooden stock had been cut back and tacked with padded cloth so that it was little more than a nub; the barrel appeared to have been shortened crudely with a hacksaw. Looking at it, the Superintendent had the vision of a hideous insect, a giant black mantis maimed and kicking under the blazing light on the smooth wood of the worktable.

'Beautiful, is it not?' Walker said, his eyes shining.

'What in the Lord's name is it?'

Walker scooped up the weapon, 'This is a Winchester Model 1893 slide action shotgun,' he said, pumping the wooden handle. The cracking sound it made was ominous, like the trapdoor of a gallows falling open. 'Twelve-gauge, it holds five shells in the magazine here, which can be fired as rapidly as the pump can be worked.' He racked the slide again to make his point.

'Five shells?' Rizby's fox face cocked to one side.

'Brass casing so that they will eject effectively when the handle is pumped,' Heaton said, placing a live cartridge on the table. It was the same type of shell that Rizby had found at the *kongsi* murder scenes.

'The shells that were loaded into this weapon hold shot used to hunt large to medium-sized game. Double-aught buck shot, nine pellets per shot. At close range they would cause incredible trauma to flesh,' Heaton spoke dispassionately, handing one of the live shells to Rizby for his inspection.

'That would explain how three men fired fifteen shots so rapidly as well as the immensity of the damage that they caused,' Hawksworth mused aloud.

'The gun appears to have been modified,' Rizby said, pointing.

'The stock and barrel have both been cut down, rather clumsily I might add. As you can see it shortens the weapon considerably, which is good for concealment but completely ruins the accuracy.'

'But for firing rapidly at close range with intent to kill multiple targets rapidly, I can think of nothing better,' Walker added with a note of admiration in his voice.

Hawksworth exhaled heavily. Except for the upper echelon of the *kongsi,* who could afford modern firearms, Chinese street gangs' weapons were mostly tools and utensils repurposed: knives and clubs and cleavers and chains. Occasionally they would capture a thug with an old pistol but anything more powerful was a rarity. But now, with such weapons as the Winchester in their hands, street violence would increase dramatically. Hopefully, the murders of Low Teck Beng and Lau Chi Man were not a harbinger of things to come. 'Where did you get it, Sergeant Major?'

'A suspect dropped it last night.'

'Dropped it?' Hawksworth could not conceal his surprise.

'I was at Magazine Road going for my evening perambulation when I espied five or six Chinamen huddled together. What struck me as suspicious was their standing with their backs to the street, as if they were sharing a secret.'

Hawksworth noted Walker's hands trembled while he spoke; he gripped the shotgun tightly to keep it from rattling. The man was fifty-five years if not older, and once the trembling started, Hawksworth knew, it did not stop. What will become of the Sergeant Major, the feared marksman, when he can no longer hold his rifle steady? Hawksworth wondered.

'I yelled for them to disperse,' Walker continued. 'Seeing me approach, they broke up and ran in opposite directions. I gave chase to one of them. As he was running, I saw that he had something heavy in a gunny sack that was slowing him down. He ran toward the river where the gas lamps give out and in the moonlight I nearly lost him but finally got him cornered where he had only two ways out, one past me, the other into the water. Then, all of a sudden, he shrieked like he had seen the devil and dropped the sack and jumped in the river.'

'You did not swim for him?' Rizby asked neutrally.

Walker took the question badly, answering in a surly tone. 'I did not because instead I picked up the gunny sack and felt the weight of the weapon and thought it was of more interest than the man.'

'Any idea as to why he jumped into the river leaving behind what must be a very expensive and hard-to-come-by piece of equipment?' Hawksworth asked earnestly.

'At first I thought it was me that scared him but then as I was examining the gun I noticed that there was someone else up the road. I could not see very well, as I said there were no gas lamps down that way and the moon was not bright, but he was dressed like a Chinaman.'

'He was too far away to pursue?'

'I yelled for him to stop but he turned tails and ran for it and I was too winded from first chasing the other to catch him. He moved very quickly for a man his size. Or I should say he hopped.'

'*Hopped* did you say?' Heaton interjected.

With his arms held straight out before him, palms down, knees bent slightly, Walker jumped forward. 'Like a rabbit.'

'I see.'

'He smelled terrible, too. Even from that distance. I thought there must be durian stored in a nearby godown.'

Hawksworth narrowed his eyes, 'Smelled like a corpse?'

'Exactly like a corpse, yes. But he moved quickly. I did try to chase him but as I said I was already winded. He must have slipped down an alley or into a house for he disappeared just around the next corner.'

'I do not suppose you looked up?' Rizby asked.

'*Up*? No, I did not think to. Why would I?' Walker snarled.

'The Detective Inspector is asking because *jiangshi* are believed to be capable of flight.'

'What is a *jiangshi*?' Heaton asked with a note of amusement in his voice. He knew Hawksworth's reputation for being too-close-for-comfort to native superstitions.

'A *jiangshi* is an undead corpse, risen from the grave. I remember hearing stories about them when I was a boy in Penang,' Hawksworth spoke vacantly, as if disowning the words.

'They say that a magician can control a *jiangshi* to do his bidding,' Rizby added in a helpful tone.

'Rot!' Walker bellowed, unconsciously pumping the Winchester. 'Chronic rot. You two are always prattling on about ghosts or werewolves or some such nonsense. Been too long in the East, Hawksworth. Starting to think like a native.'

'I am sure there is a perfectly reasonable explanation, Sergeant Major. Perhaps a trick of light and shadow, nothing more,' Hawksworth said evenly, but he could see that Rizby was agitated.

'Be that as it may, I will store this,' Walker lovingly cradled the shotgun, 'in the armoury. I assume you will need it for evidence at some point in the future, but for now it will be most secure here.' He did not appear willing to let go of it anytime soon.

Once again in the Superintendent's office, Hawksworth propped his right foot on a footstool, staring absently at the oblong of azure sky framed by the small high window. 'Where would a Cantonese street gang member get his hands on such an exceptional American weapon?'

'It is easy to smuggle things into Singapore,' Rizby replied while leaning with his back against the wall.

'True, but I wonder who procures such weapons for such people? I wonder, were they supplied merely to murder Low Teck

Beng? Or is someone plying expensive foreign weapons to the gangs for some other reason? Or perhaps they stole them?'

'Where shall we start to look?'

'What is the largest American import into Singapore?'

'Legal? Earth oil and other petroleum products, though our works in Sumatra may soon catch up. As for illegal imports, both opium and people.'

'Start with the legal imports. Find out if the Americans guard their shipments with Winchester shotguns or if there are other legal channels by which they will enter the settlement. I will look into the illegal channels.'

'And what do you think of the Sergeant Major's encounter last night? I have not heard of a *jiangshi* in Singapore before.'

Hawksworth narrowed his eyes at Rizby. 'If I had to guess, the true explanation is far more frightening than the superstition. It is possible that a cholera victim was wandering the streets in a fever. The putrid smell and strange movements and lack of response would all suggest someone quite ill. A quarantine may be inevitable.'

Rizby studied Hawksworth's face closely but could read nothing there. The man's ability to both believe and disbelieve simultaneously never failed to amaze him. He smiled at the seated man, then spoke casually, 'I will start with the American Consul. Where will you be, sir? In case I need to reach you on short notice.'

Hawksworth did not stir while he spoke, though his voice had a sharp edge, 'I will be at Outram Prison, asking our friend Mr. Hoi what he knows about *ah kuahs* and Winchester shotguns.'

*   *   *

'Jeremiah, with me, now,' he barked at the young detective – the first member of the Native Crime Squad that he came across while preparing to leave.

'Yes, sir!' came the hasty reply as the rangy younger man scrambled to catch up with the figure striding with his cane. 'Where are we going, sir?'

'Outram Prison. Interrogation of the suspect we brought in yesterday.'

Interpreter Heng was waiting on the street with a carriage. Along the way, Hawksworth sensed that Jeremiah was at a loss for words. 'Is this your first interrogation, detective?'

'Yes, sir, it is.'

'In that case you are to remain silent throughout. Do not utter a sound. Stay out of the suspect's field of vision but make sure he knows that you are near him. If I ask you a question, you are to reply honestly but as briefly as possible. Do not string out long sentences. The idea, Jeremiah,' Hawksworth paused while the carriage bumped over something in the road causing the passengers to judder in their seats, 'is to intimidate him with your presence only.'

Old Noorhakim Bin Mohamed Noor let them into the prison, his black eyes blue from cataract, nearly blind from standing all day beneath the blazing equatorial sun, peering into the faces of visitors to determine if they were honest men or not. He recognized the sound of their voices; Hawksworth's he had known for years; Jeremiah's he had heard for the first time the day before.

'New recruit with you today, Superintendent? He came yesterday with a boy bound for the Stews.' The Malay voice was slow and mellow.

'Did you keep our suspect suitably comfortable, Hakim?'

The molasses voice crackled into brittle laughter. 'No mortal man can take more than three days in there and you left the young Chinese in there for twenty-four hours already. He will sing like a *murai* for you now.'

They waited with Heng in the anteroom while guards brought Hoi to the interrogation room. He was blinking in the brightness, shivering in a wooden chair beside an empty table, his wrists and ankles shackled when Hawksworth and Jeremiah came in. As instructed, the younger detective took up position behind the suspect while Hawksworth strode toward him, cane rapping ominously against the stone floor. Heng lingered off to one side, barely visible to the seated boy.

'You stink, Hoi,' Hawksworth spoke with evident disgust, leaning heavily on his cane, towering over the shaking form. There was no reply, so the Superintendent smacked him once in the face. He saw Jeremiah flinch but kept his attention on the suspect.

'I am speaking to you. Answer when I speak. I said you stink.' He slapped him again.

'Yes,' was the croaked reply.

'Yes?'

'Yes, sir.'

'Better.' Hawksworth nosily pulled out the chair opposite the suspect and placed his cane within easy reach on the table, the knobbed end that had felled Hoi the previous day pointed now directly at him.

'Why did you kill Low Teck Beng?'

Hoi sniffled once, a look of complete terror filling his face. Jeremiah looked surprised, too, but kept his mouth shut.

'I asked you a question, boy.' Hawksworth raised his hand to slap but Hoi cowered and uttered unintelligibly. The Superintendent lowered his hand, 'What was that? I did not hear you.'

'I did not kill him.'

'But you helped, did you not?'

Hoi fell into an uncertain silence, eyes fixed on the empty table before him. Hawksworth knew that the silence was not born of recalcitrance but fear…and not fear of the Caucasian man threatening him now but fear of something far larger and more nebulous. Fear of the Chinese mass out there who would consider him a traitor. The Superintendent had seen this many times before and knew how to turn it to his advantage.

'Understand that the minute I let you out of here, your friends will have their turn. They will torture you to learn what you told us. Then they will kill you.'

He saw the fear in Hoi's trembling eyes. There was no braggadocio now. The tough guy exterior had melted away to reveal the frightened boy beneath.

'Your only chance is if we release you in secret. We will give you an escort to a ship that will take you to Batam Island. From there you can make your way back to whatever shit-hole in China you come from. Otherwise, I will open the door of this prison and send you straight into the waiting arms of your partners in crime.'

Hoi's mouth moved but no sound came out.

'I do not have all day. Tell me what you know and I promise you safe passage to Batam, or stay silent and face the wrath of your criminal associates. Choose. Now.'

Hoi nodded and then began to speak, wiping his nose with the back of his shackled hand.

'I did not mean for Meng Hwee to die,' he sniffled. 'He was my friend, too, not just a….'

'Meng Hwee is the female impersonator you sent to Low Teck Beng?'

He nodded.

'Is that how you treat your friends? As a means to an end?'

'No,' the answer was a whisper. Hawksworth sensed the heaviness of the regret.

'He was more than a friend to you, was he not? He would keep you company when you grew homesick, did he not? You two were very close, indeed.'

Hoi jerked in the shackles, 'No! Not like that!'

'He was your closest brother, your secret sharer, and you sent him to die like a dog. Admit it!'

'If I knew that they would kill him, I never would have told them about it,' the boy sniffled.

'Told who about what?'

The shackled boy sniffled again and Hawksworth sent Jeremiah to fetch him a glass of water. It was time to apply the velvet, not the iron.

'Tell me who killed Meng Hwee.'

'I do not know who killed him, but I know who knew where he was when he was with Low Teck Beng.'

'Who?'

'Yueng Ha Sau, leader of the Tiger Claws.'

'The very gang you aspire to join?' Hawksworth spoke confidently to hide his speculation. He had never heard of the Tiger Claws.

Hoi nodded meekly, his smooth face dejected in defeat. 'Yueng knew that we were providing boys to Madam Koo for Low Teck Beng. He laughed and did not care, but about a month later he asked me to tell him the next time I arranged a boy for Teck Beng. He wanted to know when and where. Koo does not tell me where Teck Beng takes the boys, but since Meng Hwee was my friend, he told me where they were to meet. It was the Plum Suite.'

'Meng Hwee told you that they would meet at the Hotel

Formosa, and you told Yueng. This was the same night of the murders?'

Silent tears started on Hoi's cheeks.

'I need you to be clear with me, Hoi. You told Yueng that your boy Meng Hwee was with Low Teck Beng at the Hotel Formosa the same night that they were killed. Is that accurate?'

He nodded affirmatively, wiping tears and snot from his face, his shackles rattling.

'Do you know if Yueng killed them?'

He looked at Hawksworth now for the first time, his eyes red rimmed, the shame brewing inside him, 'I do not know.'

The Superintendent pushed the knob of his cane across the table at Hoi as he stood. 'If you are lying to me, boy, I will find you and I will not be so forgiving. Do you understand?' He rapped the knob once hard on the table, causing both Hoi and Jeremiah to jump. 'I will arrange for your passage to Batam. You will be released tonight under cover of darkness. Get out of Singapore and never come back. If I see you here again, I will put this cane through your skull.'

In the carriage ride back to the Central Station, he noticed that Jeremiah was especially quiet. 'Do you think I was too fierce with the boy, Detective?'

'Did you mean what you said about arranging for his passage to Batam?'

'I did indeed. Hoi is young enough that he still stands a chance. If he heads home now, he may face some shame, but he will live a longer life.'

Heng nodded at Jeremiah to confirm what Hawksworth had said. As the carriage rolled through the Chinese Quarter past the very spot where they had taken Hoi the day before, Hawksworth said grimly, 'This Tiger Claw gang that Hoi aspired to join will have to prove themselves in order to move higher up the clan hierarchy. Hoi's torture would have been extreme. Any violence with which I threatened the boy pales compared to what they would do to him if they caught him.' He turned from the window to face Jeremiah, who seemed to be contemplating the Superintendent's words. 'Are you sure this is the line of work that is best suited for you, Jeremiah?'

Tensing his jaw, the young detective spoke in a deep voice meant to show his resolve. 'Teach me everything you know.'

\* \* \*

After dinner, while Fon washed the plates and Ni dandled Fenella on her knee, cooing at her in Siamese and tickling her nose, he checked the bottom of the Shanghai jar in the brick bathroom. There was no snake in the room, only a brown frog with a broken back leg that caused it to leap pathetically sideways when it tried to hop away. A gecko, known as *chickchack* for the chirping sound they made, scurried on the wall beside his head. Five successive chirps were considered good luck. Tonight he only heard two.

Later, after Fon had tucked Fenella into bed and had retired with her, Hawksworth and Ni sat on the veranda together, a glass of arrack in the man's hand. It was a damp night, and despite the high temperature, Ni shivered. She went inside to retrieve a shawl when a carriage rolled up before their house. It was late to be travelling and he knew immediately that something was amiss.

Hawksworth was out of his chair and striding across the darkness of his front lawn, his cane stabbing the grass, when the carriage door opened and a Chinese boy in plain cotton pantaloons and smock bounded out. A messenger from the Mother-Flowers, but such a late night visit, and by carriage no less, was unprecedented.

The boy stood at the edge of the property, his feet never leaving the dirt of the road. He murmured good evening to Hawksworth in Hokkien, and said nothing more. Before him he held a piece of paper, folded twice.

No sooner had he taken the paper from the boy's hand then the lad raced to the waiting carriage, which immediately sped away, lamps burning orange as it receded in the darkness.

He unfolded the note under the yellow light of the paraffin lamp on his veranda. It was in English, badly written in block letters, some of which were skewed as though the writer were drunk while others were reversed completely, but he was able to interpret the message.

The note was from Tan Yong Seng, and it provided information to Hawksworth a full twelve hours sooner than if he received it through official police channels.

Chong Yong Chern, the *samseng ong*, the big boss of the Mother-Flower *kongsi*, had been shot to death along with two bodyguards in their safe house across the straits in Johor Bahru.

The killers were Cantonese armed with shotguns.

## CHAPTER VIII

# Johor Bahru

IT WAS HIS FIRST TIME visiting the bungalow that Yong Chern built as the house he would share with Shu En in Tanjong Katong. Knowing that he would be spending most of his time away from home attending to business, Yong Chern had spared no expense for her comfort. The seafront plots were already sold, but he was able to buy one behind these, on the unpaved dirt track they called Syed Alley Road. The land had previously been a coconut planation owned by old Dunman, Singapore's first Superintendent of Police, but was now being parcelled out to Peranakan families who wanted to live near the seashore, and European and Jewish families who wanted weekend homes near the popular beach off Grove Road. It was one of the few beaches that was safe for sea swimming as a sandbar kept the sharks out of the shallow water. A plain white obelisk pointed skyward from the middle of the sandy stretch shaded by coconut trees, marking the eastern limit of Singapore harbour. Fort Tanjong Katong sat at the other end of the beach; when its two big Armstrong guns engaged in target practice, they shook the loose sand all around the fort and were known to knock glassware off shelves a quarter mile away.

The two-story bungalow was nestled in coconut trees, the parcel bordered by rhododendron shrubs and tall croton plants to increase privacy. A gravel walkway led to the entrance, elevated several feet from the ground in the Anglo-Malay style. Walking toward it now, the fronds in the palms above him ruffling in the salty sea breeze from the shore less than a half mile away, Hawksworth could not help but recall when he first met Yong Chern, when the Mother-Flower *kongsi* were housed in a one-storey shophouse on Hokkien Street. Now he could afford to build a bungalow with a second floor veranda and a tile roof in the most expensive suburban district in the settlement. Or he had been able to afford: now he was stiff in Johor Bahru and the Mother-Flower fortune would be run by Yong Seng…and perhaps Shu En herself.

Hawksworth could hear horses whinny as he walked up the front steps. There were stables behind the house. A young female servant in a plain cotton smock, a *sinkeh* not long from China, opened the door after seeing the police shield he flashed. Inside, his cane rapped hollowly against the fine wood beneath the fringed Persian carpet. The foyer was elegant, with mirrors in ornate metal frames reflecting the somewhat weather-beaten clothes of the tall European. The mirrors were hung at a height designed to reflect the visages of shorter people: he could not see his own face.

A voice sounded in Hokkien from a farther room and he recognized with an unexpected frisson the soft purling sound of Shu En. The servant called in response, identifying the visitor, then led him forward. Hawksworth was unpleasantly surprised to find himself nervous as he approached the half-open door to the sitting room.

Shu En was sitting alone at a mah-jong table, idling playing with the colourful ivory tiles, her eyes on him as he entered. An Edison Motor Phonograph, its brass trumpet standing like a flower on a stalk from a polished dark walnut case, was on a side table beside her. The music of a clarinet and piano was audible above the crepitating surface noise of the rotating wax cylinder; it would be a four-note figure on the clarinet that would play in his mind whenever he recalled this moment: her seated in the brilliant room, petite fingers toying with a mah-jong tile, her moon glow face turned toward him, her rook-black hair in a loose chignon, as if she had been expecting him.

She was dressed all in white, a simple smock with loose cotton pants, to signify that she was in mourning, but the whiteness of the clothes only added to the beguiling ambience of the space. The sitting room was cheerfully bright, decorated in pastels of sea green and lavender and furnished in the Western style, with a daybed and matching bolsters upholstered in dun-coloured corduroy. A carpet woven from bleached cotton shreds, with a pattern in a lighter shade of white, covered most of the floor. There were fresh flowers, too; magenta rhododendrons with dark green leaves and woody stems from the garden, exuding a clean fragrance whenever the gentle sea breeze blew through the open window. The mah-jong tiles clacked peacefully as she toyed with them; the duet on the Edison cylinder filled the room.

'Good morning, Superintendent,' she spoke in accented English, much to his surprise. She knew very few words when he last saw her. 'Yong Seng is not here.'

'I came as soon as I heard the news of Yong Chern. Please accept my condolences.'

'How good of you to come,' she smiled at him now, her teeth white and compact. She had switched to Malay, which she spoke imperfectly but better than the English that sat uncomfortably on her tongue.

'You are alone? Are there no guards?' he asked with alarm.

'They are here. You were seen long before you stepped on the property. One upstairs, I think, another pissing behind the stables, two more roaming around, treading dirt on my floors. Yong Seng ensured that his best men are here. I made sure that they were armed with pistols,' she said archly, her coral pink lips pursed.

He noticed that she had become slightly plump in the two years since he had seen her. The provocative razor sharp curves of her petite body had been shrouded with a domestic weight around her thighs and breasts that in no way detracted from her allure. Yet the pitch-black eyes that gazed at him intently could still conceal any cupidity; in that she was unchanged. Hawksworth knew that not yet twenty years old, she was considered by many to be the most dangerous woman in Singapore, and with good reason.

'Yong Seng has gone to Johor Bahru?'

She nodded, pushing a tendril of stray hair behind her ear. The Edison cylinder had stopped, creating a sudden vacant silence.

'I shall not stay long. I am also on my way to Johor…for Yong Chern.'

'You need not concern yourself with his passing,' she spoke assuredly, then added offhandedly, 'We will quickly take care of that business.'

'I am sure you will, but his death is related to my investigation and I will head to Johor Bahru regardless.'

The female servant returned with coffee in a silver carafe and a silver filigreed *bang* pipe, with a small pot of the narcotic in a matching silver pot. Shu En daintily packed the pipe with the tar-like stuff, a sticky substance derived from the unfertilized buds of the female cannabis plant. She struck a match and ignited the mass in the bowl while the servant poured the hot brew for Hawksworth into a ceramic cup.

Exhaling a cloud of blue smoke that filled the room with

a coniferous scent, she smiled at him, 'Coffee is your favourite beverage, is it not?'

'How did you know?'

She laughed a light chromatic laugh, 'Yong Seng tells me all about his adventures with his *ang-moh* police friend.'

He grimaced, displeased that he was an object of conversation when not present.

Seeing this reaction, she quickly added, 'I hear that you have a daughter now? They say that she is very beautiful.'

'She is the pride of my life,' he said, sipping coffee, feeling like an awkward schoolboy in her presence. It was strange to speak of his daughter with a former lover during a *tête-à-tête* brought about by Yong Chern's violent demise. The coffee was strong; he could feel his pulse quickening. With it came a rush of desire. If he reached for her, would she stop him? He shut down the impulse, watching yet another blue cloud of exhalation turn gold as it drifted across the sunlit window.

'I see that the After Eight club is doing well,' he said.

'Ah! Now you bring up the pride of *my* life,' she said, her words becoming detached from her facial expression – an effect of the *bang*. The nightclub, known for its discrete offerings, was something that she opened in the aftermath of Hawksworth's last case as Chief Detective Inspector. In a way, he had helped her by removing the competition. 'I now have much interesting information on European officials and businessmen. Did you know the Assistant Colonial Secretary is a fetishist?' she giggled.

Amused, Hawksworth asked, 'And what, pray tell, is Mr. Winstedt's preferred method of intercourse?'

She again laughed the high chromatic laugh, only this time it was warbled by the narcotic, 'He does not indulge in intercourse. What Mr. Winstedt enjoys is having young girls press their unwashed feet into his face.'

'What?'

'Young pretty girls who are otherwise immaculately clean but have not washed their feet for several days, their soles stinking and black with filth, rubbed and pressed against his face,' she could not repress another laugh. 'The girls tell me that he moans in ecstasy then spews his jam when they stuff their dirty toes in his mouth. They enjoy it, too. It is easy work for them, and the fat *ang-moh* is harmless and silly.'

Hawksworth knew the man professionally and now dreaded the next time he would see him, knowing that it would be impossible to keep the image of dirty toes out of his mind.

'Do you ever supply *ah kuahs* to your *ang-moh* clients?'

A mischievous grin broke across the pixie face, her black pupils twinkling from the *bang;* it made her almost intolerably delectable. 'Are you asking out of curiosity or because you want to know something about the killing of Low Teck Beng?'

'A little of both.'

'Ever the policeman,' she said, then lit the pipe again, the mass glowing in the bowl as she sucked in the smoke. Finished, she knocked the ash into a porcelain ashtray on the mah-jong table, then tucked her legs up beneath her on the chair seat so that her petite frame was held in a lotus position. Her head swayed slightly. 'Do you know about Teck Beng's cousin, Liu Xiao Hun? The one that has gone missing?'

'I do not. Do you think she is involved with these murders?'

Shu En shrugged, running her fingertips along the polished edge of the mah-jong table. 'He put her in charge of distributing girls to their brothels, then she disappeared.'

'When?'

'About a week before Teck Beng was shot. There are rumours

that she had taken up with a Cantonese and he did not approve.'

'A Hai San?'

She laughed lightly, then looked straight at him, face muscles slack, eyes wide open, the black irises big as she gazed at him: she was excited to ecstasy from the *bang*, and, he thought, she looks ravishing when she traipses through paradise. Seeing him stare at her, she smiled gently and warmly, 'I have no idea if he is Hai San, one hears so much nonsense these days...' her voice trailed off.

He watched her sliding a mah-jong tile back and forth on the table. Emblazoned on it in bright crimson was a Chinese character that resembled a sabre pointing downward. 'Do you play?' she asked.

He nodded his head no, taking another sip of coffee. The caffeine was going to his head; he felt the energy flowing into his system as he shifted in his chair.

Shu En held the tile up, 'This is the red dragon, the character is *hong zhong,*' she brought the tile close to her face to study it more closely, 'this tile represents the centre.'

He leaned on the table, placing his head closer to hers, to better examine the ivory piece.

'And this one,' she plucked up another, 'is known as the plum tile. The words for plum blossom are *mei hua*. Say *mei.*'

'May.'

She laughed at him with the Chinese laugh that means light condescension, as used with young children learning a lesson or foreigners who are friends. 'No, no. You must say it like *m-e-i*, with the sound in the middle going like this,' and she made a wave in the air with her fingertip.

'*Mei,*' he said hesitantly.

'Very good!' she clapped, then gently placed the tile in his palm. 'The plum brings the spring and innocence.' Her voice was dozy and she was not speaking clearly. Both fell silent as he studied the tile. There was a simple, stylized plum blossom etched into the ivory, over which he ran his blunt fingertip.

He could stay there forever in that bright, white room with her, the sea breeze caressing her jet-black hair, but time was growing short – he needed to get to Johor Bahru as quickly as possible and the journey from Tanjong Katong would take several hours, at least. 'I must go soon,' he said, placing the plum tile on the table between them.

'To Johor? You will find Yong Seng...or he will find you. He is now *samseng ong* of the Mother-Flower *kongsi*.'

'And you, Shu En? Where does Yong Chern's demise leave you?' he asked boldly, the coffee propelling him to impertinence. One should not speak so directly of the recently deceased.

She sat up straight now to look out the window so that her thin stalk of a neck was arched provocatively. 'You have a child now, Superintendent. You have made something that lasts, something with...meaning. Now I too want something that will last.'

'I am afraid that I do not understand.'

A faint smile crossed her pink coral lips, the curving bow her only reply.

He stood to go, 'Thank you for the coffee. I will see you again soon. We should not let so much time pass.'

'Superintendent Hawksworth,' she turned to him, but now her face had lost the far-away softness and had resumed harder lines. She was sobering quickly, climbing down from the high. Her tolerance for *bang* was considerable. 'Did you know that the Lows want to open a bank?'

'I had heard. According the Protector of Chinese, it will take them quite some time to do so.'

'I want one,' she said sternly.

'You want...a *bank*?'

Arching her back so that her breasts pointed at him, her chin held at the same angle, she said evenly, 'I want a bank. We will let the Lows open a bank and let them fail. We will learn from their mistakes. Then we will open a bank of our own.'

'The Bank of the Mother-Flowers?'

'A bank for Hokkiens,' she said in an indomitable tone as she reached to refill the pipe's bowl. He said goodbye once again, then turned to leave. She said to his back, softly in Malay, '*Sesuatu akan selama-lamanya.*'

'Something that will be forever,' he translated in his head.

\* \* \*

Some long-time residents still referred to Johor Bahru by its original name, Tanjong Putri, when it was merely a coastal fishing village at the foot of the Malay Peninsula. Since 1866, when Sultan Abu Bakar decided to locate his capital at the mouth of the shallow Segget River at the narrowest point of the straits across from Singapore, the village had grown into a booming border town. The Sultan himself spent most of his time either in Singapore or abroad and, through a generous concession program, had convinced many Teochew and Cantonese families to develop the land around Johor. The result was a sizable enclave of Chinese living semi-autonomously in a Malay sultanate a long cannon shot from a British colony. The Sultan had formed a police force, but the Chinese, because of their wealth and power, were largely left to run their districts on their own. Beyond the reach of the British officials, yet a short distance across calm water from Singapore, Johor Bahru had become the base of vice operations for the local *kongsi*.

The legal business links were strong between the two towns as well, and there had once been talk of constructing a bridge so that the Singapore steam tram could travel unimpeded between the two places, but nothing ever came of these plans. There was a scheme on the books to build a railway from Singapore's centre to the north coast at Kranji, where steam launches would take passengers directly from a jetty at the railhead across the straits to Johor, but the railway had been held up by political wrangling for years and ground was not yet broken, though every year it seemed it would be. Excepting the telegraph and telephone lines, the separation between the two places was as it had been for centuries.

Hawksworth's carriage rolled beneath the coconut palms lining Tanjong Katong to Geylang Road, the junction not far from his own bungalow, then headed over the river into the city centre to connect to the Bukit Timah Road that wound another seven miles through the vivid multi-hued greens of planation and jungle to the village of Kranji, where both steam launches and native sampans ferried passengers across the straits. The weather was turning darker in the interior, heavy storm clouds passing overhead, and the Superintendent hoped it would rain just long enough to tamp down the red dust of the laterite road. By the time he reached Kranji, the rain had started, but it was only a brief shower that spattered on the roadway and stirred the air without cooling it.

No steam launches were on the Singapore side when he arrived at the jetty, and not wanting to wait in the heat, he negotiated passage on a single, short-masted Malay sampan. The air was soupy with barely a breeze and the young lad who took him had to row much of the way, sweat glistening on his body. Across the bathtub-warm water, on the dark green of the Johor shore, they passed rows of misshaped plank houses on stilts, makeshift fishing *kelongs*, jetties built from discarded flotsam, protruding from the mangrove that lined the shore. The sampan passed close to the Sultan's Istana, his luxurious palace, surrounded by manicured gardens in the European style, situated on a hill overlooking the straits. The tall buildings of the Stulang steam sawmills at the mouth of the Segget River at the foot of the town hove into view, and then Hawksworth was disembarking at the pier. Hailing a rickshaw, he made his way directly to the police station. He wanted facts before he went looking for Yong Seng.

\* \* \*

'Yong Chern was shot so many times his body was nearly severed in half, which is impressive, considering his girth,' said the Johor Police Supervisor, a bulky middle-aged Malay with a thick neck and a face pitted with acne scars that he attempted to conceal with a prodigious moustache. 'So many shots were fired so quickly that those who heard them thought it was a single explosion.'

'Where was he when he was killed?' Hawksworth asked as he sipped tepid tea in the Supervisor's office.

'He was in his office in the shophouse owned by his *kongsi*. Witnesses say three Chinese men walked in without any restraint and simply opened fire. Other than the body, we recovered fifteen of these....' He handed a brass shotgun cartridge to Hawksworth, who held it up in the amber light of early evening pouring through the Supervisor's windows. He could see the market on Pulau Segget at the mouth of the river, piles of silver fish skin glimmering in baskets.

'This is a cartridge used in an American weapon, a Winchester shotgun. It allows one man to rapidly fire five shots in close proximity to his target. The same weapons were used in the murders of *kongsi* headmen in Singapore.'

'*Ya ampun*!' the man exclaimed in dismay. 'Someone is killing the *kapitans* of the clans? We had heard rumours, but were not sure what to believe.'

'It would appear they are true, but we have no idea who is doing the killing nor why. They have now proved that they can reach Johor,' Hawksworth sighed, placing his teacup quietly into the saucer. 'Is there any other information you can give me about the murder? Descriptions of the killers, for instance?'

The Supervisor's curly hair was slicked down with hair tonic and did not move as he shook his head negatively. 'Nothing. The Chinese do not like to announce themselves as witnesses. However, if anything else comes to light I will let you know.' He stroked his moustache then asked, 'You are to take the body back to Singapore?'

'I am.'

'The Mother-Flowers are making inroads here in Johor Bahru. The Cantonese are losing power as they age and the Teochew are increasingly moving into legitimate businesses. The Cantonese still dominate most of construction and gambling here, but much of the illegal trade in town is in the hands of the Hokkien gangs, and the Mother-Flowers control most of them.'

Hawksworth stared for a moment at the Supervisor. He had the rough edges and the hard eyes of a man who had seen action yet he spoke of the Chinese gangs who operated in his town – indeed, right outside his very window – as though he were viewing them through a telescope on some distant shore. Which *kongsi* was paying him? Probably all of them, Hawksworth realized. And he was probably told to keep his nose where he was told to keep it: everyone from the Sultan down to the street sweeper did not want to jeopardize the annual fortune they made from the Chinese activity, legal and illegal.

Rising, the tall man stuck out his hand, 'Thank you for your help. It is late now. I will stay in Johor tonight and escort the body back to Singapore in the morning.'

'May I recommend the Hotel Casablanca?' the Malay said, pumping Hawksworth's hand, 'It is located near the jetty and is popular with European visitors who...' he caught himself before he mentioned money.

Catching his meaning, Hawksworth smiled. 'I require nothing fancy, I assure you. I am here on police business, not on holiday,' he said coolly. Was the Malay Supervisor aware that he would have to pay for the hotel himself?

\* \* \*

At night he sought Yong Seng. The area under Mother-Flower control was to the north of the traditional Cantonese zone, known as Kampong Wong Ah Fook. When they first started their operation there, Yong Seng had told him, the Mother-Flowers had paid a tithe, a sort of right-of-way fee, to the Cantonese gang running the zone for the Hai San. That their direct competitors would allow this set-up at first amazed the Superintendent, but then he saw the prescient practicality in the scheme. In this way, the dominant gang would earn money even if their rivals supplanted them. Now that the Cantonese were running the big construction projects the Sultan was undertaking, laying a grid of new roads over the snaking river, the Mother-Flowers were allowed their own territory, even if this meant dominating local vice. But the tithe was still paid, so everyone was content.

The architecture of the shophouses was no different from what he was used to in Singapore – or Penang, or Malacca, for that matter – the same one- or two-storey narrow buildings with a sloped tile roof, the peak running parallel to the façade, not perpendicular as in European houses. The same red laterite roads, the same sweaty shirtless rickshaw coolies, the branches of the occasional banyan hanging low into the street, the air roots tied up in knots so traffic could pass beneath.

But the similarities ended there, for this was, more than any town he had experienced before, a Chinese town, and without British rules and regulations, the street life propagated relentlessly. In the fluid darkness of the kampong at night, it was like moving through a carnival. Striding while watching two men drunkenly push each other as though waltzing, he nearly tripped over a legless man begging in the streets from a wheeled board. Cursing at the tall European, the beggar tossed a fistful of filth at him then pushed himself laboriously over the unpaved road.

A screech called his attention to a monkey with a rope around its neck. Its owner squatted behind a sharp-faced creature dressed in a tattered Pierrot costume with a conical hat, snapping two miniature cymbals together while making hideous noises supposed to resemble human singing. A crowd of men – for everyone around him was a man, and Chinese – had gathered to watch. They laughed, pointing. When the monkey fell quiet, his owner jerked the rope around his neck viciously to make him start again. Despite the crowd, the spittoon for coins that the monkey held out at the end of his performance was nearly empty – it would be a long night for the pathetic creature.

Durians hung in great spiky profusion from a stall cobbled together from scrap wood. Behind the durians, in the light of an oil lamp, he could see a rough table had been set up next to a wire cage filled with cobras. The durians' rancid stench filled his nose as he stopped to watch a man behead a snake.

A thin boy reached fearlessly into the cage, scooping out one of the long forms slithering inside. Stroking the top of the snake's head to calm it, he held it down to the table where his companion whacked off its head in one chop of a clever. The body jerked then began to coil around the boy's arm, who held it forward to drain the blood into a glass. Only inches away, the head on the table still moved, snapping open and closed, the white fangs showing. The blood drained, the boy began to peel the skin from the flesh, the body continuing to coil around his arm as though fighting him. A grill and brazier stood on the other end of the table, where the snake meat would be strung in little slivers onto short bamboo sticks then roasted. Hawksworth watched a man buy the glass of snake's blood, tip it back and gulp it down, sticky and warm, while handing the boy two coins. The blood supposedly made men virile.

A gunshot pulled him back from the spectacle, his body reflexively adjusting its balance so he could use his cane as a club. But no pistol could be seen and no one behaved as though they had been shot. Where the gunfire had come from, he had no idea. It would not be the last time that night he heard a shot but could not identify the source.

The end of the street was an empty void where the road and buildings and lanterns stopped and the complete darkness began. A shadow puppet stage had been set-up on this last stretch of road, a miniature *wayang* opera. The red cloth of the little proscenium was worn in places, and the leather skin of the thin puppets appeared tattered on the backlit scrim. The humble spectacle matched the clanking toy-like music made by an orchestra of four skinny men of indeterminate age playing gong and cymbals, rattle-drum and wooden clapper, and a badly tuned *erhu*. Despite the grotesquerie, or perhaps because of it, a small crowd of boys and men had gathered in the dim circle of light cast by the oil lamps to watch the show.

Standing on the edge of the crowd, he could see over all their heads to the small stage where imps played out the imperial romance. He did not recognize the story, only the character types, denoted by the colour of the paint. The harlot's white face signified her wicked and deceitful character; the scholar's face was painted violet to show his upright character and sophisticated mien. The unseen puppeteer made a nasal singing noise to accompany the movements of his characters, but no words were sung. It was only an approximation of the melody. The audience would be familiar with the story.

The smell of opium was strong – the building behind the stage was probably a smoking house – and it mingled with the sweat of the bodies around him and the pungent aroma of cooking grease wafting from the street stalls. The air took on a hallucinatory density, as though he were submerged in still water.

Hawksworth did not notice the tip of the knife blade in his lower back until it had pressed deep enough to cause pain. Balancing on his good foot, he whirled around, the heavy end of his cane swinging like a club through the thick air.

He just had time to redirect the strike when he recognized Yong Seng's face grinning at him.

'Good lord, man, I nearly knocked you cold.'

Laughing, Yong Seng gripped his elbow, 'Not a chance. You are not that fast! One thrust and the knife would be in your kidney.'

Recovering his poise, Hawksworth asked, 'How did you find me?'

Yong Seng shrugged, 'You are not only the tallest but also the whitest man on the street.'

Hawksworth smiled wryly then his face fell. 'I am very sorry about Yong Chern.'

Yong Seng's face turned stoic, then taking Hawksworth by the arm, he said quickly, 'This is not a good place to talk. Come with me.'

'Where?'

'You have wandered past the edge of the Cantonese kampong into Hokkien territory. We own all the houses from here to the river. Our *kongsi* house is over here.'

He walked quickly beside the shorter man, who was, he saw by his speed and purpose, completely sober. The *kongsi* house was nothing more than a shophouse on an adjacent street, its back directly on the river's edge, so that from the high rear windows the slap of water against stone was audible, the stench of the water potent.

There were at least three guards that Hawksworth could see and probably more upstairs. They sat in an austere front room: this was a frontier house for the Mother-Flowers and it was furnished simply with rough wood tables and a simple altar. The decorations on the walls consisted only of hand painted scrolls and an image of a sampan from a European illustrated magazine. The opulence of their Singapore holdings would be out of place here.

Nonetheless, the usual hospitality was observed, hot tea and steamed buns served. No alcohol, Hawksworth noticed; also no indication of mourning, only readiness.

Given the gravity of the changed situation, Yong Seng's first question surprised him. 'You saw Shu En before you left Singapore?'

'Yes, at the bungalow in Katong.'

'She is safe?' he asked tenderly.

'Very much so, it would seem. She told me that there are armed men surrounding the house and grounds,' Hawksworth spoke casually, studying Yong Seng's face. There was genuine concern there, and something more.

Then it hit him like a bolt: they were lovers.

While Yong Chern was in Johor Bahru, Yong Seng stayed in Singapore and the soft pale flesh of the girl had been too much to resist. How long had the amours been carried on, he wondered. Had they already begun when Hawksworth and Shu En shared their intimacies that morning years before? Jealousy now stabbed at him, his thoughts running through the situation. Yong Seng had given her to me, he thought, and she at that time was freshly in the hands of Yong Chern. Could she have already been with Yong Seng then as well?

The complexities of the human heart overran his sensibilities but he stiffened his back and concentrated on the matter at hand. 'It would appear that Yong Chern was murdered by the same men who killed Low Teck Beng and Lau Chi Man.'

Yong Seng nodded solemnly, facing the table top.

'The Johor police have no leads and seem content to let the matter rest. We are on our own.'

Nodding again, he looked up to face Hawksworth with red eyes. Yong Seng was holding back tears. 'I was not here when it happened. My people tell me only that Yong Chern was sitting at his desk when three men walked into the room and shot him. Not more than two feet away. He never even got out of his chair.'

'They spoke Cantonese, like the others?'

'That is what my men tell me.'

'No one fought them?'

'No. Yong Chern was expecting a visit from Cantonese, about our lottery operation here. No one suspected a thing until it was too late.'

'We will find the men responsible.'

Yong Seng snorted derisively. 'The three most powerful *kongsi* in Malaya are looking for them. Do you believe that the police will find them first?'

Hawksworth stayed quiet and sipped his tea rather than concede the point. The bigger concern now was that the *kongsi* were being drawn into a three-way war. 'You must give me time to find them and bring them to justice.'

'*British* justice? Fair and slow. Let the Chinese handle their own business.'

'We usually do. But if the *kongsi* fight among themselves, you know what will happen. Eventually the army will be called in and they will not hold back from slaughter. Give me time before you seek vengeance.'

'Time? Yong Chern was not given time.'

Again Hawksworth stayed silent. After a moment he spoke softly, 'Shu En told me that you are now *samseng ong* of the Mother-Flowers.'

'I am,' he said without pride. 'There is no satisfaction, no honour. The cost of attainment was too high.'

'One way or another the killers will be brought to justice. You must believe me, old friend.'

'I have sworn this on my cousin's blood,' he said with steel in his voice. 'There were pieces of him on the wall in his office. It is desecration. He will be avenged if it is the last thing I do.'

'And I will do my utmost, Yong Seng, do not doubt that.'

A servant entered and noiselessly removed the empty tea tray.

'Where will you stay tonight?'

'Here in Johor, at the Hotel Casablanca. Tomorrow I will take his body back to Singapore.'

Yong Seng grunted. 'I cannot join you tonight for I am too busy *keeping the train on the rails*,' he used the English expression, 'however I will not let my friend sleep alone. If you want company, we own a house over the road, near the puppet show. Pretty girls with slender fingers and good quality rice wine and a private room, with large cushions. I will bring you there…and make sure one of ours is on hand to see you to your hotel safely after. Johor Bahru has become a dangerous place, even for you.'

'Thank you, Yong Seng,' Hawksworth said sincerely. He was unsure if female companionship was what he desired, but a bottle or two of rice wine would be most welcome.

## CHAPTER IX

# Father, Mother, Orphan

THE DAY BROKE hot and brown and harsh through the thin hotel curtains. Hawksworth opened his gluey eyes, swung himself over the side of the bed and stretched, his spine crackling like burning kindling. His mouth was furry and dry, but the water in the brass pitcher by the bedside smelled questionable and he dared not risk drinking it.

He pulled the bell cord and shortly a rail thin Chinese boy appeared to see about his *sarapan*, his morning meal. Moments later the boy returned with a tray which he set on the dresser – there was no table – so that Hawksworth dined standing up and alone, gazing out the window at the hectic morning activities of the wet market on the triangle of Pulau Segget. He had no doubt that his own food had been fetched from there earlier that morning before being heated in the hotel kitchen; simple fare, white rice, whole steamed fish with head and skin and bones, sliced cucumber, a teaspoon of *sambal* sauce: the quick satisfying meal of the market. He followed the plate with two cups of black coffee and a fistful of fresh jackfruit. The caffeine, vitamins, and grease seemed to do the trick and though he still felt as though he had been trampled by the previous night's rice wine, the breakfast got him on his feet and energized for the melancholy visit to the police station and morgue to fill out the paperwork and arrange for Yong Chern's body to be transported back to Singapore.

There was no trouble in making the arrangements – mere formalities – and he had an hour to kill while waiting for the body to be delivered to the jetty for the ride across the Straits. Near the main passenger jetty was the Nuri Biru café, popular with the European expatriate community who had washed up in Johor Bahru, beyond the ordered world of Singapore; beachcombers, planters gone bust, struggling mercenaries, and assorted dropouts and undesirables who hoped to earn a few dollars as day labourers or worse. Hawksworth decided a beer would raise his flagging spirits for the boat ride back and strode into the place, his cane gripped lightly under his palm – in case he needed to swing it suddenly.

At that hour the place was nearly deserted. The only light came from the glass windows at the front so that the back of the room was left in hot dimness. He could discern a few men hunched over a low table toward the back, evidently looking over a map or schematic and speaking quietly to one another. There were two men sitting at the Western-style bar that ran along the side of the wall, slouching on stools and looking vacantly at nothing. The bartender was a tall man, his red checked gingham shirt the only colour in the otherwise colourless room.

A newspaper had been abandoned on the bar top, the page open to an advertisement for Kupper's Beer, Chop Payong. *Ini Beer sahja yang dapat bintang di Chicago Exhibition.* Hawksworth had forgotten about the slogan, but now that he had read it again, it annoyed him anew. 'Chop *payong.*' Quick umbrella? What the devil could that possibly mean?

The bartender was turned away from him, sopping at some

spilled liquid with a dirty rag. Hawksworth barked, 'I would like a glass of Kupper's Beer,' then he added clearly, 'Chop *payong.*'

The bartender turned a bony face to Hawksworth. He looked as though he was about to fall flat from a wasting illness, consumption, or Addison's disease. 'You want something, matey?' he asked in a raspy Australian voice. A long jagged scar on his face was livid in the murky light of the bar; his dull grey hair clung damply to his scalp.

'Kupper's Beer. Chop *payong.*'

'You can chop all the *payong* you like, mate, but Kupper's you will not get. The Johor supplier died of black water fever two weeks ago. Have Becks pilsner and Guinness stout. Fancy one of them?'

'Becks.'

He watched the thin back, the spine visibly protruding beneath the gingham shirt, the bar apron knotted just above as though a red bow had been tied to a vertebra. The man took a large bottle and pulled the cork, tossed ice cubes into the bottom of a glass mug with a thick handle, then poured the flat liquid until the mug turned golden. The first sip was supremely refreshing in the rising heat of late morning.

'Chop *payong,*' a voice next to him said in a gravely French accent.

Hawksworth found that it emanated from a short bald man who appeared to be in his early sixties sitting at the bar next to him. The man's linen clothes were clean and had once been expensive but were now worn nearly threadbare, the collar of his shirt frayed, the buttons mismatched; his skin was leathery and tough – years in the tropical sun, Hawksworth surmised.

'Do you know what that phrase is supposed to mean?' Hawksworth asked.

'*Oui, bien sûr*. Buy me a pilsner and I will tell you,' the man croaked.

After studying the face for a moment trying to judge if the old fellow was still sane or had already gone around the bend, Hawksworth ordered another Becks and placed it before him.

'*Merci bien*, Monsieur.

'And who might you be?'

'I am Jules. Arrived from Phnom Penh last week.'

'Superintendent Hawksworth, Straits Settlement Police, Singapore.'

The fellow's grey eyebrows went up in surprise, but he laughed, 'My papers are not in order, but as we are not in Singapore, *grâce à Dieu,* there is little you can do.'

Amused despite himself, Hawksworth wiped his mouth with the back of his hand, 'And what do you know about this "chop *payong*"?'

'Ah, *très bien*. You see, we have a similar expression,' he quaffed back the Becks in two swallows then gestured for Hawksworth to buy him another, which the tall man did. He drank half the mug in a single draught before explaining, '*Chope de bière. Vous ne savez pas*? Translation: a pint mug of beer, but in our, eh… argot…it means a fast beer, a quick beer. Chop chop beer!'

'What about the umbrella?'

'*Quoi? Parapluie?* What umbrella is this?'

'"*Payong*" is the Malay word for "umbrella".'

The Frenchman looked blankly at Hawksworth a moment, then shouted angrily, 'I live in *Indochine*, not in Malaya, *hein*? I do not speak Malay! *Imbécile*! The next time you want an answer, you had better ask someone else, *ça c'est sûr*!' He swilled back the last of his beer before storming away from the bar on bandy legs, muttering and swearing to himself as he passed through the swinging doors.

'Better check your pockets, matey,' the bartender said to him after watching the scene. 'Frenchie is known to have the fastest fingers in Johor.'

All the items in Hawksworth's pockets were as they should be. Even Frenchie would not dare to pick the pockets of a police superintendent.

'He said he was just in from Phnom Penh,' Hawksworth said defensively, patting down his clothes.

'Oh and I am just arrived from Paris myself!' the Australian laughed in a grating har-har, 'The City of Lights! Call me Frère Jacques!' he brayed loudly until the laugher became a hacking cough that doubled him over.

Hawksworth asked curtly, 'And you? Any idea what this Kupper's "chop *payong*" is supposed to mean?'

Recovering from his coughing fit, his thin frame still convulsing, the man replied with a shrug, running a moist hand through his lank hair. 'I only pour the beer, mate, I do not think about it.'

\*   \*   \*

He had Yong Chern's body in Singapore at the dead house at Sepoy Lines just after tiffin time. Back at this desk at the Central Police Station, he found a terse message from Theophilus Green, the Chief Librarian of the Raffles Museum and Library, waiting for him. 'Code deciphered' was all it said, but Hawksworth knew what it meant.

About six months earlier he had deposited with Green a journal that had been handed to him in the town of Gading, outside of Malacca. He had been told the diary belonged to his mother – the mother he had spent most of his life believing to have died and placed him in an orphanage before he was five years old. The woman was named Isabella Lightheart and the evidence that she was his mother was circumstantial, though powerful. He hoped the journal would provide the answer, but it was written in code. He knew it to be a book cipher, but try as he might he could not break it. So he took the journal to the only person in the settlement he knew could not only break the code but could also be trusted to keep the contents secret.

The rickshaw ride to the library was pleasant. It was one of those rare days in Singapore when the humidity seemed to vanish at the encouragement of a slight breeze. The sun was high and bright, a few white cirrus clouds texturing the cobalt sky, the atmosphere splendidly limpid. Even the stench of horse dung and the blowing red dust of the laterite road did not detract from the happy afternoon languor.

He saw the dome of the museum shining grandly when they rounded the corner on the slight rise of Stamford Road. The wooded slope of Fort Canning hill rose up behind the building, framing the neoclassical façade as though it were Grecian ruins found squatting in the jungle. The rickshaw wallah dropped him in the forecourt, then seeing no other passengers around, rotated his conveyance to rest on the back of the chair, pulled the canvas cover lower, plopped himself into the seat with his feet planted on the cross bar, lowered his head, and dozed off.

The interior of the museum's rotunda was cool and mild. No one stopped him as he strode toward the library wing, which felt, as the rooms darkened, as though he were descending. When he finally reached the main book repository, the stacks reaching to the ceiling, it felt as though he had reached the bottom of a cave.

Green was seated behind a massive desk piled high with books and ledgers and loose paper, the end of a nibbed pen pressed to his lips as he poured over a manuscript. Seeing Hawksworth approach, Green put down his nib and looking straight at him spoke in a sonorous voice, '"And Jesus saith unto him, The foxes have holes, and the birds of the air have nests; but the Son of man hath not where to lay his head."'

'A sermon, Theophilus? But today is not Sunday.'

'Perhaps you should attend church more often, Superintendent,' Green spoke dourly before reaching across his desk to pull the Lightheart diary from beneath a stack of papers. 'Do take a seat.'

'Your message said that you have broken the cipher?' the tall man asked as he sat, leaning his cane against the edge of the overflowing desk.

Green smiled thinly. 'As you believed, the code is based on the New Testament, though discovering which book took some effort. Luckily the author was fond of quoting entire passages, which helped a great deal.'

'Which book?'

'Matthew. Standard King James version.'

'You are certain?'

'See for yourself.' Green slid his notebook along with the leather bound journal and a copy of the King James Bible across the table to Hawksworth.

'Here is the code from the journal. Take this first number, 691. It refers to Matthew chapter six, verse nine, first word,' he flipped through the Bible until he found the page, then read ruminatively, '"After this manner therefore pray ye: Our Father which art in heaven, Hallowed be thy name." So the word in the journal is "after". Or this number, 123710, which corresponds to chapter twelve, verse thirty-seven, word ten: "For by thy words thou shalt be justified, and by thy words thou shalt be condemned." The word in the journal is "by", and so on. Further, there are Roman letters, sometimes singularly, others in pairs. These would appear to be initials of people and place names. The names "Georgetown" and "Penang" do not, rather obviously, appear in the New Testament, so the author abbreviated them as GT and P.'

Hawksworth stared at the lines of handwritten numbers on the page, then back at the printed pages of the Bible. 'How much did you decipher?'

'Only two pages, to test my hypothesis. There is an added difficulty in that the author seems to have not used a consistent code but revisited the key text at each instance of need.'

'I am afraid I do not follow your meaning.'

Green rubbed his knuckles against his temples as he spoke, 'For example, if the author wanted to use the word "I" in the journal, then she used an instance of "I" found randomly in the source book. In this instance, "I" is coded as 12185, corresponding to chapter twelve, verse eighteen, word five, yet here it is coded as 5202, corresponding to chapter five, verse twenty, word two. Quite clever. Why are you smiling?'

'Do you not see, Theophilus? It was not part of a plan. She must have prayed before she wrote her journal. The source code word is random precisely because she was letting her eye fall randomly on the page before her.'

'How can you be sure?' Green asked, arching his eyebrow.

'Detective's intuition.'

'Then perhaps your intuition can shed light on why this journal was coded in the first place. There is little here that seems to be secret.'

'What do you mean?'

'I mean, from the small portion I deciphered, it would seem to be nothing more than a daily journal of a mundane passage from Liverpool to Penang.'

'The secret must lay within the text itself.'

'It will take much effort to decode the entire journal, but now that you have the key it should not be difficult work, merely tedious.'

'Tedious only to the disinterested, Theophilus.'

Green studied him a moment as he would a book, with a look of sharp intent crossed with intrigue. 'Whoever wrote this code did so because they wanted to keep the journal secret. The code itself is highly idiosyncratic. I doubt if the author ever intended anyone to bring the true text to light. Perhaps this is one secret you should leave in the dark?'

By way of answer, he took up the Bible. 'May I borrow this until I finish deciphering the code? I do not have a copy at home.'

'Of course,' Green said, leaning back in his chair to look up at the standing man. 'I wish you good luck, Superintendent.'

Hawksworth tucked the books under his arm then rose to leave, 'I am curious about one thing. You said that the author quoted entire passages from the book of Matthew, which helped you decipher the code. Can you recall the first passage she wrote?'

Green recited, '"For as the lightning cometh out of the east, and shineth even unto the west; so shall also the coming of the Son of man be." Why do you ask?'

'A prime rule of investigation: the first clue is usually the one that uncovers the rest.'

\* \* \*

Hawksworth's front room was filled with the piquant aromas

of homemade fish sauce, the tartness of lemongrass, the sharp hotness of chili padi. Ni and Fon had cleared the plates and put out mint tea that mixed pleasantly with the lingering liquorice flavour of the *bai horapha*, the Siamese purple basil. He had Fenella propped on his lap, her fat little fingers banging about on the table while he adjusted the wick on the lamp. The notebook and pencil were centred, the journal to the left, the Bible to the right; he would change the arrangement throughout the process so that by the end he understood why the Chief Librarian's desk always looked a mess: there was an underlying order and method, but it was only perceptible to the user of the materials.

It was arduous work deciphering the journal. He had to account for frequent mistakes in the coding, for Lightheart often miscounted the number of words in a verse. Nonetheless, she had managed to construct readable sentences from the limited vocabulary provided by the source. The first sentence read, 'Departed Liverpool in clear weather and calm sea.' This he constructed from the transcribed text 'departed Liverpool clearly weather sea calm' deciphered from code '276030/ Lp/7518/16217/18637/82630'.

The slowness of the transcription meant that the detective was reconstructing not only the text but also the journey itself in painstaking detail. That the descriptions were of his own hidden life meant that the frustrations increased with the slowness of the velocity of transcription.

The starkest moment of recognition, the one that brought the situation most forcibly home, came when he realized that the little boy in the book, whom Lightheart symbolized with the letter M, must have been named Matthew. This journal was her own Book of Matthew, of her son and 'man,' as in 'son of man'. The family name – his father's name, *his* name – was rendered simply by the letter 'E'. Not 'H' for Hawksworth, but 'E'.

He had been David Hawksworth his entire life and now he discovered that at least for a time he had been someone else. Or was he still that same person? His body aching in the uncomfortable chair, he struggled to decode the story of Matthew, the story of himself, anticipating the moment when Lightheart would place him in the orphanage, hoping that some explanation would be given for the event that changed his own biography. His forensic mind compelled him to keep going, to unravel the mystery, even if it meant losing himself completely into this other person that was both he and not he. And he knew that by deciphering the journal he was calling forth ghosts that perhaps should have stayed quiet, and he knew that after the dead are resurrected, the living will never be the same again.

But why had she decided to code her journal in the first place? Why go to such lengths to keep the contents secret? Who was she afraid of? He worked all night, seated at the table, the yellow circle of flickering light causing him to hold the pages of tiny text close to his nose.

He was able to piece together from her reminiscences and anecdotes that Isabella Lightheart had met the devilishly handsome 'E' on a sunny day on the Chain Pier by the pebble beach at Brighton and, it seems, instantly fell in love. She was a London girl on a weekend to the seaside. 'E' was working there in a commercial capacity that she did not elaborate upon. Nor did she, to Hawksworth's immense frustration, explain any details about her own family or his: the history of their lives began with her meeting him. Nonetheless, it seems she moved to Brighton to be near him and soon after they married came baby Matthew. She did not, in her reminiscence of this event in her travel journal, provide a date or place.

Years went by and they were happy, but money was always short and they frequently struggled, so when an offer came from Jardine Matheson and Company for 'E' to travel to the Far East to work, she felt that her prayers had finally been answered. He accepted the offer and the family made preparations to travel. The final destination was Singapore.

And here came the first premonition that all was not well. In the journal she indicates that when they first met, 'E' never mentioned that he had previously lived in the East. He now said that not only had he previously lived there but that he had connections in the opium trade that would help to make the family rich. Jardine Matheson had hired him to return to Singapore to help coordinate the transhipment of their trade in legitimate opium between the manufacturing sources in India and their distribution depot in Hong Kong. Yet, he hinted to Lightheart, his previous job involved the smuggling of illegal opium and that he intended to re-establish his connections once the family arrived in Singapore. Most distressingly, he told her that when in the East previously he had used an assumed name and that once they returned, he would once again take up that name.

The future missionary woman was already given to a religious frame of mind and was firmly opposed to the opium trade and was none-too-pleased that her new husband was involved with the business; but it was this stuff about smuggling and fake names that frightened her. She describes several arguments they had prior to departure, but he insisted that she and the toddler join him. The more she remonstrated, the fiercer he became; though she eventually relented and agreed to go with him, she was now afraid.

The coded journal, Hawksworth realized in the steamy heat of his dark bungalow, was really her record of fear, coded to keep it safe from 'E', and her trepidation increased the closer they drew to Singapore.

His heart leapt into his chest when Lightheart described landing in Penang. He had been told as a boy – and had believed all his life – that his parents had perished when a contagious fever broke out aboard the ship while it was off the southern tip of India. They were the first to die, their bodies buried at sea. The ship was held in harbour at Penang until deemed safe and he was taken ashore, soon to be adopted into the care of the Jesuit brothers at St. Joseph's Orphanage.

Now only did he learn that his parents both survived the passage but that there was no fever, the ship was never quarantined. The entire family had stepped ashore at Penang. He had been lied to from his earliest age. But why? And by whom? He had known the false history for so long that it had merely become part of his consciousness, the first link in the chain of cause and effect of the narrative of his life.

And now that first link was shattered as if forged of glass. Why had he been lied to? Was it to intentionally hide a bitter truth? Or had the Jesuit brothers simply not known the truth and made up a story to offer some comfort to the child?

Transcribing further, he learned that once in Penang, 'E' spent much time with business partners, as he called them, leaving her and the boy in the hotel near Fort Cornwallis in the sweltering heat in the strange land. Inevitably, she came down with fever and convalesced with her son in the cool damp of the hotel garden (he imagined a brick-lined path and benches shaded by the soft green leaves of tree ferns).

In the garden one day she meets a missionary named 'NC' (Nathaniel Cooper, he surmised, the man with whom she will one day live) with whom she can find confide. 'E' is increasingly distant. She and Cooper share religion. He tells her of his plans to travel to the interior of Malaya to open orphanages. Her desire begins to shift to this man as 'E' becomes ever more strange.

'E' seems oblivious to the changes in her heart. He tells her that he is setting up an operation with locals that will make them fabulously wealthy, far more than he would earn from Jardine Matheson. These locals, whom she codes as 'east men' he knew from his previous sojourn in this perfidious land where the heat sapped one's strength, the mosquitoes buzzed about the ears and ankles, and a mere scratch could turn fatally septic. He tells her the name of the local he is working with, and Hawksworth came to a dead stop when he transcribed it, for she had recorded the name as '112915,' chapter eleven, verse twenty-nine, word fifteen, 'lowly'. 'E works with east man named lowly.'

Did she mean 'Low Lee', or merely 'Low', for the word 'low' does not appear in the gospel? The name appears only once more in the journal, several pages later. 'E afraid east man lowly Judas.' 'E fears local Low will betray,' is how Hawksworth read the line. Could the same Low family of Singapore have been involved in the opium trade in Penang with his father forty years before? Or was he importing his own current investigation into the text?

It was nearly dawn. His eyes were growing tired, his head heavy, and he could not go on. Exhausted, he mouthed words from the page before him, speaking into the solitary silence, the words echoing in his head as he slumped over the kitchen table while the lamp's flame turned pale as the room brightened with the light of dawn.

'All things are delivered unto me of my Father: and no man knoweth the Son, but the Father; neither knoweth any man the

Father, save the Son, and he to whomsoever the Son will reveal him.'

# CHAPTER X

# Quarantine

NOT LONG AFTER breakfast that morning, about an hour after the sun had risen, a Chinese man was discovered lying upright against the post of the gas lamp at the corner of Synagogue and Macao Streets. His body had been propped against the pole with a hat pulled low over his brow and his hands folded under a red handkerchief and in the tumult of the busy morning, the passers-by thought he was asleep, a drunk blacked out or an opium addict still under the influence. Eventually someone tripped over his legs, causing his body to tumble sideways, knocking off the hat. His ears and nose and fingers were all missing, which told the investigating detectives that he had been killed by the Lows. Such mutilation, often performed while the victim was still alive, was their calling card. As the body was dumped near the Hai San *kongsi* house, it did not take the police long to figure out that he was a mid-level operator in their organization.

A little more than an hour later, another Chinese body was discovered, this time near the shophouse of a Low family enterprise on Keng Cheow Street. The arms had been bent backward, then the scalp cut away, which indicated that he had been killed by the Hai San – a quick investigation revealing that he had been a mid-level operator, this time in the Low family *kongsi*.

By midmorning, another Chinese body was found, this

one with the ears, nose, and fingers cut away. He had been, the detectives determined, a member of the Hai San *kongsi*, a junior enforcer with one of their affiliate gangs. His body was thrown from a carriage as it passed a noodle stall owned by the brother of the first man found dead that morning.

Inspector-General Fairer sent a note to Hawksworth. The colonial elite were already nervous about the possibility of a cholera epidemic, the last thing they needed was another *kongsi* war. Fairer wanted him to handle this personally. Put a stop to the conflict before it escalates. Hawksworth's personal quest into his family history would have to be suspended for the time being.

'Superintendent Hawksworth, Straits Settlement Police,' he said, showing his shield to the clerk at Teck Seng's business office in Waterloo Street. 'I want to see your employer.'

The clerk stared gormlessly at the shield, then at the white man's face before slipping away wordlessly. Hawksworth waited, leaning on his cane, surveying the place.

Two men dressed in Western suits discretely lounged on either side of the entrance. Thick bulges under their jackets showed that they were armed with short-barrelled revolvers. One locked eyes with Hawksworth then made a subtle gesture to the other, thinking that the Superintendent would not notice. It was the sort of voiceless communication required to keep their presence unobtrusive while covering the changing situation in the room. Their level of sophistication impressed him: these were not local street-level bullyboys but professional gunmen.

Upstairs, he found another armed guard outside Teck Seng's office door, a giant of a man wearing a cuffed shirt without a jacket, his hair cut short in the Western style. His guns were Western too: two short-barrelled double-action Colt .45 revolvers, worn in a shoulder holster rig. They were sophisticated weapons, and expensive. The bodyguard made no effort to conceal them. Low Teck Seng was taking no chances.

'He is expecting you,' the guard said in perfect English that twanged with an accent Hawksworth recognized as American.

Once inside, Teck Seng motioned for him to sit where he had before.

'Bringing in professional gunmen from outside Singapore? Do not trust the local boys anymore?'

'We live in parlous times, Superintendent.' The man seemed agitated, but he put on a cool facade for Hawksworth.

'Are you also bringing in American shotguns? Winchester pump action guns?'

'Hardly. Though I will tell you that if I knew where to procure some, I would. Have you made any progress in catching my brother's killers?'

Hawksworth pursed his lips to restrain himself from shouting. 'I am here to learn why you broke our agreement. The Lows are now killing Hai San.'

'We are not.'

'First Lau Chi Man is murdered then middle level Hai San start turning up dead. They strike at you in retaliation. The implications are clear.'

'No....'

'That is how the police read the situation.'

'The police are wrong. We did not strike at the Hai San nor are we fighting in retaliation, however if they go on killing our men, that situation may change. We are exercising restraint because of the understanding that I have with yourself. Am I now to consider that understanding to be breached?'

'Not at all. Yet I need to know what you know if I am to be effective. If you are not behind this round of slaughter, then who is?'

Teck Seng sighed heavily, drumming his fingers on the table. 'I wish I knew. It might be a faction or a minor gang. Now that your laws have forced us to operate in this piecemeal manner, it is far more difficult to control them. Smaller gangs can run amok.'

'There is something you are not telling me. You know the name of this minor gang that is running amok.'

Teck Seng's fingers stopped drumming. 'We hear rumours, nothing more.'

'Who?'

'A Cantonese gang, once controlled by the Hai San, now working independently.'

'The Tiger Claws?'

Teck Seng shrugged the Chinese shrug that indicates both lack of knowledge and lack of interest. 'Perhaps, perhaps not. The outcome is the same: the Hai San believe that we attacked them so we will, in time, have to defend ourselves. Unless of course the police do their jobs and apprehend the true murderers.'

Hawksworth clenched his jaw so hard his teeth hurt.

'Superintendent, the organization that my father created, the one that my brother so impressively managed, is now coming to the end of its usefulness to us in Singapore. It is my intention, as it always has been, to move our business into more, ah, salubrious ventures.'

'Like banking?'

Teck Seng nodded affirmatively. 'The Hai San are antiquated. They represent the old way. When that way is extinguished once and for all, we can stop expending our energy on pointless fighting. I trust that you believe me when I tell you that I want this killing to end as quickly as do you. It costs me men...and men cost me money.'

Hawksworth narrowed his eyes as he studied the man opposite him, the slicked down hair and high collar framing the slim face. Teck Seng may be vicious but he was, above all else, a businessman.

The question in Hawksworth's mind was whether Teck Seng truly believed that this round of killing was needless, or maybe he merely thought it a quick way to extinguish the Hai San once and for all.

\*   \*   \*

That afternoon, about an hour after tiffin time, the Principal Civil Medical Officer declared that all ships arriving at the settlement were to stay at anchor in the roads until health inspectors could board them. Passengers were to be examined for symptoms of cholera and were not to be allowed ashore until they were given a card declaring that they were free of the disease. Passengers leaving Singapore by steamship were required to obtain a similar card.

In addition, the entire lesser town, including the traditional Chinese Quarter and the immigrant Kling districts, were placed under immediate quarantine. Any persons exhibiting signs of ill health were to be confined to their homes, which were to be marked with an X in red chalk. Restaurants, cafés, theatres, and other places where people gathered, even the unlicensed brothels, were to be shut. Regular patrols in the affected districts were to be increased and ad-hoc search, seizure, and detainment powers were temporarily allowed to uniformed police under the direction of European officers. Near certain cases of cholera were to be immediately taken by official vehicle to an isolation camp hastily erected on the grounds of the General Hospital, in which they were to be kept until cured.

The announcement did not state that just outside the isolation camp, equipment and men were readied for the digging of mass graves. The army was placed on a state of heightened alert in case the denizens of the lesser town tried to break the quarantine by force. According to the official tabulation, based on the current intake of cholera patients into the hospital, about three in ten of the Chinese in the lesser town had the disease. At thirty percent of the population, the PCMO told the hastily arranged meeting with the Governor and the Executive Council, epidemic was no longer an imminent threat – it had already begun.

Their immediate concern was to confine the disease to the affected native districts and more generally to confine it to Singapore. Given the high volume of traffic in the port, ships from the island could spread the disease throughout the Indian Ocean ports to the west and the Pacific ports to the east in a matter of weeks. There were already reports of increased cholera cases in Hong Kong and Macau, and even Adelaide was reporting a spike in cases, while the situation in Port Said on the Suez was said to be so bad that the city was implementing its own quarantine measures.

'This quarantine will place walls around the Chinese Quarter that will only increase the violence of the *kongsi* war,' Hawksworth said to Yong Seng.

They were sitting in the townhouse on Neil Road that Yong Chern had bought for Shu En several years before. After they moved to Katong, the Neil Road house served as a gambling den and high-end bordello for the Mother-Flowers themselves, but now only Hawksworth and Yong Seng along with a single kitchen servant were in the place. The quarantine measures had already made the Chinese Quarter feel as empty as a ghost town.

'At least it will keep people off the streets during the day, but the patrols will not be able to maintain as much control at night,' Hawksworth continued, speaking with a frown.

'The people are staying home at night anyway. They are afraid.'

'Of cholera? Or the police?'

Yong Seng shook his head negatively, 'Both of those, yes, but something more. There is a rumour that a *jiangshi* is preying on the coolies. They say the cholera was introduced by British doctors either as a way to cover for the deaths caused by the *jiangshi* or to appease it, or both.'

'Chronic rot!' Hawksworth raised his voice to a brassy shout. 'We are faced with the beginning of a *kongsi* war and a cholera epidemic and the *sinkeh* coolies are worried about superstitions!'

'It is not just the *sinkehs* who are talking this way,' Yong Seng replied coolly.

'What do you mean?'

'Even the *kongsi* are afraid. They say that it is Low Teck Beng retuned from the dead. They say that Guan Yu has given him power to avenge his death. Others say that the family angered the immortal by holding the funeral on his day of worship, so he is punishing Teck Beng by making him walk the earth instead of resting in peace. Some say it is both of these.'

Clucking to himself, Hawksworth muttered, 'Sergeant Major Walker thought he saw a *jiangshi* the night we recovered the Winchester shotgun.'

'You see!' Yong Seng clapped triumphantly. 'Even the police are haunted by the vampire!'

'Bosh! This is imagination run wild. Cholera victims may appear like vampires.'

Ignoring him, Yong Seng continued, 'In most people's minds,

the *kongsi* killings, the cholera quarantine, and the *jiangshi* have all become one and the same thing. It is a curse on Singapore.'

'I can do little about the cholera epidemic and nothing about superstition. My immediate concern is quelling this nascent war. The Lows say that they are not behind the killing, though they are protecting themselves by bringing in professional gunmen. Perhaps elements within the Hai San hierarchy are fighting for domination now that the *kapitan* is dead?'

Yong Seng shrugged the Chinese shrug that showed genuine indifference to the topic. 'We do not care. Let them kill each other. The Mother-Flowers are ready to take over all their operations.'

'But who is murdering the upper echelon of the *kongsi*? What about the killing of Yong Chern? Your street contacts tell you nothing about this?'

He shifted uncomfortably. 'The powerful weapons are American guns, this much we know…from our sources in the police,' he added quietly. 'Otherwise, it is like phantoms. I tell you my friend, this is not the Singapore that I grew up in. People used to respect the *kongsi*. No one would dare kill a *kapitan*. Now they respect no one,' he made a slow waving motion with his palm, as though swatting away invisible moths: a sign of resignation.

'Tell me about Yeung Ha Sau and the Tiger Claws. Could they be behind all this?'

Yong Seng laughed loudly, a combination of a snort and a guffaw. 'They are a low-level Cantonese gang under the heel of the Hai San. They mostly loan shark and run prostitutes, a little black market opium dealing on the side. Small fish. Why do you ask?'

Hawksworth spoke flatly. 'Their leader used the *ah kuahs* to learn when and where Low Teck Beng would be the night of his murder.'

Yong Seng thought for a moment, scratching his head. 'They were feeding information to someone higher up. Perhaps the Hai San were behind Teck Beng's killing after all.'

'I am going to bring in Yueng for questioning to find out.'

'When?'

Hawksworth popped open the cover of his pocket watch. 'In about an hour.'

'But you have no men or weapons with you!' cried Yong Seng in dismay.

'I will meet my men at the Tiger Claws' house. As for weapons,' he rapped his heavy cane on the wooden floor board twice, 'this is all I need.'

* * *

Darkness came fast. When Hawksworth arrived in Pagoda Street, the evening sky was distended with clouds swollen purple and black, a ribbon of crimson shining along the horizon like the rim of a wound.

At his signal, uniformed officers, big Sikh men with heavy rifles, barricaded both ends of the street.

'One good thing about this quarantine,' he said to Rizby as he boarded the wagon that would take them to the Tiger Claws' house, 'we can raid whoever we want under cover of medical inspection.'

'It may be that the suspects have cholera,' Rizby said apprehensively. 'I have taken the precaution of instructing the men on what to do should we discover infected persons during the raid.'

Lightning flashed in a great sheet across the sky, a sudden wind snapping down the empty street as Hawksworth and the others leapt out of the wagon. The gale and downpour would be on them in moments. The house was tightly shut, but yellow lamplight was visible through the window shutters.

Rizby had brought four others from the squad, including Joseph Jeremiah and the veteran detective Anaiz Bin Abdul Majid. All were armed with service revolvers and truncheons. 'Jeremiah, with me,' Hawksworth said as they massed outside the front entrance under the five-foot way.

The first fast drops of rain lashed at the side of the shophouse as Anaiz kicked in the front door. The detectives poured in, pistols drawn, Hawksworth at their centre, a full head and shoulders taller than the rest.

The front room contained half a dozen Chinese men sitting around a table drinking and smoking, frozen in place as the police piled in. A young woman in a loose silk robe was halfway down the stairs; when Hawksworth looked up at her with menace in his eyes, she screamed with her mouth fully opened then turned and dashed up into the darkness.

'Rizby, the girl!' he yelled, running toward the foot of the stairs as the room exploded in a frenzy. Some of the men grappled with the detectives, others ran for the back room.

Rizby reached the stairs before he did, racing at top speed. A shot sounded in the front room. Hawksworth did not stop to look, instead following Rizby up the stairs, his cane thumping on each step.

When Rizby's head popped up at the top of the staircase someone shot at it, the round splintering the wood beside his ear. He pulled back, his Tranter .32 in his hand. The taller man reversed direction slowly; the downstairs room was secure. A dead Chinese was on the floor, Jeremiah standing over him, his pistol in his hand. The other suspects were on their knees, hands on their heads. He heard Anaiz shout at someone in the back room, then he heard a shot above as Rizby returned fire.

'Yeung Ha Sau, surrender now. We are the Straits Settlements Police. You have no chance!' Rizby yelled. The response was another shot.

'Jeremiah!' Hawksworth yelled down at the detective below who was trembling above the man he had just killed. 'Up here, now!'

The young man jerked from his reverie and took the stairs two at a time. 'Give Rizby covering fire,' Hawksworth said as he passed.

Jeremiah reached the top step to open a rapid fusillade while Rizby dashed past him into a narrow hall with doors on either side. He slammed through one while Jeremiah reloaded. Two more rounds came from the end of the hallway, at the foot of a small staircase that led to a third-floor loft room. To judge by the amount of return fire, the adversaries were armed with only one revolver.

Hawksworth climbed the stairs past Jeremiah, striding with his cane down the hall as Jeremiah fired behind him. As in most shophouses, above the peaked third-floor room was most likely a skylight of some sort, and that would be Yeung's route of escape. Pinning the police down at the second storey was giving him time to get away over the rooftops.

He strode past the door Rizby had smashed into when a man with a revolver appeared at the end of the hall. Hawksworth did not break stride, heading like a juggernaut toward the assailant, his cane rapping rapidly. The man fired without aiming, the bullet zipping past Hawksworth to burrow into the wall at the end of the hall. The gun fired again, only three feet from him. This time the round grazed his abdomen as it sailed between his torso and arm. A quarter inch either way and he would have been down.

Then he heard the hammer click: the revolver was empty. The gunman turned to flee but Hawksworth was already upon him. He balanced then swung his cane, bringing the knob down hard on the man's skull.

Behind him, he heard Rizby yelling at a woman who was screaming and swearing foully in Cantonese. He turned back to see her slapping and clawing at him, Jeremiah rushing to Rizby's aid. Behind them, he saw the head of another detective emerging at the top of the first-floor stairs.

Then he moved with all possible speed up the stairs toward the darkness of the third floor.

Halfway up the stairs on the third floor, an iron bar swung out of the gloom toward his head; he caught it painfully with his free hand. He let out a grunt as he gripped it, then yanked it out of the man's hand. He heard the man stagger back into the room, stumble into furniture then fall. In a flash of lightening, he saw the skylight, no larger than two feet square. It was propped open, rain cascading in. Taking the final steps in a bound, he smashed the iron bar against the man sprawled on the floor. The wet thwack of the impact told him the man would not be standing again anytime soon.

Dropping his cane, he grasped the edges of the skylight and with great effort pulled his upper body into the space. The edge was slippery, the rain pouring into his eyes as he pulled his belly onto the roof. Kicking his legs and pulling himself forward, Hawksworth finally managed to hoist himself up. In the wind and rain he could just make out the figure of a man on the thin edge of the roofline of the adjacent building, trying to balance on the rain-slick tiles. 'You! Stop!' he yelled, out of breath.

The figure turned back toward him in the downpour, wind

buffeting him, trying to escape. But the storm was vicious and the man moved in slow motion. He fell on all fours, trying to scamper like a squirrel.

Hawksworth stood unsteadily, instinctively grasping for his cane. There would be no way he could balance then move quickly enough over the rooftops in the flashing storm to catch the fleeing man. He looked back at the skylight and saw Rizby looking up at him, yelling something. Leaning down, he heard 'The girl said the man on the roof is Yeung. Do you see him?'

'Quick, my cane! On the floor, there!' he pointed.

The knob was in his fist and he pulled it through the skylight then was upright again, holding it horizontally for balance, like a tight-rope walker. Using his bad foot like a deadweight to anchor himself, he used the other to propel himself forward, moving crabwise but quickly along the roofline. The rain streaming from his soaking hair filled his eyes so that he had to stop to wipe it away and rebalance, but he was gaining on Yeung, who had missed his grip and was now sprawled on the roof tiles on the adjacent building.

Another sheet of lighting flashed above him, and he was atop of Yeung. Hoping his bad foot would keep him in place, he swung his cane hard into Yeung then awkwardly dropped the knee of his good leg into the small of the man's back. Crooking his cane under his arm, he pulled his shackles from his belt and snapped them closed over Yueng's wrists, then yanked him upward on his knees.

The slick tiles slipped under his tread as he tried to haul the man up without tipping them both over the edge to the street below. He yelped in pain as the bones in his foot ground against each other as he pulled Yeung up; his cane dropped from under his arm, sliding down the tiles to lodge on the eave of the roof.

He saw Rizby's head then shoulders rise up on the roof ahead of them, and he shoved Yeung toward him. 'His arms are shackled but watch his feet,' he yelled. Rizby moved deftly across the slippery surface to catch hold of the soaking suspect. Hawksworth inched forward while Rizby pushed the man down through the skylight.

The Superintendent was now alone on the roof.

Stooping to retrieve his cane, Hawksworth leaned forward then locked himself stock-still. From the corner of his eye he saw a silhouette standing on the edge of the roof on the building across the street. The figure stood at an impossible angle, as though he were perched halfway in mid-air, only his heels on the tiles. Straitening himself, Hawksworth slipped, his posterior slamming on the tiles, his legs splaying. Accidentally, he kicked his cane, which clattered over the edge into the muddy street. Cursing, the tall man twisted himself around to secure his grip on the slick surface and look again at the silhouette.

To his shock, the black figure was now on the edge of the same roof, only a few feet from him, facing him as motionless as a statue. Its eyes were two blank orbs of silver, shimmering like liquid mercury. Lightening burst noisily, and in that instant of electric whiteness Hawksworth discerned the features of Low Teck Beng glaring at him, hideously bloated with rot yet weirdly animated, the bare white teeth clenched beneath lips curled back by rigor mortis so that the terrible face grinned at him in a rictus in the bright flash. Two needle-like fangs protruded from the upper jaw, curving downward over the lower lip.

Hawksworth's legs kicked reflexively as he tried to crawl backward up and away from the figure, knocking loose a tile so that he slipped and quickly slid toward the edge. His legs were over the side to his knees and he braced for the fall when his fingers instinctively grasped a narrow vent pipe protruding from the roof. The metal was hot and it burned, but he could not let go. Straining painfully, he finally pulled himself up then wedged his boots against the tiles. His breath came in gasps as he craned his neck to see if the black figure had somehow managed to get above him. He was expecting a boot in the face, a swift kick to plunge him over the side, but the horrible apparition was no longer there.

Rain lashed his face as he scanned the horizon for the figure, but he was alone on the slippery rooftops, sprawled and panting, his heart beating so hard it hurt.

CHAPTER XI

# Fizzy Water

SHIVERING IN THE TORPID heat of Geylang, he sat at his desk under a blanket, a strong brew of herbs and honey cupped in his hands. He was sore all over, his bad foot throbbing. The fever was slight, but combined with the beating he had taken the night before, it wore him down. And with the threat of cholera in the air, he decided that the best course of action was to stay home to rest. Yeung could stay in the Stews for another twenty-four hours while Rizby worked the case – he was still trying to discover the source of the Winchester shotguns.

Despite the physical exhaustion, Hawksworth's mind was restless. In the light of day, he disregarded the phantasm as a product of the fear and rain and lightning, though the image of those terrible blank silver eyes and curving feline fangs remained vivid in his mind. He had witnessed many strange things in his life and, though he remained a rationalist, he had nonetheless learned to be comfortable with the unexplained; but Low Teck Beng's dead bloated face hanging so close to his own in the storm was beyond anything he had previously known.

The diary and Bible beckoned, and he sat in discomfort before them, tediously transcribing the handwritten code. Rendering the script comprehensible helped to banish the blank silver eyes from his thoughts.

He picked up where he had left off, the strange line that seemed to indicate that the Lows were mixed up with his father. The doubt lay in his transcription of the code and in his interpretation. Lightheart had coded 'E afraid east man lowly Judas.' He read this as 'E fears local Low will betray.' The word 'lowly' was not cited again in the code – and perhaps she had not meant lowly as a signal to a name.

Switching between pencil and mug of broth, Hawksworth continued the slow transcription. Lightheart continued to write about NC, the minister Nathaniel Cooper, to whom she increasingly turned for succour as 'E', the husband and father, became a different man.

'E' was seldom with her now, spending days away from their hotel – he told her that his business with Jardine Matheson required him to travel to the hinterland with his secretive Chinese business associates. She did not believe him completely, but alone in the foreign land, she feels she has no choice but to stay put and wait. They no longer even argued – they are leading separate lives.

Then one day he simply did not come home. She waited at the hotel and inquired at the local office of Jardine Matheson, but they also had not heard from him. He was due to sail to Singapore in a few more days. If he does not appear soon, they told her, they would assume he has resigned his position.

And what about her? And her child?

She is free to do as she pleases, they said. Return to England, sail to Singapore, stay right here in Penang. She and the boy were not their concern.

There is some cash, not much, that 'E' left in a strongbox along with all his luggage. Cooper suggests that he can help with some money for her passage home, but he is due to travel to Gading, near Malacca, to establish an orphanage, and he asks if she would rather not go there with him.

Her mind is made up by the arrival of an envelope containing her husband's ring and a gold coin. It also contains a lock of hair that did not belong to 'E'. It belonged to young Matthew, her son, the man Hawksworth.

He stopped transcribing. It was now late afternoon. His body ached from sitting on the hard chair at the wooden table, hunched over the small print. Ni and Fenella were out at the market. Fon had brought him more broth, but he did not notice. It had grown cold.

Lightheart took the envelope to the police along with her story of her husband's strange friends and history of opium smuggling. The interpretation was that her husband had crossed the wrong men and was most likely dead. The lock of her son's hair meant that she was no longer safe; if they could get close enough to snip his hair, they could get close enough to slit his throat. The coin would indicate that she was to buy passage and leave town as soon as possible. The police would investigate, but they told her that given such slim evidence, they would probably not turn up much. As Hawksworth knew, there were no detectives in Penang in those days, and the police were notoriously corrupt. They offered advice: the Chinese secret societies were not something a woman and child all alone in a foreign country wanted to tangle with. They recommended, none too subtly, that she leave Malaya and never return, the sooner the better for all concerned. Once the clans mark you, you are marked for life, they told her.

The minister Nathaniel Cooper gave her different advice. Providence had brought her to Malaya to do good work, to atone for her husband's crimes and sins, to help the local people by spreading the Gospel. Come with me to Gading, he said. Use your maiden name to stay safe from the clans. But be warned that the going will be tough. The land around Gading is wild. The town itself little more than a mining camp, a rough and tumble settlement of Chinese miners and cutthroats.

Her boy could be looked after in the orphanage here in Penang. The Jesuit brothers would take him in. She would come back for him once they had established a safe home in Gading.

Full of tears, she brought him to the orphanage. 'I suffered and cried when I placed Matthew, my firstborn, in the children's house. Then I went away,' he transcribed the words then paused. She left his clothes and the two framed profile silhouettes with him, one of her the other of 'E'.

A fresh mug of hot broth steaming in his hands, sweat beading on his brow, he recalled the rows of wooden beds, the snores and shouts of the boys in the narrow dirty hall. He had the top bunk. Two different boys in the bunk beneath him died while he was there. The first was only a vague memory, for he had been young, but the other was a playmate and they became friends. A fever took him away. Hawksworth had seen his ragged exhalations, the jerking rise and fall of his chest as he struggled for breath in the sweaty bed in the sick room, his lips whitish blue. They did not let him stay longer than to squeeze his dying friend's hand. They buried him in the corner of the cemetery reserved for unclaimed orphans, unmarked and unnamed. Even at that young age, he understood that the same fate could have just as easily befallen him.

The day she placed him at the orphanage, Lightheart wrote, 'I will return to him.' Why did she not come back? Why stay in Gading to run an orphanage for other people's children? Was it the new life with Cooper in which he had no place? Or was there some other fear, for either her or him, that if she returned it would expose their identity to the Chinese clans? She indicates that she kept track of him as he grew into a man, into David Hawksworth of the Straits Settlements Police. Why did she not reveal herself then?

His detective's intuition kicked in: a dead man's ring, a gold coin, a lock of a child's hair. His mind flashed to the coin in the cigar box on his dresser, the gold half-sovereign that had been pressed into his hand two years before. He had been told it functioned like an evil eye. He thought also of the statue made of coins, some quite old, some quite new, which he had seen on the altar at the Low family house. Perhaps the police in Penang had got the symbols wrong? The ring, the coin, the hair, perhaps they were not meant to be interpreted as signs but were altogether something else, totems or talismans.

He wanted to let the questions go, to find a release – learning more would not change the past, so what good would the knowing bring? His brow burning, the fever reaching its peak, he stopped transcribing and fell into his *charpoy*, drained.

But the questions would not stop revolving in his mind and he knew he could not relent until he had uncovered the truth. He would have to finish the diary, which stretched into her years in Gading. His next step would be the office of Jardine Matheson. He would learn his father's name, 'E'. The question of the involvement of the Lows, if true, he would deal with later.

*   *   *

The business offices of Jardine Matheson and Company were in a three-storey building on Queen Street, not far from Low Teck Seng's office. In fact, like all the new buildings in this section of town, the two were nearly indistinguishable. They presented a stolid façade meant to project seriousness and clarity of purpose, concentration on the art and science of business. Ornamentation, if there was any, abjured the fanciful in favour of a conservative pattern of faux-Greco-Roman columns and faux-Gothic arched windows.

Cool and quiet, the building's interiors matched the single-mindedness of purpose of the exteriors, with Western-suited clerks, both native and European, moving smoothly as if on tracks. Hawksworth noted that this building had been wired for electricity and telephone, with brass-bladed fans on the desks swirling the hot air without cooling it. The old method of the *punkah* suspended from the ceiling was more effective at cooling a large space, but it required the hiring and keeping of a team of pullers. Electricity neatly did away with that unattractive human encumbrance.

Hawksworth approached the front desk where a scrubbed youthful Tamil with a stiff collar and hair slicked close to his head with fragrant clove oil greeted him in a clipped voice meant to approximate an Oxbridge accent. The tall man had seen this type beginning to appear in greater numbers in the business district, the local youth graduating from English-language training schools, their clothes and hair and entire deportment geared to integrate them as closely as possible into European companies. Hawksworth found the effect unnerving: would everyone soon dress and talk like supercilious English clerks?

He explained the purpose of his visit, and the dark Tamil face was politely replaced by a young white one, ginger haired and freckled, nose and cheeks and ears pink with perpetual sunburn. His eyebrows matched the ruddy tone of his skin so that at first glance he seemed to have none. Nonetheless, the pale blue eyes that appraised the tall man were full of the vitality of youth. He had the look of a man who enjoyed his current station in life. 'I am Chief Clerk Thomas Powrie. How may I assist you, sir?' The voice was clear, with an Irish lilt that had been smoothed over but not polished out.

'Police Superintendent David Hawksworth. I am searching for information about one of your employees.'

'Hopefully nothing serious, Superintendent?'

'Most likely not. He would have been in your employ sometime in 1854 or 1855.'

The clerk's blue eyes widened in surprise. 'Well, that might make things more difficult. What do you need to know?'

'I need to know all the information you have. Full name, work history, position, everything.'

'Of course, sir. That information would be available, assuming we still have the records. The company shifted offices years ago and many of the old files were destroyed. What we retained is stored in a warehouse near our wharf at Telok Blangah, but last I checked, the files are very poorly organized. Mostly stacked pell-mell. It will take time to go through them. What can you tell me about this man?'

'Not much, I am afraid. I know he sailed from Liverpool, though I believe he had been living in Brighton. I know that he stopped in Penang and it is quite possible that he died either there or en route to Singapore.'

The clerk whistled low. 'It would be easier if you had more information to give me, at least a family name.'

'Only a letter. "E".'

'Right. Give me some time to search our warehouse. Even if he died en route, we would have a copy of his work contract, assuming, as I say, that it was not destroyed when we shifted the office. You said 1854 or 1855?'

Hawksworth nodded. 'If possible, I would like the information as quickly as you can get it. Once you have it, please telephone the Central Station.'

'Police Superintendent Hawksworth,' the clerk jotted down the name and information. 'Hopefully it will not be more than a day or two, assuming that we find the records in the warehouse,' the man said, before adding in a tone meant to sound solicitous, 'Forty years is a long time, sir.'

\* \* \*

In his own office with a plate of spicy *nasi goreng*, rice fried with spices and vegetables topped by an egg fried in a perfect circle, and a fourth cup of hot strong coffee, he tried to push the thoughts of his family from his mind, bringing his focus to the case at hand. But the patterns of the two puzzles kept blurring into each other, so that the mosaic of clues formed a single picture that jumbled elements from his mother's diary with the *kongsi* murders. No matter how he tried, the liquid mercury eyes of a *jiangshi* kept insinuating themselves into his thoughts as well. He blamed his own exhausted mind for this lack of control over his imagination.

A knock at the door pulled him from his reverie. Rizby entered, pausing before taking a seat. 'Late breakfast, sir?'

Studying the plate a moment with his head bowed, Hawksworth said, 'Truth be told, I am not sure what meal this is. I was hungry, so I called for it.'

'You need to regain your strength,' Rizby said, taking his seat. 'Eating rice between meals is an ideal way to do so.'

Hawksworth smiled at the small man nestled in his chair, which looked big around him. He closed his eyes and immediately the bloated face appeared, unbidden. Hawksworth sighed, opened his eyes to take in Rizby's fox face, then spoke quietly, 'Allow me to ask, when we were on the roof in the storm, did you notice anything...unusual?'

'Unusual, sir?'

'I thought...I mean to say...after Yeung was apprehended, I saw something....'

Rizby's agate eyes narrowed on Hawksworth before he said in an abstract voice, '*Jiangshi* are said to be attracted to violence and bloodshed, appearing where these are most intense.'

Hawksworth nodded meditatively. 'It was an intense squall, with much thunder and lightning.'

'And you were of course under great strain, having just been shot and lightly wounded,' Rizby added with a hint of mischievousness in his voice.

'Yes, very much so, Detective Inspector,' Hawksworth agreed, pointing the sharp tip of his aquiline nose at Rizby. 'There is always a rational explanation for such seemingly incorporeal things.' His tone indicated the subject required no further commentary.

'Not always, sir,' Rizby retorted seriously before cracking into a toothy grin, 'Love is a case in point. I have asked Soe Soe Aye for her hand in marriage.'

Hawksworth's eyebrow arched in surprise; he did not think Rizby had the romance in him. 'And how did she reply?'

Sighing sumptuously, he said with relieved triumph, 'She has said "yes".'

'Congratulations! Well done Rizby! Well done indeed! Once this case is finished you must allow me to stand you to a celebratory feast.' Hawksworth spoke with genuine cheer, glad that good news was finally coming to him.

'Thank you, sir. There are still details to be worked out regarding her current employer and other nuisances but these are minor things.'

'If I may be of any assistance in any way, never hesitate to ask.'

'Thank you, sir, it is very kind.'

'As much as I would like to celebrate with you now, we must unfortunately go to Outram Prison.'

'Time to interrogate our suspect?'

Glancing at the clock on his desk, Hawksworth said, 'He has been nearly thirty-six hours in the Stews. That should soften him up.'

'Shall I find Sergeant Major Walker?'

'Let him be. What I would like very much are two bottles of carbonated water from the canteen.'

'Somewhat early in the day for whisky and soda, is it not, sir?' Rizby cried in genuine surprise.

'In that case, Detective Inspector,' Hawksworth said with a tight smile, 'I shall only require the soda.'

*　　*　　*

The day had grown overcast with the coming of an afternoon storm so that the sky appeared as heavy as the granite walls of the prison. Grey light filtered through the window high on the wall that looked out onto the European exercise yard below, a grey that suited the oppressive atmosphere of the place, Hawksworth thought.

As was the regular method, Yeung was already shackled in the chair behind the empty table when Hawksworth, Rizby, and Heng entered the room. He had been changed out of his wet clothes and put into blue serge prison garments that were a size too big for him. From the look on Yeung's face, Hawksworth could tell that his time in the Stews had exhausted but not broken him. This was not, almost assuredly, his first time in gaol. It probably was not even the first time he had been interrogated.

Rizby walked behind Yeung with Heng, who then sat in a chair against the back wall, out of sight but clearly audible. Hawksworth placed two drinking glasses and two bottles of soda water on the table, then sat on the edge as he uncorked a bottle and poured out two sparkling glasses.

'You must be thirsty. Care for fizzy water?' he politely offered one.

Yeung made no reply, his face immobile, staring straight ahead.

Hawksworth shrugged then put the cork back in the bottle. Taking up his glass, he sipped his water. 'Disappointing news. The Tiger Claws are no more. Your companions are either in custody or dead. You are finished.'

Yeung said nothing.

'I believe that you know who killed Low Teck Beng, Lau Chi Man, and Chong Yong Chern. I do not believe that you killed them because I do not believe that a low-level street thug like yourself would be capable of such a feat. What I want from you is information. Tell me, who killed Low Teck Beng?'

The man stayed dead silent and stock-still. Hawksworth sighed with resignation, then took up the bottle, turning it over to examine it.

'This rather funny-looking thing is called a Codd-neck bottle. After the manufacturers inject the gas into the water, the glass is twisted at the neck around this marble, here,' he pointed, holding the bottle in front of the immobile face. 'The marble acts as a stopper that allows me to pour out very exact amounts of carbonated water. Very inventive, is it not?' he said cheerily, shaking it until the water became frothy in the bottle. 'Sure you do not care for some?'

Rizby pulled the man's head back so his nose was pointed at the ceiling. Hawksworth held the bottle to the man's face then swiftly pulled the cork causing soda water to ejaculate explosively into Yueng's nose. He writhed in the chair, jerking his head from side to side, his shackled feet stamping.

'The carbonic acid in the water causes intense pain in the soft tissue of the nostrils. I am not sure exactly how the process works, I am not a chemist,' Hawksworth calmly explained as Rizby let go of the man's head. 'I understand it is an intense burning sensation. Is that true?'

Yueng's head lolled forward, the water running out of his nose followed by strings of snot. He swallowed hard as the rest poured down the back of his throat.

'I asked you a question,' Hawksworth barked, slapping the man's face as Heng translated. 'Does it burn?'

Yueng nodded affirmatively, his eyes watering and red. The tears were involuntary.

'Who killed Low Teck Beng?'

He nodded negatively. Hawksworth reached down to yank the man's head back by his hair. 'I asked you who killed Low Teck Beng. Answer me.'

The fear glistening in Yueng's eyes told the Superintendent that the man knew the answer but was scared to death to tell him.

'If I keep pouring water up your nose, you may drown accidentally.' Hawksworth let go of his head, frowning. 'Your death is of no consequence to me, except that if you give up the ghost too soon I may not learn what you have to tell me, so do forgive me, but this is for your own safety.'

He snapped his fingers and Rizby again pulled the man's head back. This time Hawksworth slapped him hard. 'Open your mouth.' He slapped hard again then grabbed Yeung's lower jaw, jerking hard on it. The teeth parted and with his other hand, he jammed a rag into the man's mouth, stuffing it tightly. Then he picked up the Codd-neck bottle and shook it. Yeung's eyes went wide with fear and he tried to twist his neck to escape the geyser but it was unavoidable: the fizzing water slammed into his nostrils, pooling deep within his nasal cavities. He jerked wildly, his entire body spasming.

After half-a-minute, Rizby pushed his head forward to allow the water to pour out. Once it was drained, he inhaled deeply: when the water was in his nose, he was unable to breathe. The panic was as unnerving as the pain.

'What is nice about soda water, other than the fact that it will leave no scars on your body that you can claim as war trophies, is that your flesh does not become accustomed to the pain it causes. In fact, every time I fill your nose, the pain will only increase as the acid burns again the skin already damaged.'

Yeung's torso heaved.

'Careful not to vomit into the rag. We might not get it out in time then you may well drown in your own spew. Better tell me now. Who killed Low Teck Beng?'

He shook his head negatively. Hawksworth sighed, reaching again for the soda bottle. 'Nearly half empty already! Luckily soda is cheap and plentiful. Amazing to think that something as innocent as fizzy water could break such a toughed criminal as yourself,' Hawksworth smiled at Yeung. 'Last chance. Save yourself the agony. Who killed Low Teck Beng?'

The bloodshot eyes glared at him with pure hatred.

'Once more unto the breach...' he said, and Rizby pulled Yeung's head back again. This time he left the water in for a full minute before allowing it to drain out. When Yeung opened his eyes, Hawksworth was sitting at the table, casually sipping fizzy water from one of the glasses. 'It is refreshing. Unfortunately, we do not have any whisky to go with it, but my colleague has admonished me that it is apparently too early in the day for alcohol. Tell me, who killed Low Teck Beng?'

Yeung tried to cough, gagging around the rag in his mouth, mucous and saliva and water running out around the edges and down his chin. He glared at Hawksworth, who was pouring more fizzy water into his glass, which he then held close to Yeung's face so the gas from the exploding bubbles rose into his nose. He flinched in pain, his body clenched.

'Ready to talk, are you? Or shall I again use your head for a drinking glass?'

After a pause, his eyes screwed tightly shut, Yeung nodded affirmatively.

Hawksworth reached forward and tugged the soaking rag from the man's mouth. 'Who?' he asked again, tossing it on the table with a wet smack.

'Wong Dai Long,' the man said, leaning forward in defeat.

Hawksworth glanced at Rizby who shrugged and shook his head.

'Who is Wong Dai Long?' Hawksworth asked.

'I do not know.'

'Come come, Yeung. Tell me, is he Cantonese or Hokkien? Malaya-born or China-born?'

'Cantonese.'

'What was the nature of your business with him? He was in another gang?'

'I do not know what gang he was from. He never told and we never asked. Sometimes we sold goods for him and sometimes we got goods for him.'

'Goods?'

'Weapons. He gave us weapons to sell to other gangs. Sometimes we helped him with shipments, helped to transport the cargo from one place to another.'

'Did he ever show you American weapons? Pistols, shotguns?'

Yeung grimaced, 'Shotguns. Very expensive. We helped him cut them down. Sawed the barrels and stocks.'

'How many?'

'Five.'

'He asked you to cut five expensive American shotguns and you honestly expect me to believe that you have no idea to which gang this man belonged?' Hawksworth reached for the soda bottle causing Yeung to jump in his seat against his shackles; but the Superintendent merely filled his own glass.

'I am telling the truth,' Yeung pleaded through the translator. 'He always met me alone. I thought he only sold weapons. I did not know that he was a killer.'

'Why did he kill Low Teck Beng?'

'I do not know. When he learned that we were using Hoi to supply boys to Low Teck Beng, he asked me to tell him more.'

'And you told him that Teck Beng was at the Hotel Formosa the night he was killed?'

'Yes.'

Hawksworth sipped more water, sloshing it around in his mouth before swallowing. 'Where is Wong Dai Long now?'

'I do not know. He always came to me. Except for one time when I met him at a hideout, in a swamp in Jurong.'

'Jurong? That is far, indeed.'

'They use the location to store goods when they are being transhipped.'

'So he is little better than a pirate. Give us a detailed description of the location.' Hawksworth sipped the last of the carbonated water in his glass, then smacked his lips loudly in satisfaction. 'We will keep you in protective custody until we capture Wong Dai Long and his cohorts. You will be safe with us. I suspect that if your former friends were to find you on the street, they would use something much worse than fizzy water.'

CHAPTER XII

# Attacked!

THE SEA WAS PATROLLED by reef sharks, the mangrove verge by crocodiles. Crisscrossed with creeks that came and went with the rainy season, pirates and marauders had made the swampy estuary a nest site for centuries. The pirates hid their shallow-draft boats in the dense vegetation then sprang out from behind the low islands around Selat Sembilan to attack ships heading up the straits toward Malacca.

Inland from the mangrove coast, the land rose in small hillocks that provided hard soil for building hideaways amidst the morass. The quagmire had been called Jurong, from the Malay word for shark, *jerung*, long before the arrival of the British, but no one knew who had named it. A road had been cut into the jungle in the middle of the century but the land was useless for planting and the road tailed into a muddy track. It connected to the main Bukit Timah Road via a dirt lane that washed out half the year; otherwise, Jurong was inaccessible from town. The pirates had been driven out during Hawksworth's youth and now the area was the terrain of smugglers who used the old network of creeks and trails to move their contraband.

Yueng had drawn a map with the creeks marked with dotted lines, the trails with dashes, and the hillocks with circles, which indicated that Wong Dai Long's hideout was on one of the mounds of hard land. The abstract squiggles would be all they had to go on: the colonial authorities had yet to survey the deep swamp of Jurong.

A large contingent of men would immediately call attention to itself. Surprise was the order of the day, so only three Sikh riflemen, handpicked by Sergeant Major Walker for their bravery and reliability, accompanied Hawksworth and Walker into the bush. The Sikhs were trained for jungle fighting and kept their beards trimmed short; in place of the colourful turbans they wore in the city, here they merely wrapped their heads in black cloth, knotted tightly at the back, with a short loose tail to cover their necks.

To avoid being seen, the men stayed in the foliage, moving parallel to the trail. The ground was spongy, their boots sinking an inch into sucking ooze with each step. The vegetation around them was so thick that often their visibility was only a foot in any direction. A flash of red through the dim green caught Hawksworth's attention and he crouched, drawing his Webley. One of the Sikhs moved swiftly through the growth in a fast duck walk, his carbine cradled in his arms, only to find that the splash of red was a lobster claw blossom longer than a man is tall, dangling from a *Heliconia* plant.

The soil became firmer and the vegetation thinned as the ground sloped upward. According to the rough map, they were at the base of the hillock on which was situated the hideout. A cluster of *Alocasia* plants, some with leaves more than six feet across, ran alongside a muddy streambed at the base of the hill: perfect cover. They crouched in the mud, peeking through the leaves up the woody slope. Hawksworth could see the crown of a tree towering far above them. Such growth would require stable soil: near the base they would find the smugglers' den.

It was decided that the men would break into teams. Walker and one Sikh and Hawksworth with the other two would charge the hill from opposite directions, with Hawksworth's team coming from the direction of the trail and Walker's team sneaking around the back.

The climb was short but slippery, the mud stinking of vegetable rot. They needed both hands to scramble up the slope, Hawskworth using the handle of his cane like a piton hammer, their weapons slung and holstered. If they came under fire now they would simply let go and slide back under the broad *Alocasia* leaves.

By the time they crested the top, Hawksworth's trousers were coated with a thick film of slime, the cloth at the knees torn. Once up, he palmed the Webley, following behind the Sikhs who pushed swiftly through the underbrush, keeping low. He was amazed at the agility of the big men. He had once watched a troop of long-tailed macaques move with the same speedy silence up and along the top of a bamboo fence; the fierce-faced Sikhs moved with the same uncanny skill. Hawksworth felt especially clumsy, lagging behind them, using his cane as much for balance as for support.

Their way was blocked ahead by the giant buttress root of the tree Hawksworth had seen from below. The roots radiated in massive fins around the trunk of the tree, some reaching three stories tall. A rough-hewn shed with an *attap* roof, little more than a lean-to, was snug in the crotch of one. They approached silently, their weapons cocked. Remembering that there could be men inside with pump-action shotguns, Hawksworth's heart pounded so loudly he could hear it. A twig snapped under his foot and he nearly leapt into the air. The Sikhs crouched, raised their carbines to their shoulders ready to fire, but no one appeared.

They rushed the structure but it was empty, though it had not been for very long. Outside a pit fire still smouldered. Inside they found two pallets with bedding beside a table cobbled from scrap wood, and on that was a dented teakettle beside a chipped teacup, half filled. The metal was still warm to the touch.

'They heard us coming and escaped,' Hawksworth spat.

Shouts came from the other side of the giant tree, the Sergeant Major's voice barking orders. They dashed in the direction of the noise, not bothering to conceal their sounds. One, then two crevices created by the root buttresses were empty; in the third they found Walker pointing his Webley at the skull of a man squatting over a narrow hole in the ground, his trousers around his ankles, a pile of stinking shit beneath his bare ass. A revolver lay in the mud just beyond his reach.

'Found this one doing his toilet,' Walker said, grinning. 'He was squeezing so hard that his eyes closed and that is when we sprang on him.'

'Their shed is on the other side of the tree. There might have been one more but he seems to have slipped away.'

'Too bad for this one his bowels betrayed him.'

'Wong Dai Long?' Hawksworth asked.

The man did not answer but to judge from the hatred in his eyes, Hawksworth guessed correctly that they had their man. 'Wong Dai Long, I am arresting you for the murders of Low Teck Beng, Lau Chi Man, and Chong Yong Chern.'

The response was a steady stream of oaths in Cantonese. Walker raised his arm to pistol whip the squatting man but Hawksworth yelled for him to stop. 'Get him to stand. I will shackle him then we will walk him back to the carriage. You take the front and I will follow. Keep two of the men on either side of him at all times.'

Walker grabbed a fistful of the man's hair and pulled him

to his feet. They let him raise his trousers slowly, two carbines pointed at him. When Hawksworth twisted his arms behind his back, Wong struggled, kicking as Hawksworth snapped the shackles on his wrists. They had no chains, merely a hinge, so the suspect's hands were closer together. If he fell, he would land face down.

Once the shackles were in place and Walker's pistol back in its holster, Wong turned toward Hawksworth and spat a gob of green snot on his shirt. Reflexively the tall man punched the short suspect in the face, flattening his nose and knocking him backward into the root fin. Walker's pistol was in his hand in a flash, the hammer cocked. Hawksworth punched again, this time in the gut, doubling Wong over. 'We need him to walk out of here, otherwise I would knock him unconscious,' he muttered to no one in particular. 'Blindfold him then we march.'

Tediously, the six men moved along the dark mud of the trail, reaching the carriage just as the sky turned as black as the ground, the downpour imminent, low swirling clouds the colour of midnight stretching ominously over them like giant hands. Hawksworth hoped they could make Bukit Timah Road before the track washed out. He wanted Wong interrogated as soon as possible, and having to push and pull the carriage through the mud was not a delay he relished.

On the long bumpy ride back into town, the interior of the carriage grew steamy like a glasshouse, stinking of mud and shit. The men rode in silence, the smattering noise of the heavy raindrops pounding the roof like incessant hammer blows. Hawksworth studied Wong's face. There was dried blood around his nose. A dirty leaf clung to the unkempt hair. There was not a trace a fear.

The Superintendent had spent his life around criminals

toughened by prison and men hardened by combat. He had watched whores die slowly from venereal disease that ate them from the inside out, their flesh dissolving while they screamed. He had seen men on the scaffold, seen the look in their eyes when the final moment was upon them, holding fast their last thought before crossing over. He had been close enough to men he had killed to taste their blood when it splashed hot and brassy on his lips. He had seen depthless remorse in a sober killer's eyes when confronted with his drunken crimes, and he had seen the mirthless joy of the psychotic when his crippled victim was called to testify.

He looked now at Wong Dai Long and saw the face of a man who had also spent his life among hardened criminals and merciless thugs. He saw a face that stared back at its captors with utter disregard for their authority and total disdain of their persons. How many times had he been shackled before? How many times beaten? His finger bones snapped? He feared no man. The face staring back at Hawksworth, pockmarked and beetle-browed and blood-stained, swaying not more than a foot from him in the narrow confines of the bouncing carriage, was the face of a man who could casually kill a roomful of people then sit at his breakfast in peace. Breaking him would take more than threats and fizzy water. Breaking him, Hawksworth knew, would require reaching Wong's own deep threshold of cruelty, then going one step further.

*   *   *

They returned to find the normally frenetic town quiet as a tomb. An army checkpoint had been set-up on Outram Road near the golf links north of the hospital. Close by, to the south, was the

Chinese Quarter; to the north lay a native Chinese kampong on Burial Ground Road.

A trio of uniformed soldiers with rifles strapped to their backs stopped the carriage; barrels filled with sand had been placed in a zigzagging obstacle course across the road. The rain had stopped, leaving everything wet with the woody smell of rot. Hawksworth pushed open the carriage door, stepping out then rising to his full height. 'Police Superintendent David Hawksworth.' He handed his shield to the nearest soldier who appeared to be the man in charge. 'What is the disturbance?'

'Coolie riot, sir. They attempted to march on the hospital and barracks,' the soldier examining his shield said. He was older, a career army man and obviously not very impressed with his current duty. Manning checkpoints was for new recruits.

The youngest of the three, a blond boy who appeared too young to be in uniform, spoke excitedly, 'There was a large number of cholera deaths last night. They were bringing the bodies into the hospital grounds for burial when suddenly a column of coolies with torches and tools came marching up the road. They were chanting something about...well sir, I was told that some blamed the police for poisoning the water and others that a... sounds ridiculous...'.

'A vampire.'

'Yes, sir,' the young solider was taken aback, 'They claimed that the police had somehow let this beast loose in the Chinese Quarter and that it was responsible for the deaths. The state of the bodies, cholera victims appear, well, drained, sir.'

'Did they breach the hospital grounds?'

'No,' the officer in charge said, handing back Hawksworth's shield, 'the local guard was able to hold them back along with assistance from men from the barracks and prison. The

Protector of Chinese is meeting with their leader now to quell the uprising, hopefully.'

'I take it that in the meantime the Chinese Quarter is not only under quarantine but is now under martial law.'

'Yes, sir. Several doctors said that they spotted cholera victims among the rioters. You can imagine what would happen if they overran the hospital. It would be worse than the clan war!'

Far worse, Hawksworth thought, envisioning the bloodletting that would occur if any respectable European civilians were harmed at the hands of a coolie mob.

The third solider, also young but stout with a bass voice, peered into the darkness of the carriage, 'Who do you have there, sir? He looks in rough shape. Does he need the hospital?'

'Prisoner being transported for questioning. If the road is blocked, we will take him the long way around to the Central Station,' Hawksworth explained, then added in a rasp, 'No need for hospital. His wounds are only superficial.'

Inside the carriage, Walker asked what the checkpoint was about. Hawksworth explained, staring out at the empty streets sliding past in the murky evening. No one seemed to be about. He knew that they were at home, ensuring that the larder was full in case of siege, checking that the mechanism of the revolvers they had not touched in years still functioned and that the ammunition that had lain for so long at the back of the drawer was still good. The precarious calm that the settlement had grown so accustomed to was eroding, revealing the fragile skeletons upon which it rested.

*   *   *

Fenella was seated on his lap, clapping her hands playfully while he combed her hair, the brush moving smoothly through the fine strands.

'Sit still, child,' he gently chided her, 'we are nearly done.'

It was a task he enjoyed more than any other, tugging the bone comb through his daughter's tangled hair until in ran like silk past her tiny ears, down her slim neck. When Ni tried to brush her hair she squirmed and pouted, but when her father's big rough hands held her fast, she relaxed her body back into his and offered no resistance as he pulled the teeth of the comb repeatedly through the rook-black cascade. When they were done, he would wind a few ribbons of hair around his fingers into his fist and tug slightly while she remained quietly staring forward, the slight pain a pleasant sensation. He knew that soon she would be too old for this nightly ritual, and felt a tinge of regret. Someday not long from now, she would insist on combing her own hair: her mother would probably still be allowed to plait it but her father would be forbidden into the women's domestic sphere. Then the soft silky ribbons in his fist would simply be a memory. But now, while she still allowed it, he gathered two fistfuls of hair, rolled them into flat ribbons between his thumb and fingers, and tugged gently on them so that her head tilted back until she was staring at him upside down, smiling up at him with her baby teeth. 'All done. Bed time for you. Go to your mother,' he said before releasing her.

She hopped off his lap onto fat toddler legs, moving through the world of big furniture to Ni, who was at the table with Fon, talking in Siamese.

Hawksworth watched as Ni scooped her onto her lap, the child's arms wrapping around her slender neck. Then he watched the three females rise and head to the bedroom. Now was his time, the only time he had alone during the long days. He glanced at the books and papers neatly stacked beside his *charpoy*, Isabella

Lightheart's journal, Saint James Bible, loose pages of notes. Not tonight, he decided. He was relaxed and in a good mood and not ready to burrow into the obsessive mental space required to decipher his own past.

It had been more than twenty-four hours since they brought Wong Dai Long into town. They had not bothered with police paperwork, booking, cell assignment. He had been taken directly to their unofficial interrogation space on Pulau Saigon, a disused godown where Sergeant Major Walker had been working him over, a translator and Rizby on hand to ask questions. The three Sikh rifle guards were there as well, patrolling outside, carbines plainly visible. They were there as much to keep Wong captive as to keep his cohorts away. They reasoned that the gang was aware of Wong's capture and might try to shut him up by pumping buckshot into him – and anyone else nearby. Hawksworth would go down in the morning to see if the suspect was tender enough for him to finish the interrogation, but the Superintendent suspected with a grimace that twenty-four hours, even with Walker zealously tenderizing, might not be enough. Wong looked as if he had the soul of a crocodile and a skin just as tough.

He stretched himself then rose to fill his nightly glass of arrack.

In the darkness of a starless wet night the toads beyond the door loudly filled the air with throaty music. Pungent smells of the delicious dinner still hung in the bungalow and as he sipped his arrack, Hawksworth felt at peace. He wished he could take Ni into his arms, slide into her soft moistness, but that one desire would have to be thwarted awhile longer. He sipped more then set about closing the house for the night, window shutters and door locks.

He had set the empty glass on the sideboard, too relaxed to

wash his face or clean his teeth, and was sitting in his nightshirt on the edge of his *charpoy*, the mosquito netting draped over the side parted by his knees, when he became aware of the change. He froze, immediately alert, his mind straining to detect the alteration in his sensorium.

The toads had stopped croaking.

The recognition came at the same instant as the gunfire. The buckshot slammed into the wood of his front door, sending splinters flying through the room.

Hawksworth dropped to the floor, rolling as the next shot tore through the shutters of the front window. He had time to realize that it came from the same direction as the first as he frantically groped under the bed for the Snider-Enfield, his fingers snatching at the hard metal.

He heard the roar of another shot, the heavy pellets slamming into the wall outside the bedroom – the room where Ni and Fon and Fenella were. So there were two shooters; his mind raced, envisioning their positions outside in the dark. On his back, the rifle held close to his chest, he watched as the next shot blew in the shutters, shattering the wood, smashed into the wall opposite him, sending plaster raining down on the *charpoy* – a third shooter, or had the first shifted position?

His fingers worked the metal breech lock and the .577 cartridge slipped into place. Now the women were screaming in the bedroom and he was running toward it, the heavy rifle in his arms. The next shot hit the front door again, taking it off one hinge, the splinters sailing through the room: were they trying to shoot their way in?

He used his bad foot to kick the bedroom door open, pain lancing through his leg. The two women were huddled over Fenella and they shrieked when they saw him, their faces contorted into sheer terror. He was shouting at them to stay down, then on his knees to check for blood – there was none, no one had been struck – and then stood up just as another shot impacted the window of the bedroom, ripping away one of the shutters.

This time he saw the muzzle flash in the darkness outside. The Snider-Enfield was against his shoulder. He squeezed the trigger, the kick staggering him – he had not braced. The box of cartridges was still under the *charpoy*, in the next room, and he ran back, his bad foot dragging, diving hard as the next mass of buckshot smashed into the room. There was not much left of the door or window shutters to deflect the rounds now, and this one slammed into the framed silhouettes of his parents above the sideboard, obliterating them.

The box of cartridges was now in his hand, loose shells rolling across the floor as he worked the breech block – the brass of the first cartridge stuck – he could only load one at a time – when buckshot slammed into the opposite wall, shaking the frame of the bungalow – three shooters, now he was certain. The empty brass finally clear, another round fitted into the breech, the block flipped shut, the hammer back, and he sent a wild shot out the shattered wood of the front door in case the bastards were moving toward it. Breech open, rifle flipped to shake the smoking brass, he jammed a fresh round in place.

The pocket of his night shirt was stuffed with loose cartridges – the women were still screaming hysterically – and back on his feet, the pain like hot wire in his foot as he ran out of the front door half expecting a load of shot in his face. Instead, the shot whistled past, ploughing into the doorframe beside his head. On the veranda, he ducked behind a wooden post then raised the heavy gun to his shoulder. He sent another round in the direction of the bright yellow muzzle flash in the darkness.

Shooter one was near the banyan tree on the front lawn. Hawksworth's ears ringing from the gunfire, he reloaded and capped off another round before running across the mud of his own lawn toward the banyan in the blackness. Emerging in the gloom ahead of him, he saw shooter one fumbling with a firearm – jammed or out of ammunition. Hawksworth heard shouting in Chinese but could not tell which dialect; the figure by the banyan started running down the road, yelling to his companions. He raised the Snider-Enfield and fired, the flash blinding him momentarily in the night. He crouched, waited for his vision to clear. Straining he could see no body in the road. He had missed.

He ran back around the house, the rifle already flipped in his hands so the dense stock could be swung like a club to smash a skull, the pain in his foot causing his leg to go numb to the thigh. Outside the bedroom wall he found a pile of brass shells where shooter two had stood. He heard the women still shrieking and ran, slipping once and landing painfully before regaining his feet, to the opposite side of the house where shooter three had been, but he knew before he got there that he would only find a pile of brass shells, still smoking hot in the mud. The men had vanished into the darkness.

He yelled in fury. The blood was rushing in his temples, the adrenaline coursing through him, then his bad foot gave way and he fell to his knees in his own garden, the rifle gripped so tightly his hands hurt. He was going to tear and shred and pull these bastards apart with his teeth, he was going to crack their bones and eat them alive and fling pieces of them all around him, but all he could do was bellow like a wounded animal, his inarticulate noise emanating into the indifference of the still and silent night that enclosed him.

CHAPTER XIII

# Golden Lotus

HE WAS IN his office before sunrise, writing his report on the attack on his house. Three uniformed – and armed – officers were now stationed there a round the clock, including a British sergeant, by order of the Inspector-General of Police, who issued it from his bed after he was roused from sleep to be told of the attack on the Superintendent.

Hawksworth was more angry than afraid – never before had anyone struck at his home. All of the years of trust he had built with the Chinese seemed to have been blown away as quickly and easily as the frames of his windows. There was no longer time to wait until the long investigation came to an end. By hook or by crook, he would extract all Wong Dai Long knew before the sun set. Those weapons needed to be out of the hands of the mysterious gang as quickly as possible. If they did not fear the most powerful *kongsi* and now proved that they did not completely fear the police either, there was no telling what havoc they were willing to cause. As to their purpose in perpetuating this mayhem, that would be uncovered once the weapons were securely in police custody.

For once Hawksworth was in his office before Ah Fong the coffee boy arrived, so he made do with weak tea as he filled out his report. As the sky broke crimson with the earliest rays of dawn, Rizby knocked at his door.

'Are you all of one piece, sir? Ni and her sister, Fenella are all safe?' he asked before stepping fully into the room.

'I am and they are, though they are badly rattled and would rather I had stayed with them.'

'There are officers on guard there now?'

He nodded, 'Stevenson and two of his best men, armed with revolvers and carbines.' Appraising his former adjutant, he added with concern, 'You look rather wan, Detective Inspector.'

'Bit drained, to tell you the truth. Myself and the Sergeant Major were interrogating Wong all night long.'

'What did you learn?'

'Nothing.'

'All night and you got nothing from him?'

Rizby moved to speak but wobbled on his feet. Hawksworth dashed to catch him, but the shorter man steadied himself. 'Better sit down, sir.'

'Take the remainder of the day off,' Hawksworth said gently. 'I do not need my top detective coming down with cholera. I would rather lose you for a day or two than for several weeks, or worse. Best if you stay far from the miasma of the Chinese Quarter. Go home and get some rest.'

'I will be fine, Superintendent. A few hours sleep is all that is required.'

'Detective Inspector, I insist. Take two days leave, more if you require it. If I need you urgently, I will send for you. In the meantime, rest and sleep and eat well. Perhaps you can rendezvous with your Burmese paramour,' he said with a playful hint of mischief in his voice, trying to lighten the mood.

Rizby merely smiled weakly, then rose to take his leave, apologizing.

'On your way out, send someone to fetch the Sergeant Major, I would like a word.'

Fong arrived with a pot of coffee, hot and bitter and reviving. He felt the energy returning before he finished his second cup. Before Hawksworth started on his third, Sergeant Major Walker was standing in his office, ramrod stiff despite his drawn face.

'I understand that an attempt was made on your life,' Walker spoke impassively.

'If they had wanted me dead they would have burst in and shot me in the face. No, they were sending a message. They want to me, us, the police, to break off our investigation. They know we have Wong. Rizby informs me that despite your best efforts, he will not talk.'

'Tough bastard. Tear out his fingernails and he will still keep his mouth shut.' Walker said matter-of-factly, daubing sweat from his brow. The heat of the day was rising.

Hawksworth thought for a moment, tapping his cane on the floor of his office. 'There is probably one way to get him to talk.'

'What is that?'

'"Be stirring as the time; be fire with fire; threaten the threatener and outface the brow of bragging horror."'

Walker's exhausted face went tight with anger. 'Come, man, tell me what you mean. I have no time for your nonsense.'

'I am suggesting that we "fight fire with fire", as the Americans say.'

Studying his face for a moment, Walker considered the implications then said incredulously, 'You do not mean....'

'We deliver our recalcitrant suspect to our Celestial brothers of the Mother-Flower *kongsi*. They will surely make him talk.'

'Savages! They will merely torture him to death.'

'No, no, the proper arrangements will be made. Our suspect

will talk and he shall live to testify.'

Walker merely looked away, the disgust apparent on his face, but he nodded in assent. 'We do not have much time.'

Hawksworth glanced at his watch pocket watch. 'I would say that we will have our suspect singing all he knows before nine o'clock tonight.'

\*   \*   \*

Wong Dai Long's mouth was gagged and his head was bagged in a burlap sack as he sat in the back of the closed waggon. He wore belly shackles wrapped round his midriff, with a chain leading from his wrists to the shackles around his ankles. He felt tired, sore and stiff from the beating. He was famished and parched, but still his confidence was high. They might torture him, imprison him, cut his flesh and break his bones, but he would not tell them what he knew.

He recognized the *gwei-lo* voices of the two police officers in the back of the wagon with him, the bald one with the cruel eyes who beat him during the interrogation and the tall one with the sharp face and cane who arrested him.

He reasoned that they must be transporting him to the big prison at Outram. Stupid British! Instead of snapping his ligaments or cutting off fingers one-by-one, which is what *he* would do to get someone to talk, these *gwei-lo* clowns would smack him around some more then lock him up with food and water. They would keep him until the trial then hope he would talk. How stupid!

He could hear the sounds of the Chinese Quarter outside the waggon. It was quieter than usual because of the quarantine but still recognizable by the call of the voices, the odour of the cooking food. It smelled like dinnertime, stir-fry garlic and pungent oyster sauce, fresh-cut *kailan* sizzling in a pan. His mouth watered. How long since he had eaten? No matter, they would feed him in prison. He would live fat and happy until the trial, and he would not say a word. Good jolly British justice!

The carriage came to a halt sooner than he had figured. It sounded as though they were still in the Chinese Quarter, not outside the big prison. Then he heard the tall *gwei-lo* step out, and voices outside of the waggon speaking in English and Malay.

Then he heard Hokkien.

Cold fear shot through him. Involuntarily, he began to quake, trying to work his mouth around the gag, hoping to beg them not to hand him over to other Chinese … anything but other Chinese.

Then the bald *gwei-lo* kicked him hard in his side so that he toppled over, tumbling still shackled out the back of the waggon, landing with a thud in the dirt. Someone kicked him in the head, a clumsy kick aimed at the burlap bag. It caught him painfully in the ear and he tried to howl, but the gag caught in his mouth and he choked. Then rough hands jerked him up and he was whisked, feet barely touching the ground, into a house.

It was a Chinese house, he could tell by the smells, the joss sticks and lamp oil smoke and fresh oranges on the altar; the *bak kut teh* pork fat simmering in the pot with liquorice bark, star anise, and *goji* berries; the heavy fragrance of opium wafting from a further room. His worst fear confirmed, he began to writhe in his captors' hands, but to no avail; they held him fast.

Half shoved, half carried through the front parlour, he could hear the bare floorboards creak as they moved down a hallway, then a door opened and he was pushed through. Stumbling, he fell, then was pulled up and thrown against a wooden post, the back of his head cracking hard. A thin rope was tugged tightly around his neck, and he felt them adjusting the shackles, loosening them then yanking his arms upward, snapping the metal closed. They had shackled him to the post so that he was immobile, his wrists above his head.

Then they started to rip his clothes off. The tip and blade of the knife, or knives, for at least two were working him, sliced into his flesh as they carelessly cut away the material. Still his head was bagged, the thin rope tight around his neck, but now he was naked, shivering in fear, doing all he could not to shit himself, the ice expanding in his guts. He felt the loose material of his trousers pooled around his ankles, caught on the shackles.

The bag was pulled from his head. He was in a bare room, empty except for a plain wooden table. The tall *gwei-lo* stood before him, the burlap bag in his hand. Beside him was a Chinese with the heavy face of a drinker, dark purple lips pressed into a frown, eyes black with hate. He recognized Tan Yong Seng, the new *samseng ong* of the Mother-Flower *kongsi*. Wong began to utter a prayer around his mouth gag.

The *gwei-lo* slapped him once in the face, then motioned to someone behind them. The gag was removed, the thin rope around his neck loosened.

'Wong Dai Long, I believe that you are responsible for the murders of Low Teck Beng, Lau Chi Man, and Chong Yong Chern. I want to know who ordered their murders. I want to know who supplied the American shotguns. I want to know where those weapons are now.' Hawksworth spoke slowly so Yong Seng could translate; his Cantonese was not of the first order, but the meaning clear enough.

Wong spit at Hawksworth, the gob landing on his shoulder. He glared fiercely at the detective, expecting a punch in reprisal. Hawksworth said and did nothing, merely studying the man who, bound and shackled naked to the post, was still so defiant.

'We are wasting time,' Yong Seng said in Malay.

'Proceed,' Hawksworth said, then stepped from Wong's field of view.

Yong Seng stepped forward, motioning for the gag to be replaced in the man's mouth. Rough fingers slapped Wong's face again, shoving the rag back in when his mouth flapped open.

The wire held before him was thin like guitar string. Yong Seng ran it across Wong's cheek, then pulled it taut so the man could feel how it would cut flesh. With a quick flourish, Yong Seng twisted the wire into a loop that he held before Wong's face, swinging it back and forth as though he was trying to hypnotize him.

With his left hand he reached down and gently lifted the frightened man's limp and shrunken penis; with his right, he slipped the wire garrotte around it, fitting it snugly against the base, just above the testicles. He then stepped aside, beyond Wong's view. A wire ran from the loop out of his view: Wong realized that they could tighten or loosen it slightly.

He heard the *gwei-lo*'s voice again, from behind him, speaking in English; Yong Seng translated harshly right into his ear. 'Who ordered the murder of Low Teck Beng?'

He stayed silent, squeezing his eyes tightly shut, sweat slicking his skin. He expected the wire to pull taut any moment.

Instead, he felt hands on his chest, fingers that were soft and feminine, stroking his chest from behind. Then they were gone.

'Who supplied the weapons?'

Again he stayed silent. This time the hands touched him lower down, on his belly, stroking him gently along the line of his waist, the fingertips gently brushing the tender flesh just above his pubic hair.

The blood began to move involuntarily into his penis, inflating it slightly, and he knew with sweaty certainty what they were doing to him. He drew in a breath sharply when the hands disappeared, forcing his mind through his fear to think about something else, something bad, skulls with snakes pouring from the eye sockets, rotting stinking death, anything but sex.

'Where are the weapons now?'

In the small amount of movement allowed to him, Wong nodded negatively.

This time the girl appeared before him. She too was totally nude, her black hair pulled up in a loose chignon bun, her dark eyes wide. Her body was plump and curvaceous, the dark patch of hair between her legs vivid against her creamy skin. She had breasts the size of grapefruit with eraser nub nipples; a delectable rose petal scent rose from between the globes. She pushed against him, the points of her nipples pressing into his chest, her mouth mere inches from his, blood-pink lips like a blooming orchid that she brushed against his face, undulating slowly, her hands above her head, fingers brushing his palms in the shackles.

He felt the blood rushing to his dick and now felt the first pain of the wire cutting into him, tightening as he grew bigger. If he got completely hard, he had no doubt, he would cut off his own cock. Squeezing his eyes shut, he began to whimper, trying again to force his mind into terrible places: the face of a drowned farmer they pulled from a river near his village when he was a boy, the dead man's tongue purple and swollen, eyes bulging out of their sockets; the horrible squeals of a puppy he and his friends roasted for fun, the smell of the flesh burning, the fat fizzling and bubbling. All the while the girl's soft body and delicious scent engulfed him. Despite his hunger and fear and the terrible images in his mind, his body reacted naturally to the stimulus. He felt his cock swelling, the wire cutting. He thought of the big vein that ran in a bulge along the top and imagined it popping.

Then she was gone. He was breathing quickly, nearly hyperventilating, his body slick with sweat. With relief, he felt his penis begin to droop again.

'Wong, tell me who ordered the murder of Low Teck Beng.' Hawksworth spoke again unseen, Yong Seng translating.

Wong was weeping now, tears running down his cheeks and snot streaming from his nose, but still he nodded negatively.

'Bee Geok!' Yong Seng shouted the girl's name, and she appeared again before Wong. This time she pressed not only her fragrant breasts against his chest but also her lips against his face. She ran her tongue along the line of his neck, nuzzling into him, her hands stroking his head behind his ears.

The blood flowed again to his cock, the pain biting sharply as it engorged. The *gwei-lo* spoke, 'Where are the weapons?' but this time the girl did not desist. Instead she spun around so that the roundness of her ass pressed directly into his dick; she began to rub rhythmically in a circular motion. His cock was now half full, the wire lacerating him, cutting deeply enough that he could feel the blood begin to ooze out.

'Enough!' Hawksworth shouted, and the girl slipped away again. Ice-cold water was tossed on Wong's groin, causing the swelling to go down immediately, washing the blood away. He felt weak, delirious, kept upright more by the wrist shackles than his own legs.

'Wong, spare yourself. Tell me who ordered the murder of Low Teck Beng.'

His head lolling, he still nodded negatively.

'Then go through life a freak of nature.'

'Bee Geok!'

She was back, her breasts pressed into him, her sweet breath blowing into his face. This time her hands dropped to his crotch; she fondled his sack, the tips of her fingernails gently scraping his perineum, sending flashes of pleasure up his torso. His cock began to rise again; she rolled his balls in her left hand while her right gently stroked the head of his penis, still enclosed by his prepuce.

'Who ordered the murders?'

He was now past the half-way point, he could feel the blood running down his thighs, and still she did not relent in her gentle ministrations. He was reeling, trying to fill his mind with the terrible images, graves and skeletons, headless corpses, bamboo spikes driven through hands and feet, but it was no use, the feminine softness was merciless in its cruelty. The pain was intense, worse than he could have imagined; the tears were flowing down his face.

'Almost there,' the girl cooed in an angelic voice.

'Tell me Wong, do not be a fool!'

For the first time she touched the shaft, a gentle three-finger stroke. She squatted before him on her succulent haunches, her face close to his penis while she tugged on it, looking up into his tear-stained eyes lustfully, killing him. It was too late now, he thought, he could not hold it back any longer, the blood engorging his dick, the wire sawing into him.

'Good lord man, talk before it is too late!'

Snuffling his tears, quaking in pain, his mind going blank, he nodded affirmatively.

'You will tell us everything we want to know?' Yong Seng asked unprompted.

The blood was flowing heavily now, lubricating the girl's gentle strokes; if the wire cut any deeper, the damage would be done. Wong nodded again. In one swift movement, Bee Geok stuck her finger into the loop and tugged open the little wire noose. Wong's cock sprang fully erect the moment it was free, but the man himself hung limply from the wrist shackles. When they were opened, he collapsed to the floor unconscious.

'Take him upstairs and get him cleaned up. He has much explaining to do and I have a feeling it will take some time,' Hawksworth said.

Yong Seng motioned to the guards, who scooped up the limp body like a carcass from the thin pool of blood in which it lay. They carried it strung like a hammock between them out of the room.

Bee Geok had a clean towel in her hand, wiping sweat from her brow and Wong's blood from her hands. A faint smile traced her lips as she cleaned up, unperturbed by the execution she had nearly caused.

Seeing that Hawksworth was watching her, Yong Seng placed an affirming palm on his shoulder.

'She is quite a young lady,' Hawksworth said, watching intently as she wrapped her abundant nudity in a loose kimono, her black hair falling in tendrils against her custard cheeks. With every move she made, even dressing, she could not help but stir desire.

Yong Seng laughed without mirth, 'Bee Geok is the most popular woman in all our brothels. They call her "Golden Lotus" because she so sweet and lovely and yet perfectly willing to plant herself in mud and filth– ask for her next time you pay us a visit.'

Hawksworth shook his head in disbelief, amazed at Yong Seng's casual cheer after the horrible spectacle they had just witnessed. 'You Chinese are truly the most devilish people on the planet.'

With a sidelong glance and a smirk on his purple lips, Yong

Seng merely said, 'I know.'

*   *   *

They had dragged Wong upstairs and tossed him on a bare horsehair mattress in an empty room, a cord running from his left wrist under the bed to his right so that he was immobilized. He had not fully recovered consciousness since passing out in the room below, his head lolling side to side.

Hawksworth and Yong Seng stood over him now, the Hokkien holding the bloody wire noose in his hand. 'I need to take him back. He will need to testify,' the tall man said cautiously, anticipating the reaction.

'This man killed Yong Chern! Yong Chern my cousin, my *samseng ong*, and your friend! Once you know what he has to say, I will kill him.'

Hawksworth was beginning to lose his temper, his nerves frayed. 'This same man tried to kill *me* last night. He shot at my family, at my *daughter*. I want to crack his skull with my bare hands, to smash his face against the wall until it runs through my fingers, but I cannot do that, Yong Seng. Not until we have captured or killed the ringmaster. I need to know who is behind this....'

'Who cares? Kill this bastard now. We will send his head back to his friends in a box.'

'Whoever they are, they fear neither the most powerful *kongsi* nor the police. My guess is that Wong means nothing to them, so killing him will achieve nothing. I need him alive to testify.'

'And once he tells us who is this "ringmaster",' Yong Seng used the unfamiliar English word, 'then we will kill him too.'

The two men stared each other in the eye, bodies tense. Never before, in all the years that they had known one another, had Hawksworth felt that they were on the verge of a physical fight. He knew better than to engage in fisticuffs with Yong Seng. There would be no way to win.

Hawksworth gazed down at the man trembling unconscious on the bare mattress. 'Get Wong to talk.' A towel of thick cotton had been wrapped around his bleeding groin so he resembled a giant baby in a blood-soaked nappy. Cold water was tossed at him, and when that failed, smelling salts were used. Wong opened his eyes, gazing about disoriented. He tried to sit up, but the wrist restraints keep him prostrate.

'Ready to talk, you bastard?' Yong Seng barked at him in Cantonese.

Wong nodded meekly. Yong Seng called for the servant in the corridor to bring a blanket, and one was swiftly thrown over him.

'Who killed Low Teck Beng?' Hawksworth spoke in English.

The fear flared in the man's eyes as he heard the translation. Yong Seng held out the wire noose, still sticky with his blood, a few stray hairs testament to the pain he had endured.

'Liu Xiao Hun' Wong said, then dropped his head.

Hawksworth and Yong Seng exchanged glances. The Chinese shrugged.

'Who is that?' the detective asked.

'Xiao Hun is his cousin, the woman in charge of distributing the new girls the Low *kongsi* brings into Singapore.'

Yong Seng's voice did nothing to mask his disbelief, 'A *woman* killed Low Teck Beng?'

Wong nodded, his hands involuntarily pulling at the restraints. 'She was angry with him because he would not consent to her marrying her lover.'

'Was her lover another of the gunmen at the Hotel Formosa

that night?' Hawksworth asked, the fragments of information resolving into a mosaic in his mind. He recalled what Shu En had told him about this cousin, about her disappearance a few days before Teck Beng was killed.

Wong was silent. Yong Seng moved toward him, the wire noose in his hand. 'He was there,' Wong said quickly.

'His name?'

'Lee,' Wong said.

'"Lee?" You do not have a name for him?' the detective asked.

'I only know "Lee".'

'Who ordered the killing of Lau Chi Man?'

'Lee.'

'And Chong Yong Chern?'

Wong nodded meekly.

'Why? This goes beyond a lover's quarrel. What did he hope to gain by killing the *kapitans* of the most powerful *kongsi*?'

'Lee is the leader of the Four Forty-fours,' Wong spoke plainly, as though this answer were self-evident.

Yong Seng jumped at the phrase. 'Did you say Four Forty-fours?' he asked, his voice rising in disbelief.

Wong merely nodded in reply.

Yong Seng exhaled a long breath before speaking quickly to Hawksworth. 'We thought the Four Forty-fours were only a myth. The story is that when the Hai San split up their gangs because of the government Secret Societies Ordinance, they decided to concentrate all their top muscle men – the worst of the bunch, the real killers – into a single gang. This gang was supposed to act as the enforcers for all the Hai San operations, allowing the original *kongsi* to become a friendly society. We assumed it was a story the Hai San spread to frighten the other *kongsi*,' he shook his head in disbelief.

'The Hai San supplied the American shotguns?' Hawksworth asked quickly.

Wong looked into his eyes, but it was not the defiant face that Hawksworth had seen two days before swaying in the back of the rain-lashed carriage. They had found his edge, then pushed him over. The man on the bed sighed, then said, 'The guns were provided by the Hai San. But it was Xiao Hun and Lee who decided to use them.'

'To understand,' Hawksworth spoke to Yong Seng, 'the Hai San armed their most vicious gang with these American guns, then they lost control. The Four Forty-fours became a rogue gang under the direction of Lee and, eventually, his lover Liu Xiao Hun, the cousin of their rival Low Teck Beng,' Hawksworth punctuated the air with his index finger as he spoke.

'It would seem that is the situation,' Yong Seng glanced at him then at Wong. Gesturing with his head at the door to indicate they should speak in private, Yong Seng led way as the two men exited the room, leaving a *kongsi* soldier inside to keep an eye on the prisoner.

In the hallway, Hawksworth spoke first, 'By now they know we have Wong.'

'They are cowards, they will run,' Yong Seng said angrily.

Hawksworth rapped his cane against the floorboard, 'I am not so sure. The star-crossed lovers still have the shotguns with them. They will make a stand.'

'So you send your police after them?'

'As quickly as possible. I want those weapons.'

'What about this one?' Yong Seng asked, gesturing at door.

'I will take him to gaol, place him beyond the reach of the Lows … and the Hai San.' And *you*, he thought.

'And Lee?'

A tense stare was again exchanged between the men. 'If we catch him, he will be put on trial and justice will be swift.' Yong Seng was about to retort but Hawksworth cut him short, 'And if you get to him first, then I will also expect swift justice.'

Yong Seng shook his head, 'I want Lee. You get all the others plus the Low cousin, but Lee is mine. He must pay for what he did to Yong Chern.'

Seeing his friend's vehemence and not wanting to waste time futilely arguing, Hawksworth merely nodded, then pushed the door open and walked back in the room.

Hawksworth towered over Wong and said simply, 'Tell me the order of the killing at the Formosa.'

Liu Xiao Hun had checked in as a guest in the room next door to the Plum Suite. She had asked Lee to come and bring his friends, including Wong. Her plan was to scare her cousin, and she knew that it would take a lot to scare him. Surprising him with sawn-off shotguns in the midst of his perverted amours would do the trick. They pounded on the door until a bodyguard opened it. Low Teck Beng was on his knees in front of the *ah kuahs*. He exploded in anger when he was interrupted by his cousin. There was no discussion, only shouting, mutual accusations while the bodyguards and shooters remained tense.

The statue of Guan Yu was on an altar off to one side. Xiao Hun grabbed it and smashed it, threatening Low Teck Beng with the jagged edge. At this point, the gunmen pulled the Winchesters from the sacks and instructed everyone to sit. Teck Beng refused to move and instead swore at his cousin, saying he disowned her, that she was no better than the whores they were running. Teck Beng had a rolled up copy of *Lat Pau* in his fist and raised it to strike her, as one would to train a bitch dog.

A ball of fury, she seemed to crawl up the very air to jam

the broken edge of the statue into his neck, plunging it in again and again, the blood spraying like a fountain. She rode his body down as it fell, Wong said, like a child clinging to a falling statue, stabbing all the while.

Then they opened fire and did not stop until the shotguns were empty.

'So the killing of Low Teck Beng was not anticipated. And why did you then go for the Hai San?'

Wong spoke wearily, his voice cracking as he explained. They were intoxicated with the power of the weapons and by their own sudden success. Who knew it would be so easy to assassinate a *kapitan*? Lee and Xiao Hun reasoned that if they could start a war amongst the *kongsi*, then the Four Forty-fours could take advantage of the chaos and wrest control of Singapore's underworld. Wong and the others figured that after killing Low Teck Beng, there was no way back, so they went along with the plan.

'Very ambitious,' Yong Seng scowled.

'More questions: Where is Lee now? Is Liu Xiao Hun with him? How many guns does he have?'

Wong hung his head, then spoke so low they had to lean down to hear him. They had a hideout, an old bungalow house, near the Kwong Hou Sua cemetery at the northern end of the island, the same cemetery where the Low family tomb was located. There were probably two or three more accomplices, and at least four shotguns. The Hai San had originally given them five, but one was lost when the bald *gwei-lo* policeman chased the shooter. There were also revolvers, and at least one army issue carbine. The Hai San had kept their secret gang well-armed.

Yong Seng translated Wong's Cantonese for Hawksworth. He told him where Lee and Xiao Hun were hiding, and he told him how many guns they probably had.

Wong also explained how Lee and Xiao Hun had planned to get away if the police stormed the bungalow. They had a second hideout over the straits, in Johor, and had a boat stashed not far from the bungalow.

This information Yong Seng kept to himself.

CHAPTER XIV

# Family Ties

GREY FINGERS OF CLOUDS protruded into the pink sky of dawn. A thunderstorm was mushrooming black to the south over the South China Sea. It was far enough away that the mass might miss the island, but the afternoon would assuredly be wet nonetheless. It was the type of weather that brought on sudden colds that lingered for weeks, the unfortunate sufferers constantly sniffling snot through inflamed sinuses in the tropical heat.

The sun had cracked the horizon yellow and bright to the east when Hawksworth was summoned away from his first cup of coffee to the telephone room. He pressed the hard receiver to his ear, stooping to speak slowly in the bell of the wooden box fixed to the wall too low for a tall man.

'Good morning to you, Superintendent Hawksworth,' the voice was harshly metallic in his ear. 'This is Thomas Powrie, the Chief Clerk of Jardine Matheson and Company.'

'Good morning,' he said uncertainly. He recognized the voice of the clerk, but speaking without seeing a face was still an uncomfortable experience for him.

'My apologies about the early hour, Superintendent, but I have the information you asked for,' the words kept coming from the receiver in a torrent of clicks and clacks. The younger man spoke in a chatty tone that Hawksworth disliked; it was more appropriate to lunchtime conversations than serious business, but he knew that the clerk was not intentionally being disrespectful; it was the contraption that inspired such insouciance. 'Well sir, it was hard to come by, but our boys searched the warehouse and found a copy of a shipping invoice for inbound passengers, a family of three, for a new employee en route from Liverpool. The passengers stayed in Penang while the luggage and personal effects came directly to Singapore on a separate ship. This was in 1855. The employee's name was Edgerton, with an "E".'

'No other employees from England with an "E" in their names that same year?'

'None that we could find, sir. In fact, all the other records pertaining to this Edgerton fellow are missing.'

'*Missing*? Not lost?'

'I say missing because we seem to have kept all the employment records, contracts and what have you from that year and while all the other employees' records are intact, this Edgerton's seems to have gone missing. We have wired London to see if they can find any copies of the employment records.'

'Is there a Christian name for Edgerton?' he said, his neck growing painful from stooping to the speaking bell. His hand had grown slick with sweat and was shaking slightly.

'Thomas. No names for the family. He was to be employed as an opium clerk, sir. He would supervise shipments of opium from India to Hong Kong. We tranship most of the product here.'

'He never arrived in Singapore?'

'Not that we can see from the records. I also asked some of the senior men and they cannot recall anyone of that name working here.'

'I see. You mentioned luggage. Any indication that it arrived, and if so, what became of it?'

'It did arrive, sir, because the invoice was paid, though I have no idea what finally became of it. The record of payment for the luggage was in the "received and paid" file for 1855, not in the employee record files. It is curious. If not for that one record of payment, we would not have a single trace of Edgerton. It is almost as if the employee files were intentionally purged.'

He thanked the clerk and disconnected the line. Perhaps the company record office in London would hold more information, though he doubted it.

When he returned to his office he found a plate of hot *dosai*, a thin sheet of fried rice and lentil batter with pungent coconut curry chutney waiting on his desk beside a fresh pot of coffee. Fong must have brought the food from the canteen. He tore a piece of the crêpe-like *dosai* to dip it in the orange chutney before popping it into his mouth. A uniformed officer stuck his head in the door – a messenger had arrived with a note for him. Wiping his fingers clean, Hawksworth expected to find more information about Edgerton – to his surprise he realized that he had merely been spinning the name in his head for the past half hour – but the note was from Rizby. He and his squad had found the abandoned bungalow where Lee and possibly Liu Xiao Hun were hiding. They would wait there, keeping the place under surveillance until Hawksworth sent instructions.

Less than an hour later he had met with both the Superintendent of Constables – the man in charge of uniformed officers – and Sergeant Major Walker to arrange a raid on the bungalow for late afternoon that day. He telephoned the Inspector-General of Police to apprise him of the situation, then by noon he was in a rickshaw, heading to Panglima Prang, to let the Lows know that they had one more chance to get their cousin out before she would fall into police hands, charged for murder. If that happened, the Lows' underworld connections would become very public indeed, and that was a fact Hawksworth felt he could use to control them at the present time.

\*　\*　\*

He once again found himself standing in the receiving hall of Panglima Prang, the three chairs of the Low family men arranged before him. The chair in which Low Teck Beng would normally sit was now draped in white and gold silk to signify his missing presence. As a mark of respect, no one else would ever sit in the chair again.

Low Teck Seng was in his customary seat. The room was dim without artificial light, the overcast sky merely casting a gloomy luminescence into the space.

As a servant set out the tea, Hawksworth spoke bluntly, skipping the usual honorifics. 'I believe I know who killed your brother. Her name is Liu Xiao Hun,' he paused to judge Low's reaction. The look of surprise could not be hidden, though it was quickly smoothed. 'She is your cousin and I have been told she was running girls for the brothel operations under your brother's control.'

Low Teck Seng moved to speak, but Hawksworth cut him short, 'There is no need to deny any of this now. It appears that with an accomplice, she is behind the killing of the *kongsi* headmen.'

Frowning, Low merely murmured, 'Go on.'

'Once she and the accomplice are in custody, we can publicly say that the culprits have been apprehended. That should help to calm the situation between yourselves and the Hai San. Of course,

231

if she were to go on trial, the truth about your illegal enterprises would become public and then the status of the Low family friendly society would shift significantly. You may well loose the opium licenses that are vital to your monopoly.'

'What do you suggest?'

'Suggest?' Hawksworth was taken aback. 'I suggest nothing. My presence here is merely to warn you that we plan to take her into custody and charge her with murder. Do you know her current whereabouts?'

'No. As you are probably aware, we have been looking for her extensively, she disappeared only shortly before my brother…' Teck Seng's eyes narrowed on Hawksworth. 'Why did you come here to warn me?'

'I am here to facilitate my duty to peace and justice. The warning I have to offer is not to interfere with our apprehending of her and her accomplice.'

'And the name of her accomplice?'

'No, that is not something I will tell you. Unless, perhaps, you can help me.'

Low's eyebrows arched in interest.

Hawksworth drew the gold half-sovereign from his pocket and held it in his palm. 'What do you know about this?'

Low's eyes barely moved across the object shining in Hawksworth's hand. He shrugged unconvincingly. 'It is a gold coin.'

'This coin was pressed into my hand two years ago by men who beat me. I took it as a warning but now I think maybe it is something else.'

'A coin is only a coin.'

'Tell me about the idol on your altar constructed of coins.'

Low Teck Seng looked calmly into Hawksworth's eyes,

studying him a moment. 'My father is the person you need to speak to regarding such things.'

A bell was rung, a servant appeared, and orders issued to fetch Low Hun Chiu.

The old man entered the room dressed in an elaborate house gown of embroidered silk inside of which he seemed to be sweating. His hair was pulled into a loose queue, his face drawn and sallow, dark crescents beneath his eyes. He seemed unable to focus completely on where he was; the servant helped him to his seat. The old man gave every appearance of having just been pulled from opium-induced reveries. So the father had started smoking the pernicious stuff, thought Hawksworth, meaning that with his brother out of the way, Low Teck Seng was now firmly in control of the Low family empire.

The father seated in the centre chair of the three, slumped like an animal missing its bones, his son translated Hawksworth's question. The old man appeared mildly surprised then shook his head sagely as though he had been expecting this question to come for quite some time.

'When I was a boy, my father passed that idol to me. His father had given it to him. It has no name,' he said simply.

Hawksworth held the gold half-sovereign out to the elder Low. 'What is it?'

'There is a companion to this coin on the idol. It is an old belief. The keeper of the idol can influence the man who carries the coin. It is important to use a valuable coin so the marked man will keep it with him.'

Nodding, Hawksworth said, 'So much I have been told. Why did you place the coin with me?'

Father and son exchanged glances, the son frowning his disapproval, muttering in English, 'Antique superstitions will only get us in trouble.'

His father glowered at him to mind his tongue. 'We placed the coin with you when you got too close to our operations in Gading.'

'The land around my mother's orphanage?'

The men stayed quiet, their silence confirming his suspicion.

'You knew that I was there asking questions about the orphanage land, but did you know that Isabella Lightheart also claimed to be my mother?'

Sighing heavily, the elder Low spoke ponderously, holding up his hand to stop his son from simultaneously translating. He spoke for a long time while Teck Seng listened attentively, memorizing the words so he could translate them en masse. As he spoke, the father kept his gaze steadily on Hawksworth, speaking directly to him, not bothering to check his emotions. The tone was not of an apology but neither was it of an explanation. Was it possible that old Low was disburdening himself of some long-held guilt?

Finally done, the elder Low gestured to his son to translate. Inhaling sharply, Low Teck Seng spoke in a tone of tired explication. 'We knew that Lightheart was your mother. In fact, we have been watching you since your days in the orphanage in Penang, and from when you first arrived in Singapore, we watched you. Or I should say that my father watched you. But it was not until recently that we felt the need to...' and he gestured at the coin.

'Why?'

'Your father worked for us.'

His vision tunnelling, Hawksworth felt his soul contract. 'In Penang? Edgerton?'

'Yes, Edgerton in Penang. He did not die there, as you and

your mother were led to believe.'

'You sent the letter with the coin and his ring to warn her away?'

Low inquired of his father, who looked directly at Hawksworth and nodded affirmatively.

'You knew all these years...' a rage was building inside him, casting his vision red.

'My grandfather and father were the ones who worked with Edgerton. If you had not made your inquiries in Gading, the secret would have remained hidden.'

His mind was racing, the tension growing in his muscles. He felt like rising up and smashing the faces before him, breaking the ornate furniture into twigs. His face burned hot with humiliation, anger. He maintained his exterior poise, only his voice rose into a piercing screech, 'Explain.'

'Edgerton worked with my grandfather, smuggling opium for our coolies. He used his connections to get us access to the product the official companies allowed onto the black market. When he returned to Malaya, we arranged to continue this operation but by then we were much more established. At first, Edgerton was going to keep his position with Jardine and Matheson to direct portions of shipments to us. It would give us the advantage we needed to edge out the Hai San's own smuggling operations. But the company began to grow suspicious of him – there was an informant, perhaps Lightheart herself. Then he came over to us. He became our liaison with *ang-moh* opium smugglers, mostly Americans, who brought in superior quality products. But by then, he had left you and your mother. Without Edgerton, building up our monopoly would have taken much longer.'

'Where is he now?'

The question and response were translated.

'We do not know. He disappeared while in Java about fifteen years ago.'

Thirty years or more into his own lifetime. Hawksworth's rage now ebbed into despair, and he felt incredibly fatigued, as though he had not slept for days. 'Did he know who I was?'

Understanding the simple English, the elder Low spoke, Teck Seng translating: 'He never mentioned his son to us, but we knew. As I said, we kept watch on you since your days in the Penang orphanage. We wanted to use you for leverage in case Edgerton became troublesome.'

Hawksworth sat mute for what seemed like minutes but was only a moment. It took considerable strength for him to place the gold coin on the table before the Lows. 'I thank you, Low Hun Chiu for your honesty and candour. Once this unfortunate business with your cousin is complete, I will return to you. I believe there is more I would like to learn. For now, I must hurry.'

'Superintendent?' Low Teck Seng spoke as the tall man rose unsteadily. 'The name of my cousin's accomplice?'

He tapped his cane on the stone floor. 'Lee. Cantonese. Your cousin's lover.'

There was no expression on Low's face as he nodded his appreciation.

\*   \*   \*

Uniformed officers closed off the roads and lanes a quarter mile around the abandoned bungalow. Walker and a handful of his Sikh riflemen concealed themselves in dense undergrowth within range of the building, close enough to see the paint peeling on the facade. Scattered among the riflemen were officers of the Native Crime Squad, armed with revolvers. The storm over the South

China Sea had moved closer, darkness on the horizon portending a heavy downpour at sunset – they would need to complete the raid before the sky fell.

The single-storey bungalow was set back from the main road on a winding drive, eroded and overgrown so that it appeared as little more than a path through the bush. People fleeing the cholera quarantine in the city to take residence in the farthest planation houses often travelled the main road now, but if any of them happened to walk up the overgrown path to the bungalow, they would quickly turn back. From the exterior it appeared abandoned, and its proximity to the cemetery had led to stories of it being haunted. A casual passer-by would not notice the subtle signs that the building was inhabited, the tell-tale tramping of weeds, the lingering odour of cooking fires.

Hawksworth, Anaiz Majid, and Joseph Jeremiah walked in a phalanx toward the front door. He could feel the eyes concealed in the thick foliage all around them and picture the snouts of rifles poking through the scrub, fingers on triggers. Still he felt nearly naked as they crossed the open ground of the overgrown lawn. The windows were shuttered tight, the front door had been boarded over, the house presented a blank wall behind the sagging veranda, but if anyone was inside, they could open fire without warning, cutting down the three men before the Sikhs could fire back.

They were less than ten yards from the front door when a shutter banged open and shot boomed. The round went wide as all three men dropped to the ground. The Sikhs opened fire, the rifle rounds whizzing overhead to punch holes in the walls of the bungalow.

Hawksworth and his men scrambled for cover in the undergrowth near a flame-of-the-forest tree. By the time they were behind the trunk, the return fire from the bungalow had begun. Hawksworth could tell by the sound that the suspects were using handguns and the army issue carbine. Were they waiting with the shotguns for the police to storm the house?

After only a few minutes of firing, the front of the bungalow was pockmarked and splintered by the Sikhs' rifle rounds. A lull in fire from the house, then he heard the snarling roar of a shotgun from the back: they were making a run for it through the forest.

Breaking cover, Hawksworth ran painfully on his bad foot along the side of the house in pursuit, his cane in his hand, Anaiz and Jeremiah following behind. As they ran, they saw their concealed men emerge from the vegetation like spectres rising from their graves, rifles in their hands.

Then they were around the back of the bungalow, and he saw five Chinese, including one woman, moving swiftly across the overgrown back garden toward the line of dense foliage that marked the end of the property. The men each had a sawn-off Winchester. The woman held a revolver. She looked back at Hawksworth, locking eyes with him. He just had time to register the delicate beauty and the fear and anger etched into her features before he ducked for cover as she raised the pistol in both hands to fire at him.

The men were firing the shotguns into the dim green as they moved forward. Hawksworth watched a Sikh rifleman rise from his concealment only to take a blast of buckshot at close range, his chest collapsing under his uniform as he crumpled. Walker sprang from the brush from where the man fell, a Webley blazing in each fist. The captured Winchester shotgun was strapped to his back, a bandolier of brass shells crossed over his chest.

Lee and the others had made it to the end of the property, vanishing one by one into the darkness of the thick forest. Walker shouted to his second in command to lead the troops in storming the house and capture anyone left inside – Hawksworth caught up with him just as he slung the Winchester into his hands, racking a round as he plunged into the woods in pursuit.

They got less than six feet in when the first blast flashed, the pellets buzzing past their heads like angry hornets. They dove for cover as a second blast cut the foliage above their heads.

'Can you see them?' Hawksworth hissed, his own Webley now in his hand.

'Nothing, the leaves are too dense.'

The bushes parted beside them and Hawksworth nearly fired before he saw that it was Anaiz and Jeremiah. Now the forest was quiet, their ears ringing from the gunfire, the smell of cordite thick in the air. They listened closely. There was shouting from the bungalow as the men searched. A twig snapped to their right. Then the unmistakable sound of a muffled voice to their left and Walker rolled on the ground, bringing the shotgun up and fired.

A shot was returned from farther ahead in the undergrowth, but the shooter could not be seen. The men again took cover only to return fire and pursue, drawn deeper into the forest. They found fresh blood on the palm of a fishtail tree – one of the Chinese had been hit – and followed the trail.

There were no more shots and they could see the light of open ground coming from beyond the trees and were about to turn back, believing they had lost the trail, when suddenly fire came from three directions at once, the flashes and roars lighting up the shadows, shredding the vegetation around them. Again they dropped for cover but the shooting was wild and inaccurate. Walker saw the silhouette of a shooter and took a shot with the Winchester. They heard a scream – he had scored a hit – then the sound of yelling and running.

Anaiz and Jeremiah each fired with their revolvers, offering covering fire as Hawksworth and Walker ran forward. They burst from the thick foliage onto open ground, dropping behind a grassy mound for cover as more shots rang out, pinning them down. Jeremiah appeared next to them, breathing hard as he reloaded his pistol.

'Easy, detective. We will survive this,' Hawksworth whispered to the shaking young man. Anaiz appeared next. The man they had just shot in the forest was dead; Anaiz had taken the dead man's Winchester, which he now gripped in his hands.

The shooting stopped. They sprang out from around the mound and Hawksworth realized where they were: the Chinese cemetery. He knew that beyond the cemetery was the narrow beach of Johor Strait; the gang was trying to make it to the shore, they probably had a concealed boat waiting for them. The bathtub-like Chinese graves dotting the landscape offered perfect cover: they could pin down their pursuers while moving forward. Hawksworth knew that they would need a dozen more men to cover the vast ground, but the Sikhs and other detectives were now too far behind at the bungalow to be of any use. The four men were on their own.

A splotch of red, bright on a grey tombstone, caught his attention. The wounded man was still bleeding, and they could again follow his trail. Hopefully the gang was still moving as a group and had not spilt up to confuse their pursuers.

They fanned out, moving cautiously through the graves, the mounds offering cover for pursued and pursuers alike. It was like moving through a quiet suspension, the air moist and soft in the warmth of evening, the cloudy sky casting even light that permitted no shadows on the open ground.

Hawksworth stood to get a better perspective and just had

time to dive for cover as a blast of buckshot pulverized the guardian statue on the tombstone he cowered behind. Another round kept him pinned down. The Webley in his hand felt both weightless and solid. He suddenly noticed that the arm of his shirt was torn open, blood drenching the cloth. Had he been hit? Or cut on a sharp frond in the forest? There was no pain, the wound seemed superficial, but now his shooting hand was slick with blood.

Another blast from the shotgun tore up the dirt of the grave mound. He wiped his hand then rolled from the cover, coming to rest on his belly; the Webley in his hand roared once, twice, the rounds slamming into the grave from which the shotgun blasts had come. Then his pistol clicked empty and he rolled onto his back to reload, his fingers fumbling with the shells as he slotted them into the cylinder. He was exposed on two sides, on his back like a turtle out of its shell. The Chinese popped up from behind the grave with the sawn-off shotgun, levelling it at Hawksworth's head.

A shot sounded and the man staggered, all his lines going slack, then he took a step and fell forward, the shotgun beneath him.

Joseph Jeremiah appeared from behind a grave mound, a revolver in his hand.

Hawksworth smiled up at him – the young man had just saved his life – and was pulling himself up when Jeremiah's head completely blew apart. Hawksworth screamed then fell back on the ground. He had the hammer on the Webley cocked, but the gun slipped from his blood-soaked hand as an assailant came from above him, the horrible fat hole of the Winchester barrel only a foot from his face. He could see the Chinese man grin sadistically as his finger closed on the trigger. Then his torso exploded, spraying blood and gore over Hawksworth's prone body. The shotgun dropped from the man's hands as he staggered one step then two, then collapsed in the grass beside Jeremiah's headless body.

The Winchester was smoking in Walker's hands as he slung it to help Hawksworth to his feet. The taller man coughed, then gagged, then stopped to vomit.

'Two more remain, Lee and the woman. These two were left behind to slow us down,' Walker said, his eyes scanning the horizon.

'They must be headed toward the shore, to a boat to escape,' Hawksworth spat out the vomit taste in his mouth, then stood erect.

'Is it bad?' Walker asked, gesturing at Hawksworth's arm.

'No. I am not certain. I can go on. Where is Anaiz?'

As if in reply, there was a series of shots from a depression between two hills several hundred yards away. They turned to see Lee and Xiao Hun running up the hill, the woman turning to fire with the pistol back down into the depression, where they saw Anaiz keeping cover.

The two men broke into a slow run, Hawksworth hobbling – he had dropped his cane somewhere behind him – Walker moving as quickly as his legs could carry him.

Ahead of them, the two Chinese had nearly reached the top of the hill, the highest in the cemetery and the last before the ground sloped down to the scrub-lined sand of the beach. At the top of the hill was at a large tomb; he saw Xiao Hun crouch behind one of the elaborate graves, her pistol in her hand as Lee disappeared over the far side of the hill: she was making a last stand to allow her lover time to escape.

'I will take the woman, you run for Lee,' Hawksworth

shouted to Walker, who veered away to sprint around the foot of the hill toward the shore.

The woman fired the pistol down the hill, pinning Hawksworth behind a grave mound. He saw Anaiz break cover a little down the hill, and he shouted for him to circle around to help Walker. 'Do not let Lee escape! I will take care of this one.' Anaiz slung the sawn-off Winchester over his back. Hawksworth fired his Webley up the hill to give him cover while the Malay detective ran around the other side.

Hawksworth ducked for cover again as bullets from the woman's pistol smashed into the stone of the grave. From his position he could see the Sikh riflemen and other officers emerging from the tree line at the edge of the cemetery and immediately felt relief. Reinforcements with rifles would bring this to a quick end.

Then he heard her shrieking.

Assuming Walker or Anaiz had circled back and captured her position, he sprang out from behind the grave mound, then froze in place, terror gripping him like a fist.

On the hilltop, towering above her like a colossus shrouded in black, was the *jiangshi*. Putrid bile poured from the mouth opened wide, glistening on the feline fangs that protruded from the upper jaw. The blank silver eyes shone brightly in the dimming light while Xiao Hun screamed endlessly, her hands raised in useless defence.

Hawksworth, dazed, raised his Webley and fired without aiming. His finger reflexively pulled the trigger again, but the gun was empty. The bullet tore into Xiao Hun's back between the shoulders blades, pitching her forward onto her knees. Her body wobbled then fell forward. A moment of infinite intensity passed while the blank mercury eyes of the *jiangshi* seemed to gaze at Hawksworth, then the figure shimmered, flickered, and was gone.

The tall man remained stock still, the pistol still raised, until the terror ebbed away; then he began to move awkwardly up the hill, his bad foot dragging in the weedy grass, his wounded arm limp, the empty Webley hanging like a dead weight in his blood-slick hand.

At the top of the hill he found Xiao Hun flung like a broken doll across the ornate stonework of the tomb. He placed a finger on her neck, and though it was still warm, she was dead. There was not a trace of that other thing he had seen.

Two shots rang out from the direction of the beach below. He saw Walker with a Webley in his hand taking aim at a small row boat not more than one hundred yards offshore. Lee was in the back, ducked down below the gunwale. It was not a difficult shot for an experienced marksman, but Walker had missed both times. Hawksworth recalled the tremor he had seen in the man's hand and knew his sharpshooting days were done.

Anaiz came running along the beach, then dropped to one knee and emptied the Winchester at the fast-fleeing boat, but the short barrel made the weapon inaccurate and the shots flew far wide of their target. Lee was escaping into the greying darkness of the water, and there was nothing they could do.

A bunch of Sikh riflemen had reached the bottom of the hill and were shouting up at him, but Hawksworth felt dizzy and slowly sat himself down beside the carved lion guardian of the tomb. Xiao Hun's body was at his feet, her head turned from him, a pool of blood spreading beneath her that soaked rapidly into the ground as if it were being swallowed.

Panting and exhausted, the pain now coming as the adrenaline subsided, bathed in crimson, he leaned back against the flat tombstone and felt the texture of the carved Chinese characters press into his flesh. He could not read them, but if he could, he

would have learned that he was leaning against the grave of Low
Teck Beng.

## CHAPTER XV

# No Deposit, No Return

THE *PRAHU* COASTED silently over the water. Hawksworth sat in the narrow prow, his eyes darting furtively here and there, keeping a lookout for crocodiles. They were about a thousand yards from the nearest stilt house on the mainland side of the strait, only half a mile as the crow flies from the sawmills of Johor Bahru.

The way the body had been lashed to a pole propped up in the sand reminded him of the engravings he had seen of heads on the Tower of London, stuck on spikes and set in public view to act as a reminder and a warning: cross the powerful at your peril.

The body had appeared that morning on a spit of sandy mud that projected from a dense mangrove swamp into the Johor Strait, his dead eyes gazing at the ship traffic that coursed between Singapore and the peninsula. The Johor police had rowed out to him but did not want to cut him down until the detectives arrived from Singapore. They sent a telegram to the Central Police Station, tersely efficient:

> ATTENTION POLICE SUPERINTENDENT
> HAWKSWORTH
> WANTED MAN LEE DEAD
> MATI DI SULA
> JOHOR BAHRU

After Lee had escaped from the cemetery, an urgent message was sent to the Johor authorities with a description and an order to arrest or shoot on sight. It was understood that the Lows and the Mother-Flowers and the remnants of the Hai San were also searching for him. Such a wanted man would not get far, so the telegram came as little surprise, but the phrase *mati di sula* gave him a jolt. It meant 'death by impalement'.

The sprout of the dark green *puchok nya*, the nipa palm, which flourishes densely along the inland waterways of Malaya, is a razor sharp cone about half an inch across. It grows extraordinarily fast, up to one and a half inches per day. From the autopsy the coroner in Singapore would perform, they were able to piece together that the killers had forced Lee to sit on the sprout, his wrists bound and legs spread akimbo, tethered to the trunks of full-grown nipa trees.

To judge by the wounds, he survived for several days before a combination of blood loss and severe septicaemia finally killed him. Several bones in the fingers were broken where he had smashed his bound hands against his own skull while writhing in agony; there were deep bite marks on his wrists where, the coroner guessed, he had tried to chew through his own veins in an attempt to end the pain.

After he died, the killers left him there, slumped over as though he was trying to touch his toes. The sprout kept growing into the corpse until it finally punctured the skin of the chest just below the ribs, the sharp end protruding outward. It had begun to open into separate fronds when the killers cut it from the root. They tied the corpse onto a pole with the palm tree growing from its abdomen and hoisted it on the sandy spit of land that stuck into the strait. They were sure to position him so that he faced the water, toward the island he had believed that he could conquer.

* * *

There was a stack of folders on Hawksworth's desk. The report about his trip to Johor the previous week to recover Lee's body was one more addition to the pile, another layer of administrative sediment. He sat staring at the dunes of paper before him, feeling the nagging desire to move his muscles, to burst into the humid air. Moments later he was seated in a hackney carriage, on his way to the pretty bungalow house in Katong.

Yong Seng himself opened the door, a broad grin on his face. 'Superintendent Hawksworth! Welcome!' he exclaimed, opening his arms wide in invitation. He was wearing house clothes, plain cotton pyjamas. His queue was undone, his long hair flung loosely and unkempt to his shoulders. He had not been expecting guests and already smelled of beer.

Standing unsmiling at the threshold, Hawksworth merely said, '*Mati di sula.*'

The Chinese face slipped from a smile of joy to a smile of mischievousness. 'It took three days for the bastard to die. I watched his agony for the first two. If I could have made him suffer more, I would have.' He finished by uttering a quick prayer in Hokkien in remembrance of Yong Chern.

'You admit to the murder?' Hawksworth asked in a flat tone.

Yong Seng was caught short and did not know what to say. The two men stood facing each other across the threshold. It was a fine bright hot day. From inside the house came the smell of cleaning – the astringent odours of bleach and lye and tallow soap and water.

'If you would like to confess, then I would advise you to do so at the Central Station so that a proper written record will be made. It will help at the trial. That is the way of Her

Majesty's justice.'

His face slack, the colour draining away, Yong Seng's black eyes glared at Hawksworth in dismay. There was no fear, only incomprehension.

'On the other hand, the benefit, as I see it, of Chinese justice is that one does not need to be constantly writing records and tediously keeping files. When it comes to Chinese justice, the less said, the better,' Hawksworth stated matter-of-factly.

Yong Seng's faced eased into a sly grin, his eyes shining. He tapped his forefinger to his pursed purple lips to indicate that his mouth was sealed.

'Now let me in, please, and serve me tea. I have had a tiring morning.'

Yong Seng laughed the Chinese laugh of genuine mirth and happiness. He stepped aside to let the tall man stride into the foyer. Boots came off, cushioned house slippers were provided for his feet. Shu En was resting, he was told, but as Yong Seng was sure that she would like to see him, he would go and rouse her.

He was taken to the dining room, where steaming gunpowder tea was served in a colourful Peranakan-style pot and cup that had become popular recently among Chinese born in the Straits. The translucent pastel blue of the pot and cups was emblazoned with a canary-yellow bird, a fantastic creature that looked half snake, half peacock. The crisp taste of the tea unfurled in his mouth, folding into the sharp smells of the cleaning happening elsewhere in the house.

It was quiet in the dining room, and for the first time since this investigation began, he felt his body relax. He had been so tense so constantly that he had become accustomed to the energy torqueing his body. Now the riling was gone and he felt exhausted yet calm, as though a treacherous passage had been completed and he was now on the other side.

A side door opened and Yong Seng's head appeared. He motioned for Hawksworth to follow. He found himself in the drawing room where he had last seen her. The mah-jong tiles on the polished wooden table were now set up in neat rows. Fresh-cut white and pink camellia blooms stood in a sky blue vase on the side table, perfuming the air where the scent of bleach lingered. Shu En herself was nestled into the easy chair. She appeared drowsy, but when their eyes meet, she gazed at him triumphantly.

'Good afternoon, Superintendent,' she said sweetly. Like Yong Seng, who stood a few feet away, she was wearing plain cotton house clothes. Her hair was tied up in a kerchief, and she wore no makeup. He noted that her face was puffy from sleep, and that she displayed no embarrassment or compunction about appearing before him in this way. He had disturbed them resting at home while the servants cleaned, rousing them from domestic repose, and there was not even a moment of reproach. This meant that he was considered as family.

Since Yong Seng had become *samseng ong*, they had been living together as husband and wife. He noticed the curving heaviness of her belly, the way she moved protectively, and it struck him like a bolt from the blue. How could he have missed this on his previous visit?

'Shu En, you are pregnant!'

She smiled at him, her only way of acknowledging that he had guessed correctly. It was not quite the end of the third month, Yong Seng later explained, and it was bad luck to announce the news before that time lest evil spirits become attracted to the foetus and cause a miscarriage.

Yong Seng moved behind her, placing his hands on her shoulders, claiming paternity. Together, she seated, he standing behind in the bright light of the clean room, they looked nothing so much as a prosperous suburban couple.

'Congratulations,' Hawksworth said, still taken aback by the news.

Shu En smiled at Hawksworth dreamily, her pretty coral lips forming a cupid's bow. She stretched in her feline way, arching her back upward, one hand on her belly.

'Now you understand why we want to build something that will outlast us, something that will grow with the generations.'

It took him a moment to realize that she was talking once again about opening a bank. He merely nodded in response, quietly uttering 'yes'.

She moved her hand to her belly, rubbing it gently. 'If the child is a boy, he could well grow into the man who marries your own dear daughter,' she said absently, starting at the patterns of white on white of the carpet.

Hawksworth smiled in return, saying nothing, his eyes resting on the camellia blossoms. The white room was peaceful and quiet and clean and smelled like home. Soon there would be children here. In his mind a vision suddenly opened, just a glimpse, of a history that he did not yet know, yet that seemed utterly familiar.

\* \* \*

Seven weeks had passed since Rizby had first seen Low Teck Beng's body at the Hotel Formosa. On the forty-ninth day after the event, the Low family held a Kong Teck ceremony at Panglima Prang during which they burned offerings of paper effigies and hell money. Monks chanted to plead with the Judge of Hell, Yan Luo Wang, to allow Low Teck Beng's spirit a quiet passage into the underworld.

Hawksworth stood at the back of the immaculate lawn under the parabola of clear blue sky, the chanted mantras reverberating in the air around him. The monks were dressed in opalescent robes of white and gold, some beating hand-held toms to keep time, their voices rising and merging in a wave of sound that matched the shimmering yellow and gold of the temporary altar set up under an airy shelter, where the opera stage had been.

Low Teck Seng walked forward with an armful of gold and silver paper notes which he poured onto the mound of smouldering paper on a metal platform beside the shelter. He placed the palms of his hands together into a *wai* and bent three times toward the altar, then seeing the tall *ang-moh* standing off to one side, started toward him. His mouth was curled in a slightly upturned frown – as close to a true smile as he could muster. He was in the same sombre black suit Hawksworth had always seen him wear, and he put out his hand in the Western style of greeting. 'Superintendent Hawksworth, it is good of you to come.'

'I should like to pay my last respects to your brother, and trust that he will rest in peace.' He made no mention of the *jiangshi*. Since the shootout at the cemetery, no one had reported seeing it again.

'We are very pleased that you were able to bring the investigation to a close so…satisfactorily,' Teck Seng said, gesturing for Hawksworth to walk with him away from the ceremony so the two could confer privately.

'My efforts were to bring the perpetrators to justice while preserving the peace of the settlement,' Hawksworth replied flatly.

'Nonetheless, we would like to thank you for your discretion and expediency in handling the matter and I would like to offer you a small token of our esteem for the role you played, Superintendent.'

A Chinese *sycee*, an oval silver ingot about the size of a golf ball with fins like the brim of a hat, was in Teck Seng's palm, extended toward Hawksworth. He could see the Chinese characters stamped into the silver indicating weight and value. It looked quite old.

'I suppose a gold coin would not be appropriate?' he said caustically, then immediately felt churlish for doing so.

The palm and the silver did not move. 'This token is also a way of apologizing for the abuse that you may have inadvertently suffered due to … superstitions. Now that I am the boss, the Low enterprises will follow more modern thinking.'

'You still plan to run both the Grand Opium Syndicate and open a commercial bank?'

Teck Seng's palm extended further, the silver ingot catching the light blue of the sky above so that it shone. Hawksworth's fingers grasped the metal, which was silky and smooth and cool. Not to accept the gift would be a terrible insult; and this one piece of metal would pay for Fenella's entire education. It was heavy in his jacket pocket, the weight reminding him of his reluctance to take it. After today, he hoped he would have nothing more to do with the Lows.

His empty palm now at his side, Teck Beng spoke politely but quickly. 'We have already begun the process of applying to register the business entity that will allow us to operate a commercial bank. However, I have been assured that in order for the Legislative Council to grant final approval, we will have to relinquish our licenses for the opium farms in the Straits Settlements as well as the neighbouring territories, which will of course take some time.'

Hawksworth could not disguise his shock. 'The bank is more important to you than the opium?'

'We would wish to keep both enterprises, but in looking to

the future, we are prepared to make sacrifices.'

'Who will take over the opium concessions now?' he asked, still dismayed.

'Not many Chinese friendly societies are capable of handling that volume of trade, so by default the licenses to sell opium in the legal market will surely go to the Mother-Flower *kongsi*.' The frown in the placid face curved slightly upward into a knowing smile, 'You are familiar with them, are you not?' Teck Seng's tone hovered on sarcasm.

'Very,' was Hawksworth's terse reply. The men fell silent, listening as the monks' chanting rose in volume, rolling across the lawn before cascading down the hill to the bustling river godowns beside the turbid brown river.

\*    \*    \*

He needed a drink.

Polished teakwood reflected in the wall-length mirror that hung behind the billiards bar at the Hotel Europa. The place was quiet on a weekday afternoon, with only a handful of hotel customers sipping afternoon beer to ward off the enervating heat, and local businessmen sitting in club chairs with their heads close together, cigars burning in their fingers, talking in hushed voices.

'What will it be, Superintendent?' the bartender was a young Scot, red hair nearly as bright as his sunburned skin, his apron bleached white and clean.

Hawksworth's gaze drifted over the rows of bottles on the shelf behind the bartender, alighting on the big export bottle of Kupper's Beer. 'I would like a Kupper's.'

'Yes, sir.' Pulling the cork from the brown glass, the bartender said absently, 'Chop *payong*.'

'What? What did you say?' Hawksworth asked with alacrity.

'"Chop *payong*." It is the slogan of the brewery.'

'Do you have any idea what it means?'

The bartender was fishing around beneath the bar for the correct glass, his voice muffled, 'Not a clue, sir. I assumed chop-chop, as they say in Malaya, but I have no idea as to the *payong* bit.' His head came up from behind the bar with the ceramic beer stein with the word Kupper printed on it. 'Any ideas yourself?'

'Yes, *payong* means...' he watched in fascination as the bartender flipped back the cupola-shaped metal lid of the stein, '...it means "umbrella" in Malay.'

The beer foamed up to the top of the stein as the bartender slid it toward Hawksworth, 'Why would beer need an umbrella?'

The tall man tapped the metal lid. 'What does that look like to you?'

Scratching his head a moment while he studied the thing, the bartender exclaimed in a burst of excitement, 'Losh, man! It looks like a Malayan umbrella!'

'It does indeed. A Frenchman in Johor told me "chop" means "pint". This Kupper's mug is a pint of beer with an umbrella on top. Chop *payong*!' Hawksworth spoke triumphantly.

'Chop *payong*, sir!' the bartender said, laughing.

Satisfied, Hawksworth lifted the stein with a smile. The Kupper's was fresh and cool and crisp. Smacking his lips, he was about to gulp down more when a high grinding noise unlike anything he had heard before came from the hotel courtyard. Turning, he saw the patrons of the billiards bar with their faces pressed to the window, pointing and jabbering.

'What the devil is it now?' he muttered, then drained half the stein. Cane in hand, he crossed outside.

Hotel guests were clustered around something in the courtyard.

At first he thought it was a piece of agriculture machinery, then the thing began to move, causing uproar among the crowd, which sprang back. As it began to circle the courtyard, the two riders keeping their hats held in the air, the crowd turned to cheering and shouts of encouragement.

'Is that an autocar?' he asked the man standing next to him.

'The very first in Singapore!' the man clapped enthusiastically as the contraption rolled past them, shaking and rattling and clattering so loudly he had to shout at Hawksworth to be heard. 'The Benz and Company Motor-Velocipede! Incredible feat of engineering!'

It looked like two bicycles in parallel with a large metal crate welded between them. The passengers sat on a carriage board between the smaller front wheels and larger back ones; there was no cover or screen, only a steering pedestal and two handles, one each for high and low gear. He could see the drive chains that ran from beneath the two passengers to the motor compartment. There was a stench of burning chemicals from the combustion inside the engine that soon filled the courtyard.

'It runs on benzene,' the man shouted as it rolled past again, 'and can reach up to eighteen miles per hour! Astonishing! Way of the future!'

'Sounds like a bloody great coffee grinder!' Hawksworth shouted back. The man shot him a look of dismay, then turned back to the spectacle.

Hawksworth watched as the Motor-Velo circled, then bumped its way into the street where it was promptly overtaken by a horse carriage, the horse utterly oblivious to the juddering contraption. Some of the crowd ran into the street to follow it while others stayed, talking excitedly.

He reached the bar before the bartender returned – the bar

had emptied when they all rushed to the courtyard, including the young Scot – and resumed sipping his Kupper's.

He was hailed with a hearty, 'Superintendent Hawksworth!'

Looking into the mirror high behind the bar, he watched as Mr. Winstedt, the Assistant Colonial Secretary, approached him from behind. He recalled Shu En's detailed explication of the man's fetish, and winced. As he suspected, he had trouble looking at him without picturing his mouth slavering as dirty toes were stuffed in it.

That mouth was now smiling at him, 'Did you see the autocar in the courtyard just now?'

'It seems to have captured the imagination of the entire settlement.'

'Way of the future! The motorized buggy. No more horses or bullocks…or for that matter, rickshaw coolies. Soon we will all be riding in self-propelled vehicles.'

Hawksworth envisioned a street filled with autocars, the raucous noise and horrible stench as they rattled and ground along, bumping into each other. 'Rather expensive, though, Mr. Winstedt. I read in the newspaper that one autocar costs $1,600. I think we will require rickshaw coolies for a while longer.'

Winstedt's face fell. He did not like having his enthusiasm dampened. 'They are expensive now, of course, but the prices will come down as the demand rises and manufacturing becomes more efficient.'

'If you have time, allow me to buy you a drink,' Hawksworth offered, seeing the man nettled.

Winstedt thought it over then took a position beside Hawksworth. After receiving his drink – another metal-capped stein of Kupper's beer – he made small talk. 'I am glad this terrible cholera epidemic is finally coming to an end. The disruption to business has been enormous. My office is now undertaking a study to gauge the total cost, not only of the quarantine but of missed shipments and lost labour. However, the cost to the peace of mind of the population cannot be measured.'

'The upcoming tender of the Singapore opium farm contributed to the disruption.'

'I heard that there were some murders of prominent Chinese. All blown past now, yes? I gather that the Mother-Flowers will win the bid now that the Lows have retracted theirs.'

He nodded. 'It would appear that shortly the Mother-Flower *kongsi* will control both the legal and illegal trade in opium as well as the licit and illicit trade in human labour.'

'My sources tell me they control the illegal lottery out of Johor Bahru.'

Hawksworth nodded affirmatively, staring at his beer. Did Winstedt know that they also controlled the nightclub where he went to indulge himself with the dirty toes of clean young girls?

His stein empty, he ordered another. Hawksworth recalled Shu En's wish. 'Eventually, the Mother-Flowers will step out from the shadows,' he added, 'while no doubt keeping a foot in. I wonder, when it comes time for them to open a Hokkien bank, will they too have to trade the opium concession for the bank license, as the Lows have done?' he asked meditatively.

Winstedt narrowed his eyes, the stein poised halfway to his mouth. 'Superintendent, given that they are in a position to control what amounts to almost two-thirds of the revenue of this colony, if in the coming years the Mother-Flowers want to open a bank, then the only thing standing in their way would be divine intervention.'

'What are you implying?' Hawksworth sipped a little more.

'I mean that the only thing to stop them would be the

decimation of the entire settlement.' A grim smile traced his lips before he said stentoriously, "Then the Lord rained upon Sodom and upon Gomorrah brimstone and fire from out of heaven. And he overthrew those cities, and all the plain, and all the inhabitants of the cities, and that which grew upon the ground".'

Hawksworth gulped the last of his beer, setting the umbrella stein on the table with a hollow thud. 'I did not realize that you were a religious man, Mr. Winstedt.'

'I was not, Superintendent, until I came to Singapore.'

\*  \*  \*

A Public Works road crew, a ragtag bunch of half-naked former convict Tamil workers watched over by a Malay overseer, was metaling the dirt lane that ran past his bungalow from Geylang Road. Those in the front excavated a sharp-edged trench that was to be filled with stones that had been broken up by hand to no larger than three inches; the crew behind them filled this up with still smaller stones, less than an inch in diameter, stamping them down by jumping up and down on them. Another crew working behind this one rolled a thick layer of finely crushed rock mixed lightly with bitumen across the bed of compacted stones. Finally, this layer was smoothed over by a heavy roller pulled by a line of groaning men, dark sweat-slicked skin glistening in the sun. Meanwhile, the oldest members of the crew dug a run-off drain that was lined with brick on either side of the roadway.

As of now, the dirt lane ran through the old coconut plantation, past Hawksworth's home to a Malay kampong. His house was the only solid built structure along the way and the Malays did not need a metaled road, so he could only guess that more residents would be coming soon, building bungalows.

Land was getting to be in short supply in the enclave just south in Katong. Now the construction would begin to flow north and east, and the new residents would require better roads, especially if they were grinding along in autocars.

He had completed transcribing Lightheart's journal the previous night and found no definitive answer to the burning question – why did she never return for him? What he found instead was a lifetime of regret and longing that crystalized in a daily guilt that only drove her further into her piety. The more time passed, the more difficult it became for her to face her past actions, until keeping track of his career from afar while she ran an orphanage for other abandoned children was all she could do. In her journal, she notes how she was overjoyed to learn that he was alive – a picture in *The Straits Times* revealed him to her – but by then she had been gone too long and feared the pain of reuniting. Their separation was, she said, God's will.

In the end, he felt only a great sense of relief. He was free from the questions that had plagued him since he first travelled to Gading and seen Lightheart's grave sinking into the ground. Matthew Edgerton, the name with which he was christened, was a person who never existed, a path not followed. After all the effort of search and transcription, of revealing his father to be a scoundrel, he arrived back where he had started and discovered that he was who he always thought he was: David Hawksworth, orphan from Penang, Superintendent of Police in Singapore.

From the front veranda of his bungalow, he watched as the road crew worked their slow way around the bend toward his house. He fretted for the safety of his banyan, but Rizby had assured him that no Tamil would dare disturb the old tree; if need be, they would curve the road around it rather than risk the wrath of the tree's spirit.

Rizby would be visiting the Geylang bungalow for the first time as a civilian that night. He had of course come out many times before on official police business, and had even once or twice sat on the veranda, but never in all their years working together had he come to Hawksworth's home as a guest. It was not something male colleagues did. However, when Hawksworth told Ni of Rizby's engagement to Soe Soe Aye, she had insisted that he invite his long-standing colleague to the house. She had wanted to put on a big Siamese feast for a long time and this was the occasion she had been waiting for.

All day Ni and Fon cleaned the bungalow, blowing cobwebs from corners. Hawksworth's cot and mosquito net were put away, for what he now realized would be the last time. Once again he would be allowed to spend the night in his own bedroom with Ni warm and snug by his side.

Fenella was given the task of stringing flowers into a garland, but after a several attempts her tiny fingers did little more than spray petals across the veranda, so Hawksworth found himself sitting with his legs splayed on the boards, Fenella nestled between them, helping her gently tie one flower after another on the string, her small hands in his big fingers, until a garland of red and white and pink hibiscus was ready to be strung over the front door.

Ni was up early that morning to make her way in the rising mists to the fruit and vegetable market in the mixed-race kampong two miles distant. She had not balanced a basket on her head since she was a girl and twice tripped on the way home. Both times she managed to catch herself with only a green papaya tumbling out. The fruit was bruised but not badly, she was pleased to see. She had fussed over the groceries, snapping the chillies to check for freshness, clucking over the softness of the green Siamese eggplant. It should be much firmer, she told the Malay vegetable

seller, but the older woman merely shrugged at her indifferently –
take it or leave it.

Back home she broke three coconuts that had fallen from
the plantation trees in the back garden. She would need much
coconut milk for the *kaeng tai pla*, the pungent fish entrail soup,
and coconut cream for the green curry chicken. Fon started the
milk simmering with copious shavings of coconut flesh to boil
down to the thickness required for the cream. Both women knew
that Burmese prefer their curry thicker and frothier than Siamese,
and they very much wanted to please their female guest.

In the afternoon, after she had finished crushing the tamarind
while Hawksworth was on the veranda with Fenella, surrounded
by hibiscuses petals, Ni left again, this time for the fish market
at Bedok. She wanted butterfish for the sour *kaeng som*, and
satisfied with the freshness – the fish flesh was plump and taut
when pressed – was happy to find a heaping bucketful of prawns
with legs still kicking. She bought a handful to add to the *kaeng
tai pla*.

On her return it was controlled frenzy in the kitchen.
Hawksworth knew best to keep his distance. Ni just had time to
finish bathing and tuck her hair up in the European style before
dabbing fragrant *nam oop*, which she made herself from jasmine
and citrus blossoms and sandalwood extract, on her neck when
Hawksworth called to her from the veranda. She checked herself
in the mirror once, twice, then pleased with her presentation,
made her way outside.

Hawksworth heard the carriage rolling with a hollow sound
on the metaled portion of the road, then slow to a near halt as
it bounced nosily over the stones before thudding into the dirt
roadway and coming to a dusty halt before his lawn. Rizby stepped
out first, dressed in a clean and smart linen suit, his hair neatly

parted and slicked down tightly. Hawksworth called again to Ni, who came out onto the veranda to greet their guests, dressed in her finest *pha nung* decorated with shimmering gold fleur-de-lys on a green field.

She came just in time to watch Soe Soe Aye step daintily down from the carriage, her left hand in Rizby's right. She was a lovely sight to behold, petite, even smaller than Rizby, clad in a brown skirt-like *htamein* cloth adorned with simple geometric patterns in a rainbow of hues wound around her narrow waist and a white cotton blouse topped by a lace shawl draped elegantly over narrow shoulders. There was a *gaung baung* kerchief in a matching brown cloth wrapped around her hair that topped her head in a tightly wrapped pitch-black bun.

It was her smile, though, that was most arresting. White teeth, small and evenly spaced shone like pearls from the dark honey skin of her face. Hawksworth could understand how such a beauty had captivated Rizby. As the evening progressed, more than once he caught Ni peering at her with admiration and envy. Thinking on the dinner afterward, he recalled that Soe Soe's personality was a warm and sweet as her appearance and that her and Rizby's affection for one another was obvious: he lost track of the number of casual light touches they exchanged, fingers, elbows and forearms brushing.

He insisted on aperitifs before dinner, so while the food sat steaming in the kitchen with Fon stirring the curry sauce, the fish safely waiting beneath baskets to keep the flies off, the two couples and Fenella were sitting on the veranda. Cold beer for Rizby and a sweating glass of arrack for Hawksworth; the women sipped pink *sirap bandung,* creamy milk laced with sweet rose water syrup.

He sat gazing at the first stars to twinkle red in the violet light of equatorial dusk. His daughter was on his knee; his Siamese common-law wife seated beside him. His Ceylonese colleague was leaning against the rail of the veranda, smiling shyly at his Burmese fiancée.

Hawksworth listened to the rising staccato whine of the crickets calling in the evening air, their sound riding high above the first throaty croaks of the toads plopping in the muddy soil of his bungalow nestled in a disused coconut planation on a Chinese island at the foot of British Malaya.

Sipping the arrack, he smiled absently.

He was home.

# Straits Money and the Rise of Chinese Banking

As with the previous books in this trilogy, I have done my best to keep anachronisms out of the mouths of nineteenth-century characters, but a few must have surely slipped through. I also strove to use the original names of places and streets, some of which no longer exist. As in the previous books, for sake of narrative expediency, the words *kongsi*, clan, and gang are used to refer to the Chinese secret societies; in practice, the distinctions between a *hoey*, a *pang*, and a *kongsi* are much sharper.

I would like to thank Ellen Shi Min, owner of SMART Translation, for her invaluable translation of the lyrics to the opera *Yu Tangchun*, or *The Faithful Harlot*, which appear in the first chapter. I would especially like to offer my gratitude to my dear friend Paul Bruthiaux for his selfless help and advice in editing the draft manuscripts of each of the books in this trilogy.

The history of Chinese in Southeast Asia, and specifically in Malaya and Singapore, has been exhaustively researched and there are many revealing academic works on the subject. The most vividly written and illuminating scholarly studies of life for Singapore's working classes during this period are James F. Warren's *Au Ku and Karayuki-san: Prostitution in Singapore*

*1880-1940* and *Rickshaw Coolie: A People's History of Singapore, 1880-1940*.

For much of the nineteenth century, the principal unit of currency in the Straits Settlements was the Mexican Dollar, as it was throughout the region, including the Dutch colonies. However, between 1874 and 1895, the American Trade Dollar, the newly created Japanese Yen, and British Trade Dollars, including Hong Kong dollars, were all accepted as legal tender in Malaya. This fragmented exchange was suitable for a frontier economy, but as trade increased, the need for a single currency arose, and in 1899 the government began to issue Straits Settlements Dollars. In 1904, the other currencies in circulation were demonetized, making the Straits Dollar the official unit of exchange. In 1906, the gold exchange standard was adopted.

With the exception of the Mercantile Bank, which was founded in Singapore in 1856, the banks operating in the colony were all foreign. The first to open a branch, in 1840, was The Union Bank of Calcutta. Other banks included Nederlandsche Handel-Maatschappij (1883) (forerunner of today's ABN Amro Bank), the First National City Bank of New York (1902) (predecessor of Citibank), and the Banque de L'Indochine (1905) (now Crédit Agricole Corporate and Investment Bank).

Before the government began issuing currency notes in 1899, notes were issued by the Asiatic Banking Corporation (closed in 1866) and the Oriental Banking Corporation (closed in 1884); by 1895, however, only the Chartered Bank of India, Australia, and China (today's Standard Chartered) and the Hongkong [*sic*] and Shanghai Banking Corporation (HSBC, still in business), were issuing notes. This last was also the most popular commercial bank for immigrant workers in Malaya, who used it to remit money to the Chinese homeland. Otherwise, they used 'money houses' associated with specific dialect-orientated clans and business societies.

The first Chinese-owned commercial banks in Singapore, which were among the very first modern commercial Chinese banks in history, were opened by companies closely associated with dialect groups. Although these banks would not open until after the turn of the century, Chinese business associations had begun investigating the feasibility of opening banks as early as the mid-1890s. While in theory the legitimate business and trade groups were separate from the criminal gangs (who were officially banned), in practice the distinction was often blurry.

The first commercial Chinese bank was the China Commercial Bank, founded in 1886. Though based in China, interestingly, the largest shareholder was a Java-born Chinese named Chong Chin Fen, also known as Chong Pit See or Chong Chow Set, who seems to have had connections throughout the Chinese communities of Southeast Asia, from where he earned his fortune.

In 1903, a Cantonese businessman named Wong Ah Fook, a native of Guangdong province, opened the first Chinese commercial bank in Singapore, at the time only the second Chinese commercial bank in the world. He called it the Kwong Yik Bank, which translates as 'Cantonese profiting bank'. Ah Fook arrived in Singapore in 1851 and worked as a carpenter before founding a successful gambier plantation operation in Johor and Singapore. He was closely involved with many of the major building projects then underway in what is known today as Johor Bahru. To pay his large labour force, he issued his own currency – which may have suggested to him the idea of opening a bank. The enterprise was short-lived, however, and closed in 1913, after the bank made bad loans to some of its own managers (apparently Ah Fook was not one of them). The Supreme Court appointed representatives from newly formed Teochew and Hokkien banks as well as a European chartered accountant to act as liquidators. Several of the Cantonese bank officers were jailed as a result of the affair.

The Teochew bank involved with the liquidation was the Sze Hai Tong Bank and Insurance Company Limited, opened in 1906; it was the second Chinese commercial bank opened in Singapore. It soon expanded with branches in Bangkok (it was the first Chinese bank to operate there) and Hong Kong. Perhaps learning from the mistakes of the Cantonese, the Teochews were able to keep the bank operational and independent until 1972, when it was acquired by the Oversea-Chinese Banking Corporation (OCBC), which allowed it to operate semi-autonomously as the Four Seas Bank until 1998, at which time its operations were fully absorbed into OCBC.

OCBC itself was founded in 1932 by the merger of three Singapore Hokkien banks: the Chinese Commercial Bank (1912, the other liquidator of the Cantonese Kwong Yik Bank), the Ho Hong Bank (1917), and the Oversea-Chinese Bank (1919). The original OCBC building still stands on South Bridge Road, a short walk from the location of the former Strait Settlements Police Central Station, the logo of a tongkang under sail clearly visible in a plaster medallion on the facade. It currently claims more than 610 branches and representative offices in eighteen countries. In 2012, for the second year in a row, Bloomberg Markets magazine ranked it as the strongest bank in the world, with assets totalling 100 billion American dollars. Its reported 2015 financial year net profit after tax was 3.90 billion Singapore dollars.

# More by William L. Gibson

## SINGAPORE BLACK (VOL. I)

*Singapore/Malaya, 1892*: When a dead American is found floating in Rochor Canal, Chief Detective Inspector David Hawksworth begins an investigation that quickly leads into a labyrinth of deceit and violence in the polyglot steam-cooker of turn-of-the-century Singapore. As Chinese gangs verge on open turf war and powerful commercial enterprises vie for control of the economy, a stolen statue that houses an ancient Hindu goddess becomes the object of a pursuit with a mounting body count, and its seems that everyone is suffering from maniacal erotic nightmares. Will Hawksworth be able to restore order before the colony is tipped into a bloodbath?

## SINGAPORE YELLOW (VOL. II)

*Singapore/Malaya, 1892*: Chief Detective Inspector David Hawksworth, orphaned, middle-aged and gimlet-eyed, travels to Malacca to meet a mysterious woman who claims his mother is alive, only to find a British Resident has been brutally murdered and a Singapore police expedition has vanished in the jungle. Children are being snatched from villages, sinister commercial syndicates are fighting over virgin resources, and a seductive vampiric pontianak is on the loose. When native kids start turning up butchered in Singapore, Hawksworth finds himself increasingly isolated as the evidence points to the involvement of the colonial elite. Bringing justice to the powerful perpetrators while saving his own skin and uncovering the secrets of his dark past pushes the detective over the brink in this thrilling sequel to *Singapore Black*.